UNREST

NEW YORK TIMES BESTSELLING AUTHOR
WENDY HIGGINS

BOOKS BY

WENDY HIGGINS

YA titles from HarperTeen:

Sweet Evil

Sweet Peril

Sweet Reckoning

Sweet Temptation

The Great Hunt

The Great Pursuit

YA Indie:

See Me

NA Indie:

Unknown

Unrest

Undone

DEDICATION

To Courtney Fetchko
Court/Courtster/
Cortilla and Gwennie 4-Ever

PROLOGUE

BAHNTAN ADJUSTED HIS TIE as he sat at the head of the table, surrounded by his six female advisers. He refused to show weakness. He would not let their sharp eyes pry into the myriad of feelings he had regarding what had been done on Earth. Their plans had been put into action with resounding success, and now he could only look forward.

"Towns have been cleared?" he asked.

"Worldwide, Bahntan, yes," responded his top advisor, Vahni. "However, the remaining outliers are proving . . . slippery."

He'd tried to warn them. He'd studied humanity and war all his life. There were always those who hid. Rebelled. Fought dirty from underground. His own people did not think that way, so they'd doubted. His people trusted their government and relied on it in all ways. Some humans were like that as well, but not all. The fight or flight instinct was not in his people. They now saw humans as reckless and skittish, like animals they were attempting to wrangle and cage because they didn't know what was good for them. But, of course Bahntan saw them that way, as well. He had to remind himself it was so.

"The lands are too vast for our numbers," Vahni continued. "We have taken to bombing all places where large numbers of outliers are expected to be hidden, but we cannot continue at this pace. Ammunitions are running low. It is time to gather the worthy ranks and put them to work."

Bahntan nodded. "More bombs. Make a list of supplies needed and rank them by priority. Gather Baelese to train the approved humans and oversee the projects. Our production factories should nearly be ready."

"Yes, Bahntan." She and the other women made notes. He nearly chuckled at the way their heads jerked down simultaneously to write. He'd become so accustomed to the fluid, graceful way most humans moved. It had been difficult to train the Baelese who oversaw the takeover and were expected to face actual humans each day, to woo them into submission. Their ways were so very different.

He turned his head toward Rashna, his communications specialist. "Tell me about the newest landing. Have all of the passengers of that vessel begun training?"

"Yes, Bahntan, but unfortunately there is one male missing."

He paused, perturbed. "And how did that come to pass?"

"They were ambushed by humans—FBI—and one male was captured." Her voice became smaller as she displayed something akin to guilt. "And . . . the ship was also taken."

He felt his face harden as he turned to Vahni, whose chin went up as she responded to this. "You have been under duress, Bahntan. Those aboard the vessel had limited access to our current information, so we felt no need to worry you about it."

He fought the urge to pound a fist on the table, a very human show of emotion. "That was nearly a month ago. It is not for you to decide what news I can handle." His hands splayed on the table before him, and he worked to keep his features and voice steady. "You will relay all information to me. *All*. Do I make myself clear?"

He saw the small grip of her jaw where it tightened, the only sign of her unhappiness. "Very clear, Bahntan. My apologies."

They both knew Vahni would be the one in charge under different circumstances. But as it was, he was in charge and he would continue to remind her of that fact. If Vahni were in control, humans would be obliterated from the planet. It was only his gentle, persistent urging of humanity's usefulness that caused some to be spared. In time, he believed they would come to respect the lifestyle of the Baelese, the peace it would bring. With Baelese overseeing their reproduction, education, food control, and working conditions, humans would want for nothing.

One race. One language. No poverty. Each person a useful cog in the labor wheel. There would be no more war. No more pollution. No more unhealthy lifestyles of overeating and under-exercising. Eventually they would become accustomed to the changes and be thankful. In fact, the new generations would know nothing of what life used to be.

Bahntan looked forward to seeing the day when there was truly peace on Earth. Even if it meant hunting and extinguishing every outlier on the planet.

ONE

A GOLDEN HUE OF sunrise turned night into dawn. I sat on a small boulder, staring at the sliver of sun through trees of the Nevada parkland, the same spot where I'd been sitting silently in the dark for two hours in the cold. I couldn't take Remy's whimpering and soul-crushing cries each time she fell back asleep in the tent, venturing into nightmares of what she'd seen the night before. What we'd all seen. I might never sleep again.

Mom. Dad. Abuela.

I fought back another wave of debilitating grief that made my bones feel like liquid—like I'd never have the ability to stand again. *Have to be strong. Have to be strong.* I rocked back and forth with my eyes shut tight. I couldn't afford to give in to the loss. If I did, it would consume me whole and devour my will to live. I took a deep breath in and let it out slowly.

We'd been fired up to leave the nature preserve last night and head north to the base in Utah after hearing the Morse code message, supposedly from other military personnel in hiding, like us. But we decided to wait until morning since we needed more light to plan our trip on the map. Plus, headlights in the night would be too easy to spot, and we were all worthless last night, running on adrenaline and vengeance, one step away from crashing. I never did crash or sleep a wink, even though my adrenaline was long gone.

The soft sunrise was too pretty—too majestic—for the way I felt inside. Raw. Like my heart had been grated. During the night, I'd begun to believe the sun would never rise again, and now that it was I felt as if the Earth were mocking what we'd been through, reminding me just how miniscule and un-remarkable we were. A new day was happening despite what we'd lost. The world wasn't stopping to mourn. It felt wrong.

We'd been so close to the camp yesterday where the Disas-ter Relief Initiative, the DRI personnel, had taken my parents, my grandmother, Remy's parents, and Rylen's wife Livia. We watched in confusion as those DRI bastards fled. Then we'd watched in disbelief as Air Force jets dropped a bomb on that camp, obliterating our family and the people from our town. *Oh, God.*

I pressed the back of my hand to my mouth and squeezed my eyes shut. Even while the world fell apart around us, I never imagined anything would happen to my parents. I never let myself believe it was possible, even after watching my Grandpa Tate shot and killed by a Disaster Relief Personnel—fucking Derps. Who was I without my parents? I was the daughter of an Army man and a Mexican dancer. A Green Machine and a Señorita. A small bubble of laughter worked its way through a sob in my throat when I thought about my parents' silly banter with each other. Their relentless love and devotion to me and my older brother, Tater.

The sound of a tent's zipper wrenched through the morning solitude and I quickly wiped my eyes. I looked over and saw

Rylen crouching as he pushed through the opening. The golden hue of sun made his blond hair and the scruff on his face stand out. His eyes met mine and I had to swallow hard at the sight of pain in his expression. I'd already cried so much last night.

Seeing those solemn gray eyes brought back a flood of memories: young, scrawny Rylen Fite, loved and cared for by my parents like he was their own son. And his eyes reflected his remembrance too, as if he felt their absence as prominently as I did. But he'd lost a wife, as well. Maybe she hadn't been his wife in every technical sense of the word, but he'd been trying to make it right. Every bit of his loss was reflected in the heavy way he sat on the rock beside me and rubbed his face before staring out at the sunrise.

"Are they still sleeping?" I whispered.

"Tater's awake. Just laying there. Remy's asleep."

I nodded. We sat, sharing a heavy silence until a car door shut in the distance, signaling that some of the guys sleeping in the vehicles were awake. Devon and Josh had slept in the minivan. Tent flaps began to open. Mark, Matt, Texas Harry, and Sean slowly made their way out, stretching, followed shortly by Tater and a blanket-wrapped Remy. All were respectfully quiet as we gathered around the cold fire pit. Remy squeezed onto the rock with me and put her head on my shoulder. She shivered.

"We leave this morning for Utah," Texas Harry said. "But I suggest we only take two cars. We can siphon the gas from the third and split it between the other two. Otherwise we'll run out pretty damn fast."

My heart began to accelerate. Leave one of the cars behind? But the smallest vehicle was . . .

"We'll leave the sedan," Tater agreed.

"No!" The word burst out of me and everyone turned. In a scratchy whisper I said, "That's Mom's car." It was all we had left of her. She used to pick me up from softball and volleyball in that car. She taught me how to drive in it. The thought of abandoning it made panic rise in my chest.

"Amber," Tater said softy, his eyes tired. "We can try to come back for it someday."

"Yeah right!" The words were choked. I knew I was being stupid and sentimental. The car was just an object, a material possession, but it felt like it was a piece of her. Everyone stared at me, and I couldn't take their pity. I stood abruptly and crossed my arms, walking fast down the path toward the cars. *Don't cry, don't cry, don't cry.*

When I got to mom's sedan, I spread my hands on the cool metal of the trunk and gasped for air. Mom's hugs, her support, her unconditional love, gone forever. In my adult years she'd become so much more than my mother. She was a friend. This was unfair. I wanted her back. If only we'd raided the camp sooner. God, I was going to hyperventilate.

I sucked in a heaving breath when I felt hands on my shoulders, then arms wrapping around my upper body. His lighter skin and slightly taller build told me it was Rylen, not my brother. I reached up and grasped his forearms, taking his comfort.

"She's in here, Pepper," he whispered into the top of my hair and gently tapped my heart. "They all are. We'll take them with us wherever we go."

I leaned my head back against his chest and my body shook with leftover convulsions from last night's crying fits. He held me tighter until my breathing was even.

"Hey," came a whisper from behind us. Rylen let me go and we turned to Remy. Her long, blonde waves were a mess, framing a pretty, round face, eyes sunken from crying. She pulled the blanket tighter around her shoulders. Her voice was weak. "Sorry to interrupt."

"That's all right," Rylen said. "I'll let you two talk."

He left us, and Remy came to my side. We both leaned

against Mom's car. Remy's hand slipped out from under the blanket and she ran a hand over the bumper.

"I don't have anything of my parents'. I wish I did. So I understand." She swallowed hard.

"We can't take it," I whispered. As much as I wanted to, I wasn't going to fight them on this. It would be dumb not to conserve gas. "Will you help me unpack it?"

She nodded and we set to work. Most of our camping stuff had been packed in the back of Dad's SUV. Food stores and other essentials were in Mom's trunk. Grandpa and Dad had packed it with efficiency, but we were down to only days' worth of edibles now. We pulled out a box with canned potatoes, chicken noodle soup, and beef stew. One box of square salted crackers sat with a half-eaten box of grahams and the last of the instant latte mix. Three-fourths of a case of water bottles was all we had left.

"Have we really eaten that much?" Remy asked with fear in her voice.

"Yeah." The problem was, we'd always assumed we'd be able to find more food, or that things would get better any day. Now we knew differently. We *had* to ration. We could hunt and fish, but lack of water was most frightening. I didn't trust natural water sources after so many of them had been contaminated.

Remy said, "Thank God it's winter and not summer when we're sweating to death." She opened a box that had toiletries in it and pulled out a box of condoms. I rolled my eyes at Dad's forethought.

"These would've come in handy . . ." Remy's voice trailed off and her cheeks turned bright pink as she shoved the condoms back into the box and closed the lid.

My eyes bugged. "You and Tater didn't use anything?"

Her flushed cheeks did not lighten and she wouldn't look at me. "I got the shot."

"Yeah, but that doesn't protect you from diseases." Who knew what the hell my crazy brother did while he was overseas with the Army?

"He said he always used protection. With others."

Wow. I couldn't believe they even had a conversation that night before hooking up, as drunk as they were. And ew, I didn't want to think about it anymore.

"Don't worry," Remy said, heaving the box out of the trunk. "It won't be happening again."

Okay then. I couldn't get a reading on her feelings about that statement as she walked away, so I let it go and grabbed the case of water. I would use two bottles to make the last of the coffee today. One final hurrah before we left this place.

I didn't look at anyone when we made it up to camp, though I could feel their eyes on me. I set to work pouring water into the kettle and readying all of the cups with half a scoop of the coffee powder. Emotion welled up within me when I scraped the bottom for the last dregs. I really had to stop getting emotional over coffee. I needed to conserve the water in my body and not cry it all out.

"You really don't gotta do that," Texas Harry's voice rumbled. I looked over and he nodded toward the gas fire I was lighting. "That's yours. We appreciate your sharing the past couple days, but you should keep what's left for you."

I shook my head. "We're in this together. One last treat for all of us before we hit the road."

"Well, that's mighty nice."

"Yeah," said Matt. "Real nice."

"Hella nice." Mark earned himself a smack to the back of the head from Texas Harry.

These guys . . . they were always cutting up, keeping it light, but today's banter felt heavy. No smiles.

"When's the last time you saw your families?" I asked. The

men's eyes jolted to me.

Tall Mark, with his long, slender frame, kicked a rock and shoved his hands in his pockets. His brown hair stuck out straight, overgrown. "I was in San Diego over the summer for my mom's birthday. So, six months ago. And I talked to her three days before the bombs." The bombs on D.C. and other major cities had dropped on Thanksgiving. He cleared his throat and toed another rock. "I'm sure they're okay. And my sister's family. They live close to each other."

We were all quiet. *I'm sure they're okay.* Did he really believe that? Or was he just trying to give himself hope?

I looked up at Matt. He was the shortest, only a couple inches taller than me, but his wide back and shoulders, paired with his squared face, made him plenty masculine. His dark-blond hair had grown thick. He and all the guys had scruffy faces. He caught my eye.

"I was with my folks on Thanksgiving in St. Louis, and I took my dad's car to get back to base in Arizona since the airports closed. I never made it back to them, but . . ." He swallowed hard. "Yeah, I'm going to find them once things settle. I'm sure they're okay."

Oh, Matt. He dropped his gaze to the ground.

"Same," said Texas Harry in a rough voice. "My pop wouldn't fall for that roundup shit. He probably got Mama in the cellar when those fuckers came through."

His words rubbed me harshly, and Tater too, because my brother said, "My dad didn't *fall* for anything. He was just trying to keep everyone safe until we could figure it out—"

"Sorry, man." Texas Harry stood, holding up his palms. "I meant no offense. I wasn't thinking . . ." Tex ran a hand down his patchy facial growth and sighed. Tater turned away.

My hands shook as I pretended to focus on the cups in front of me, lining them up. The lean redheaded Air Force officer,

Sean, came over and squatted next to me.

"What can I do?"

"Sean . . ." I had to know. "What about your parents?"

His jaw clenched. "They haven't talked to me in years. Since I . . . came out." He glanced up at the other guys, his auburn-scruffed jaw clenching, as if daring them to say something. Nobody reacted. Either they already figured, or they didn't care. I glanced at Remy and she gave me an *I told you so* nod as Sean continued. "But I have an older sister in Seattle who I'm close with. She's the one I'm worried about. I was near Vegas visiting . . . a friend. I left for Nellis Air Force Base when the bombs hit, got turned away, and when I came back my friend's whole neighborhood was empty. I can only assume he's dead now."

My eyes fluttered closed and back open. I looked over at Josh with his Italian features, sitting with his legs wide, poking the ground with a stick. "Nah," he said. "It's been two years. I'm that asshole kid who uses his leave to party instead of visiting his family in upstate New York." He gave an ill-humored laugh and shook his dark head. "I got two nieces and three nephews. My brother owns a sandwich shop . . ." He poked the ground harder, his lips tightly sealed now.

When I turned to Devon's tall, muscular form, he crossed his arms and shook his head. "I don't know. I never made it out there," was all he said. But his eyes were alight, probably remembering his loved ones, I think in Mississippi.

Was it possible that what was happening here in Nevada was happening nationwide? I wasn't sure what was better—not knowing and being able to hope your family was okay—or knowing they were gone. My chest squeezed and I wiped my eyes on my shoulder.

"Let me finish this," Sean said. "You can go get ready."

I gave a small nod of gratitude and stood. Rylen and Tater

were breaking down the tent and making quick work of it. They'd set my backpack outside of it next to the tightly rolled sleeping bags. When I leaned down to get my bag, Tater took my arm.

"Still mad at me?" he asked quietly. I'd been upset that my brother hooked up with my best friend, especially under these circumstances. But that was before last night's bomb. The worry in his eyes killed me.

"No." My voice was soft. "It's the least of my concerns. Do you guys need help?"

"We've got it."

I headed down the path to a patch of trees where I could get ready in private. I pulled a facial wipe from the pack and cleaned my face, then my underarms. The pack was only half full. I didn't want to think about how we'd soon be out of the things we relied on. I changed into my skinny jeans and a thin sweatshirt with a wide neck that showed my collarbones and part of one shoulder. It felt baggier than usual. My fitted jeans that were supposed to be tight were loose too. At least my sneakers still fit right.

I ran a brush through my hair and pulled it up in a slick, high ponytail. That was it for my primping. On my way back up to camp, I tossed my bag in the back of Dad's SUV where the guys were loading in the camping stuff. Rylen closed the trunk and looked me over, making me feel suddenly warmer.

"You're losing weight," he said grimly.

"We all are," Tater remarked. He pulled up his T-shirt to show the camo belt he'd had to use with his jeans, pulled tight enough to bunch the fabric.

Rylen let out a small laugh and pulled up his own T-shirt to show he'd resorted to using his work belt, cinched tight, too. My stomach gave a flip at the sight of his lower abs with a light patch of happy trail hair leading down between his V-lined hips.

I quickly turned away and walked the rest of the way up the hill to camp, shaking out my arms. I'd been checking out Rylen for years, even while he was married, which had caused me a fair amount of guilt. But it felt really wrong to do it while he was grieving a freshly dead wife. A girl who'd kind of become my friend.

The other guys were bustling around when I got there, and Sean handed me a steaming cup of watery latte. I closed my eyes and brought it to my nose, inhaling the scent. *Well, friend,* I thought, *this is it. I hope we meet again someday.* I took a sip and felt the sweet warmth down to my toes. A moan escaped me.

"Damn, that's one lucky cup of joe," Tall Mark said. I opened my eyes and caught his goofy grin, lopsided.

"Shut it," I muttered. Normally I would have smiled, but the effort was too great. The grief that had flooded my body the night before still blanketed me, stunting my muscles from exerting signs of happiness. Every time I thought of a world without Juanita and Jacob Tate Senior, my insides felt like they were being massacred. Such wonderful lives, wasted. Suddenly I wasn't even interested in my coffee.

"Enjoy it," Mark said. I forced myself to take another sip for him. He patted my shoulder and went to help the others. His tall frame looked even thinner than yesterday, camo pants hanging lower with no butt to speak of, bunching around his ankles.

In a matter of minutes, the guys had packed up the camp and shoved everything in the back of Dad's SUV and Devon's mom's minivan. We finished our coffees as we huddled around the front end of the SUV where Texas Harry had laid out the map.

"We gotta avoid all big towns, cities, and main roads," he said. "Which means we'll have to zig-zag our way northeast."

"Let's hope for clear back roads or dirt terrain without a lot of rocks," Tater said. He pointed at part of our route. "This is the county we grew up in, so we know that area pretty well."

"There's a few national forests along the way if we need to stop," Rylen said, pointing to a couple areas in Utah. He looked at Devon. "How much gas do you have?"

"'Bout half a tank."

"Shit," Tater mumbled. "It's at least 450 miles to Dugway Proving Ground. I used our spare gas to fill up and I'm at about three-quarters of a tank. That'll only get us a hundred and fifty miles or so. We need to hit that gas station before we head out."

His eyes turned downcast at the mention of the gas station, and Remy let out a whimper, quickly covering her mouth. I took her other hand and squeezed. Going there would mean seeing where the camp had been—seeing the aftermath of last night's bomb.

"All right then," Texas Harry said quietly. "Let's get a move on. We'll take lead since Matt has the binoculars. Once we get closer to your neck of the woods, we'll switch out."

Tater nodded and patted the hood. "Hooah." The guys repeated him, and we broke apart. My stomach was a mess thinking about our upcoming journey. I kept hold of Remy's hand until it was time to climb into the back of Dad's SUV with her. Tater jumped behind the wheel and Rylen took shotgun. He glanced back and held my eyes a few seconds. I gave him a nod.

Remy and I sat close, holding hands, garnering strength and comfort from one another for what was ahead. I watched Mom's car as we passed it, leaving the safe shelter of Ash Meadows National Wildlife Refuge. Remy's grip on my hand tightened as we exited into open land. Whoever killed our parents was out here. Fear of the unknown threatened to make me cry out, but I strangled it back down. We had to move forward.

We had to survive and fight.

TWO

A S WE NEARED THE gas station, I started to crouch a little in my seat, which was silly, but Remy was doing it too. She leaned over my lap toward the window and her eyes darted skyward. Mine did the same. No fighter planes in sight. But my breathing got heavier and it felt like my heart was heaving in on itself as we pulled up at the gas station and parked. None of our eyes were on the building. We all stared in silence at the smoldering valley in the distance. My body was stiff and tense.

We continued to stare as we got out of the vehicle and walked to the edge of the paved lot. The four of us stood in a row, facing the smoking ruins. It looked from afar as if someone had taken a giant bucket of dirt and rocks and dumped it unceremoniously in the valley. Nothing green in sight. Just dirt and ash covering indistinguishable rubble where hundreds of people had walked yesterday. I felt the other five guys come up behind us and respectfully wait.

Remy let out a dry sob and sucked the air back in. She shook her head hard and ran to the SUV, shutting herself in. We let her go and continued to stare. I couldn't believe it. I just couldn't, even as I stared at the proof of what happened.

Nothing substantial remained. Only a partial wall where the large building had been. The camp was gone. Tater startled me by falling to his knees beside me. He scooped dirt into his shaking hands—dirt mixed with the ashen remains of our family.

I bent next to him and took his shoulder. A tear dripped from my nose into the dirt at our feet and I shut my eyes.

"*Maldito,*" Tater whispered. *Curse them.* "We'll find them." His tone was rough and deadly. I nodded and wiped my face.

"All the goods are gone," Texas Harry said. We turned to find him at the shop's door, his hands cupped to look inside. "This door ain't gonna be easy to break."

"I'm sure we can make it happen," Rylen said. He walked to the SUV and came back with a hammer.

"Be careful," I said. "Aim for the edges, not the middle. Edges are weakest."

He narrowed his eyes as if wondering why I'd have that kind of information.

"We had to know how to break windows to get into locked buildings or cars. In case babies were left inside. Stuff like that. And all of this glass is tinted, so hopefully it won't shatter. The tint keeps it stuck together."

Rylen lifted his chin in understanding. "Smart Pepper." My heart expanded at the sound of his nickname for me. A feisty chili-pepper, just like the one he'd had tattooed on his chest when he'd been feeling homesick in the Air Force. Back before he'd come home with a wife and shattered my heart.

He walked to the window next to the door and sized it up, getting a good grip on the hammer. Then, in a ripple of arm muscles, he swung. I flinched at the loud cracks as he swung twice, three times until there was a head-sized fissuring of glass.

Just as I'd thought, the shards stuck together from the tinting. Rylen tossed the hammer to Tex and kicked the broken spot with the bottom of his boot, successfully pushing it in. He stuck his arm through the hole and unlocked the door.

"Sweet." Texas Harry opened the door and we filed in.

I looked back and found Tater still crouched on the ground, staring at the bomb site, and something inside me died all over again. I approached him, and his eyes were far, far away.

"Tater," I whispered. "Come on."

He let me pull him to his feet, but his gaze was crazed. I gave his arm a squeeze and his eyes cleared. Tater looked from me to the gas station, and suddenly became alert. He jogged forward and I stood there a second, feeling a little freaked out to have seen my brother so out of it. Then I shook it off and followed them inside.

Disappointment filled me as it became apparent that not a single scrap of food or drinks had been left behind. Just toppled boxes and empty racks. We checked every single crevice of the abandoned store.

"Hey," said Matt from down on the floor. "Found an M&M!" He stood and held up the beautiful blue circle between his fingers. My mouth literally watered. I could feel the crunch of the shell and the soft, creamy chocolate inside.

"You're the big winner," Tater said flatly. "Enjoy."

"I think I'll give it to Remy."

Texas Harry, Josh, and Tall Mark *awwwed*, making Matt's cheeks darken. "Fuck you guys. She's sad." Tater frowned as he watched Matt walk from the store to give Remy her gift. I couldn't be jealous that Rem was getting a treat, but apparently Tater could. For different reasons.

"Let's see if this pile of shit place has a generator," he grumbled.

Generators and electronics were not in my job description,

so I stayed out of the way while they looked behind the register and in the back office room, flipping switches and searching. I squatted to see if that lone M&M had any siblings. Nothing.

Matt came back in with a dreamy, small smile on his lips. He went straight into the tiny room I thought was a broom closet and said, "Generator's in here, but the juice is low. Almost out. Might be enough to switch on the pumps for a few minutes. Get the cars ready."

Tater and Devon leaped the counter and ran out to position the cars. My heart began to jog in my ribcage. *Please let this work.* I closed my eyes right there in the empty candy aisle and waited. Moments later I heard a *click* followed by a series of beeps and shouts of victory. My eyes flew open.

"It's on!" Matt hollered.

"I've got the pumps on at the register," Josh called out.

Mark stood at the window and whirled his hand in the air, signaling to Tater and Devon to pump.

"It's working!" Josh said. "The meter's going up." We all cheered and for a second I smiled until it faltered like an awkward, unwanted sensation and fell away, leaving behind a quiet scrap of gladness.

"Ah, man, the power button's blinking," Matt said. "C'mon, baby, just a minute longer."

I held my breath.

"Tater's finished!" Mark called. "Now he's trying to fill up the backup canister."

Another beep sounded and Matt groaned. "No, no, no, come on." Then a *whoosh* went through the building as the generator shut down and silence filled the air.

We looked around at each other.

"It'll have to be enough," Texas Harry said.

Hopefully we could find another abandoned gas station

along the way. We left the building as Tater was pouring the small amount he'd gotten in the canister into Devon's tank to top it off. They gave each other high fives and everyone shared slaps and knuckle bumps before climbing back into vehicles. I slid next to Remy. We reached for one another instinctively and held tight.

"Let's get the hell out of here." Tater put the SUV in drive and we were off.

Remy put her head on my shoulder and I got a small but distinct whiff of chocolate.

"I might have to lick you, Rem," I blurted.

Both Tater and Rylen turned to us, nearly cracking heads in the process.

"She smells like chocolate," I explained. Tater shook his head and faced forward again. Ry gave me one last bemused look before turning back too.

"Hey," Remy whispered. She raised her free hand to my face, and to my shock, there was half of the tiny candy pinched between her finger and thumb. "I saved half for you."

My heart lurched with emotion. "Are you serious?"

She nodded and her chin quivered as she raised the M&M to my mouth and fed it to me. She licked her fingers off while I savored the tiny morsel. My eyes watered as I crunched down and Remy said, "Good, right?"

A second later we were hugging and crying all over again.

"We have to save our water," I choked.

She sniffled and let go of me to wipe her face. "No more crying."

"Maybe try to sleep," Rylen suggested. "We'll wake you if anything happens." He gave me a reassuring glance.

I didn't know if I could ever sleep again, but I pulled our pillows from the top of the pile in the back and we snuggled against the windows, our feet and legs tangled in the middle. I looked out the front windshield and saw only dry landscape and distant mountains. Nothingness. Kind of how I felt inside.

THREE

I JOLTED AWAKE WITH a pounding in my head as the SUV swerved into rubble.

"Whoa," Rylen called. Tater quickly righted the SUV. "You okay, man?"

My brother ran a hand roughly through his hair. "I'm fine."

I glanced at Remy, who was watching him with worry. Had he fallen asleep? Or maybe his mind was wandering? He looked pissed off, so I was afraid to ask. Instead, I stared out at the sight of dry, rugged, mountainous terrain. The minivan in front of us began to slow.

"Where are we?" My voice was scratchy from sleep.

"Well, look who's awake," Tater said drily. "You missed all the fun."

I sat up straighter. "What happened?"

"Nothing," Rylen answered. "We saw one white van back in Nevada. Looked like it was going in the direction of the Air Force Base. But we were too far away to be noticed."

"We're not in Nevada anymore? How long did I sleep?"

"Few hours," said Rylen. "And we're in Utah."

Whoa. I stretched and cracked my neck.

And then Remy spoke so quietly at the window, I almost missed it. "We saw more bombed camps."

"What?" My belly tightened. I looked up a Rylen, who gave a morose nod.

"Three areas that looked like they'd been fenced off and bombed."

Oh, my God. I pressed a hand to my stomach. If they'd seen that many, just on back roads, who knew how many people had been taken from their towns and cities to these remote places to be killed? Could it really be happening all over the U.S.? The world? Horror and indignation made my head pound harder.

Tater pulled into a small lot with a sign that read: Beaver Dam Wash National Conservation Area. He followed the minivan off the pavement and into a crevice between two rocky hills.

My stomach gave a gurgle as a gnawing hunger pain struck. Climbing out of the car, I felt weaker than I had in a while. I fought against it and helped to set up the gas burner so I could heat soup for everyone. A chill in the air made me wish I had a sweatshirt or jacket. I knew as we moved north into higher elevations it was going to get cold, and I was not looking forward to that.

I handed everyone a few crackers and shoved mine into my mouth, almost choking on the dryness. I emptied all five cans of chicken noodle into the pot. That would be half a can for each of us. I hoped like hell we got to Dugway soon and that they'd have some sort of resources there. In the meantime, we had to keep up our strength, even if it was only two small meals a day. Or even one.

As I handed out tin cups of soup, I could tell everyone was just as haggard with hunger as me by the way they tipped them back and slurped until every drop was consumed. After we finished, everyone drank one-third of a bottle of water. Then we were all quiet. In fact, other than the light rush of breeze over the rocks, it was incredibly silent outside. My head felt a fraction better.

"Damn," Texas Harry said. "I could eat a whole fucking cow right now."

Tater and Rylen were quiet, but the other six guys proceeded to list all of the things they could devour at this moment. I saw Remy slip away, arms crossed over her chest. Since I didn't really want to stand around and think about all the food we weren't eating, I decided to follow. She climbed half the rocky hill and sat on a jutting red piece, leaving room for me to sit beside her. My hands were dirty from climbing, so I brushed them down my thighs.

We stared out at the spiky Joshua trees and cacti brush that dotted the barren landscape leading to distant striated mountains. So much beauty made it hard to believe there was a war going on.

"Who do you think they are?" I asked. "The DRI. They have to be some organization or something, right? But who? Some crazy, rich cult? How were they able to do this?"

She shook her head, as bewildered as me. "They look . . . I don't know . . . like your average Americans or something. Above average, actually. Or maybe Europeans? Beautiful tanned people with money. And so many of them are women."

I felt my forehead scrunching as I thought about our mysterious enemy. For the life of me, I could not figure them out.

A breeze made Remy tighten her arms over her chest. She wore a gray tunic sweater over a black tank.

"Is that the warmest thing you've got?" I asked.

"Yeah." She sighed. "I don't know what we're going to do. We'll be out of gas soon, and since we're staying off main roads there are, like, *no* gas stations anywhere."

Worry pinched my gut. Neither one of us needed to state the obvious—that we might have to end up hiking a hundred miles, in the cold, with no food or warm clothes.

"We'll be okay," I tried to assure her. "We'll make it."

She nodded and stared out. "I keep thinking of my dad. About how we were always fighting, right up until the end."

"Rem, don't do that to yourself," I said softly.

"I can't help it. He just wanted me to be good. To focus on the bigger picture of my life, but I was caught up on having fun and wanting people to like me. I did what I wanted to do and focused on me." She studied her twined fingers. "I never made him proud."

"Stop." I turned enough to look at her. "It's okay that you let yourself have some fun. You're such a good person. I know he saw that."

"I'm not telling you this so you'll say I'm good. I'm just . . . I need to change. For me. I feel like everyone but you only thinks I'm fun when I'm drinking. And guys only like me for what I'll give them. I know it's stupid to be thinking about this when the world is coming to an end, or whatever's going on here, but look at the other night!" The night with Tater. She waved her arms out. "Even when things are falling apart around us, I'm still making bad decisions. I have to stop."

"You're being too hard on yourself."

"No." She shook her head. "This morning when Matt brought me that stupid M&M, I almost kissed him. I almost pulled him into the backseat of the car with me, because I felt like I needed to thank him. Like I owed him something. Do you feel that way when a guy is nice to you?"

"Um . . ." No.

"I didn't think so." She rubbed her face.

I put an arm around her and pulled her close, putting my head on her shoulder. I'd seen the aftermath of a lot of patients whose lives had been changed after they had a near-death experience, or lost a loved one. Sometimes monumental events sparked big changes in life, good or bad. This was normal.

"I love you, no matter what," I told her. "And I support you."

"Thank you," she whispered.

We sat there, quiet under the gray winter sky of the desert. It made me wonder how many others were out there like us. Lost. Grieving. Looking for survivors. Remy pinched my arm and I jumped, then looked where she pointed. On the next hill over, Rylen had climbed and was standing, looking out. Watching him did so many things to me. I wondered what he was thinking. Probably about Livia.

I sat back and looked at my hands. Remy nudged me, trying to get me to go talk to him, but I shook my head. Alone time was scarce these days, so I would let him have his.

"Oh, my gosh," Remy whispered. My eyes flew to Rylen again to find him taking off his shirt. I sucked in a ragged breath. Remy's claws sank into my forearm as we watched him staring out at the view. Even having lost weight, he was still amazingly fit. He shook out his T-shirt, turned it inside out, and slid it back over his head. I suppose that was his version of changing into something clean.

He turned and caught sight of us, lifted a hand. We both gave small waves in return. Then we climbed down and dusted ourselves off. Time to go. Daylight was burning. Rylen met us at the bottom and walked with us. His arm brushed mine, and I wrapped my arms around my middle.

"Neither of you brought a coat, did you?" he asked.

I shook my head and Remy said, "I don't even own a coat." I did, for our rare family excursions into the mountains, but it was at home in the back of my closet. *Home.* My heart ached with longing as the comfort of the word rushed over me. Rylen said nothing, but looked thoughtful.

Around the side of the hill, the three of us halted at the sight of Tater sitting on the ground, his knees pulled in, head down. Rylen and I looked at each other, knowing we should probably let him have a minute alone, but Remy went forward as if to comfort him. At the sound of her footsteps, Tater's head snapped up. He jumped to his feet.

"I'm fine," he said gruffly.

Remy stopped and bit her lip as Tater rushed past her, back toward the others.

"It's not you," I assured her. "He just needs some time."

She swallowed hard and nodded. The three of us walked slowly.

When we returned to camp I saw Tater sitting in the driver's seat, his head leaned back with his eyes closed. The other guys had wiped the pan and all of the tin cups clean, and were packing everything away again. Texas Harry opened the map and laid it on our hood. He patted the side of the vehicle and called for Tater to get his ass out there, which he did.

"We're here." Tex pointed a thick finger at southwest Utah. "And we need to get here, in Great Salt Lake Desert." His finger trailed up to northwest Utah. "That's another three hundred miles. We can follow roads that parallel main routes, but we gotta get close enough to a city to raid a gas station. It might take a few tries to find one with gas and a generator." He looked around with eyebrows raised, as if asking if we were up for it. We all nodded. It frazzled my nerves to think about, but we had to do it.

"Luckily, Utah is mountainous," Texas Harry said. "Plenty of places to hide if we need to get out of sight."

"We gotta watch for those rocks when we're driving, though," Devon said. "Mama's van can't handle off-roadin' with all our heavy asses in there."

"Not as heavy anymore," New York Josh said, hiking up his

camouflaged pants and pulling them out to show the inches he'd lost and the top of his blue boxer briefs over a strip of toned stomach. I noticed Remy tear her eyes away and stare pointedly in the direction of the mountains. These guys really needed to keep their shirts down.

"Let's head out," Texas Harry said. "Tater, if you need anything, just signal."

Tater nodded. His face still appeared tight.

We were silent in the car as we traveled the dusty road. Remy chewed her nails and I bit my lip. I wasn't sure how I'd been able to sleep that morning, because driving was tense. An electric feeling stretched between us in the car as we each stared out of the windows, watching the distance for any signs of movement or dust clouds that would signal vehicles. The longer we drove with no sign of anything, the more I felt my blood pressure rising. Periodically, I stared from the back window to be sure no one was following.

After an hour, Devon took a dirt road turnoff and the ride became bumpy for the next twenty minutes. They drove slower, so as not to kick up too much dirt. We were surrounded by low hills of brown on one side, and a plain of shrubbery and scrawny trees on the other.

"Slowing," Tater said.

"We're coming up on a town near the interstate." Rylen had a map open on his lap.

Both vehicles slowed significantly as two small buildings came into sight. Both were nondescript, one-story box buildings, but one had gas pumps in front of it.

"Bingo," Tater whispered.

Please, please, please, I silently begged. *Let this work.*

FOUR

DEVON PULLED TO THE side of the road. I could make out Matt's stocky form leaning over in the front seat with the binoculars, scouting. Back behind the gas station were two old trailer homes and a rusty car on blocks. Everything was still and quiet. Ghost town.

Creeping forward, we made our way to the gas station and parked at the pumps. My heart pounded as we looked around. Farther down the road were more small buildings and a scattering of trailer homes in the distance, but not a soul was in sight. We quietly got out, but left our doors open so as not to make too much noise.

Matt stood outside now, looking out with the binoculars.

"We need you inside, tech boy," Texas Harry said to him in a low voice.

"I'll keep watch," Tater offered. Matt handed over the binoculars.

Remy waited in the car with her door open. I leaned against the inside of her door as the guys smashed another window to get in the building. With every loud smack of the hammer, I flinched, the sound too loud in the silence of the abandoned town.

"This place freaks me out," Remy whispered.

I agreed. A gust of wind whipped up a small funnel of dust at the edge of the road just as a shattering blast rang out from the gas station window breaking. Mutters and quiet laughter came from the guys as they pushed their way into the shop. I ran my fingers roughly up and down my legs, digging into the thin denim, trying to scratch away the antsy sensation inside of me.

"I need to stretch my legs," I said. "Want to come?"

She shook her head, so I let her be. I walked to the edge of the building and peeked around the corner. Finding nothing but dirt and broken pavement, I walked to the back where the dumpster was. Surprisingly, it didn't smell bad. I moved closer, wondering what kind of stuff might have been thrown out last when I heard a sound—the crunch of gravel underfoot. My entire body went stock still and I held my breath as a man stepped out from behind the dumpster.

He was no DRI. This was a local man, unshaven with messy strands of brown and gray hair. His clothes hung loosely over a rounded belly, which must have been a significant beer gut a month ago. I stepped back to put comfortable distance between us, but heard another crunch and turned to see a second, much thinner man come out from the other side, boxing me in between the building and dumpster.

I tamped down my instinct to scream. These were just men. Survivors who'd managed to evade the DRI round ups.

"Hi," I said, damning my jittering voice. But I couldn't ignore the gut feeling telling me to get far away.

The thin man's eyes traveled my body from top to bottom and he grinned, showing several gray teeth. That's when I noticed the baseball bat he leaned against. I inhaled sharply.

"Nothin' to be scared of," said the older guy, stepping closer. "Been a while since we seen anyone in these parts, but you look safe enough."

"I need to get back to my friends." My fleeing instinct pushed me to try to pass, but the thin man grabbed my arm and pushed me toward the other man.

"Don't touch me," I warned. This time I barreled past him, only to scream when my head was yanked backward with a sting of pain. The old bastard had me by the ponytail, and then his hand was around my face, covering my mouth. I elbowed backward, jabbing his ribcage to make him grunt. The thinner guy in front of me moved forward and I kicked out, barely grazing his thigh as he jumped away. The older guy pulled me hard against his body, surprisingly strong as he pinned my arms. That's when I lost it. I let my body go heavy as I flailed my legs and thrashed my head back and forth. The old guy cursed low. His friend swung out with his free hand and punched my stomach below where the guy held me.

My body lurched inward and I couldn't take in a breath through my nose. The older guy took this as an opportunity to lift his hand from my mouth and smack the side of my face as hard as he could. Stinging, blinding pain rang out, and his hand was over my mouth again. I finally regained my breath, huffing through my nose and letting a muffled scream die on his palm.

"Shut the hell up," whispered the skinny man, keeping his distance and brandishing the bat. "Or you're dead."

"Amber!" Remy's voice split the air. She stood at the corner of the building, staring with huge eyes. And then she was gone, screaming, *"Tater!"*

"Fuck," muttered the older man at my ear. "How many of there are you?"

I couldn't think. My face was swelling on one side. He never took his hand from my mouth to let me answer. I tried to stomp down on his foot, but he wore hard boots, and he laughed at my effort.

"They had two cars," said the younger man.

"No matter." A tell-tale click sounded in my ear just before cold steel touched my temple. "It's all ours now. Get ready, Rick." I felt my last reserves of energy draining as my body went rigid with terror. This could not be happening.

Seconds later, the pounding of feet hitting the ground filled the air before their bodies came skidding around the corner. All at once, as my friends took in the scene, their hands went up. I stared at Rylen and nearly passed out at the look of sheer panic on his face. Remy stood in the back.

Rylen took a cautious step forward, his hands still up. "Hold on now."

"You shut your mouth and listen up," the man named Rick shouted. "If you want your gal back safe and sound, here's what you're gonna do. First, drop your car keys on the ground."

"The keys are in the vehicles," Devon said with care.

"Is that so? I'll have to check that out for myself. Right now, every one of you's gonna walk down that road with your hands on your head."

Rylen stepped forward, holding his hands higher.

"Not another move!" yelled the big man, right in my ear. He pressed the gun harder into the side of my head. My heart galloped. These guys were crazy and desperate. I knew for a fact that Texas Harry kept a gun on him, but he wouldn't dare pull it while they had me hostage.

"Okay. All right." Rylen remained motionless. "Let her come with us. You can have the cars and all our stuff. Just let her walk away with us."

The old guy chuckled and pressed his belly into my back. "I'll let her go when we're done with her."

I was going to puke against his hand and choke on it.

Rylen's face turned stony and his eyes honed in on the guy. He gave a nod, which I didn't understand, until a *bang* split the air, ringing in my ears. My neck felt slick with wetness as the tight arms around me loosened and with a *thump*, the old guy hit the ground, banging into my calves. I was frozen in place. An echoing *whoosh* filled my ears, like they were clogged and I couldn't hear properly.

Rick's eyes bugged out and his holler sounded far away as he focused on something behind me. He swung the bat with his skinny arms, but a brown flash was there, grabbing the man's wrist to stop his swing, and smacking the side of his head with something metal, hard enough to make him tumble to his knees.

Tater. Grandma's gun.

I touched the thick wetness at my neck and looked at my strangely maroon hand, then down at the old man splayed on the ground. Half his skull was gaping, spilling bright red flesh onto the cracked pavement. Bodies suddenly rushed all around me, yelling. I toppled over to the ground and scuttled away.

Arms banded around me, picking me up, cradling me and running for the second time in less than a day.

"You're all right." Rylen's voice sounded muted, though I felt him all around me. "It's okay now."

I began to shake violently as I stared at my bloodied hand.

"Get it off me," I tried to say, but it sounded weird with half of my lips swollen and my ears still ringing.

Rylen ran into the gas station, back to the bathroom where a few paper towels were left. He sat me down on the closed toilet seat and together we did our best to wipe me clean. My hands still trembled, and I noticed his did too. We filled the sink with bloodied napkins until there were no more. I still felt dirty, but at least the whooshing in my ears had begun to subside.

Quick footsteps sprinted into the shop and I whimpered. Rylen looked over his shoulder.

"It's Remy."

She burst into the room and rushed me, hugging me despite how gross I was.

"Amber!" She pulled back to look at me and hugged me again.

"I have blood on me," I tried to say. She stood and looked me over, lifting my sagging ponytail and swallowing hard. Then she ran a soft finger over my cheek and upper lip.

"Turn around a little," she whispered. I did, and she took my rubber band out.

"Don't touch it," I said. "I'll do it." I reached up, but she gently pushed my hand down.

"Let me." She began picking things out of my hair and flinging them to the ground. Her breathing hitched over and over, and I knew she was trying not to heave. She pulled my hair up into another tight ponytail and wiped her trembling hands down her jeans, leaving pink streaks. I leaned my face into her belly and she pulled me close by the shoulders, rubbing my back.

We said nothing, just clung. Rylen watched us with distant eyes, his jaw clenched.

More footsteps came into the gas station, and Remy and I held each other as we listened.

"No generator juice," Matt said.

"Fine. Let's get the hell out of here and try someplace else." Rylen's voice sounded tense at the mention of stopping at another place. Reality of our lack of safety was hitting hard.

Rylen and Remy both helped me to my feet and watched me.

"I'm okay," I whispered. I touched my lip and let out a little whine of surprise at how swollen it was. My mouth still tasted metallic. But I moved forward and they followed me out.

Tater was in the car, in the passenger seat, staring forward with glossy eyes. Rylen made sure Remy and I were seated with the door closed before he climbed in the driver's seat.

"Tater?" I whispered. I wanted him to look at me, to let me thank him, but he continued to stare blankly ahead like a stone statue. Remy took my hand.

We followed Devon back down the empty dirt road to get to the original one lane road we'd been on. After our awful encounter with the first people we'd seen in days, the void was a comfort.

My skin felt tight where the man's blood had dried on me. I clenched my teeth as the memory of what transpired flashed through my mind. I'd never wanted a shower so badly in my life.

A low hum came from the front seat and turned to a groan. Rylen shot Tater a startled look as my brother slumped forward, his arms over his head, shoulders wracked with convulsions. It took a moment for me to realize he was crying. My chest constricted and Remy gasped. He sobbed for an anguished minute, the sounds stabbing at my gut. *How would Mom comfort him?*

I unbuckled and leaned over the seat to press a hand to Tater's upper back. "Esta bien, Jacob. Thank you." Two of my own fat tears ran down and splattered his T-shirt.

Tater reached back and took my hand, holding it tight.

"I can't lose you, Amber." His voice was thick with tears.

"I'm here," I whispered. "Because of you."

"But I never . . ." His shoulders shook and he sucked in a breath. "That man. He wasn't DRI." Tater sat up, letting go of my hand to wipe his face. "He was just some fucked up man. A victim, like us. But when I saw that gun on you . . ."

"You did the right thing," Rylen said. "Anyone who threatens one of our lives is an enemy, DRI or not." Ry glanced at me, then back at Tater. "I would've done the same thing."

Tater shook his head. "Everything's fucked up. They've got us all turned against each other like animals." He put a knuckle to his mouth and turned to the window. I could see the tendons taut in his neck, his arms muscles flexed with tension. Another sob wrenched out of him. "I took his gun, man. It wasn't even loaded."

God above. A sinking heaviness pressed me down. My brother had killed for me, and it hadn't even been necessary. He could have hit him over the head. Now a man was dead. Tater's trembling hand covered his face, and I squeezed his shoulder harder. I would have done anything to take this burden from his soul. It was my stupid fault for exploring by myself without my gun. Now Tater would carry this guilt for life.

"I'm sorry," I said, squeezing my eyes shut.

"There was no way to know it wasn't loaded," Rylen tried to assure us. "You couldn't take the chance."

I squeezed Tater's shoulder harder, trying to infuse my remorse and reassurance into him. I wanted to tell him it was going to be okay, my mouth couldn't form the words. Nothing was okay.

We rode in stunned silence for forty-five more minutes until it was time to try again.

FIVE

EVERY CELL IN MY body was on high alert as our cars crept down a side road and we spied a gas station ahead. It was one of the bigger chain companies with four aisles of pumps. Between my breathing and heart rate, I hardly heard Rylen whisper.

"I think everyone should stay in the vehicles this time except those who need to turn on the generator and pump."

He didn't have to worry. My exploring days were over. We inched closer, all of us swiveling our heads around at the empty rest area off the highway. The closer we got to the mini mart and pumps, the more apparent it became that the place had been looted. Broken glass. Trash strewn and shelves toppled. Everything useful had to be gone. I let out a shaky sigh.

Devon and Rylen pulled up at the pumps, facing out toward the street so we could take off at a moment's notice if necessary. Matt and Texas Harry came up to Ry's window.

"We'll check it out," Texas Harry said. "Y'all keep an eye out for our signal."

Rylen nodded and stepped out, sending a rush of cold air in through the open door. He and Devon got the pumps ready. Tater opened his door and stood inside of it, gun propped on his shoulder as he kept watch. His jaw was set hard. I looked over at Remy and found her watching him, rubbing her arms.

She abruptly turned to look out the back window, away from him. "So weird to see towns abandoned," she whispered. I followed her lead, turning and sitting on my knees, resting my arms and chin on the back of the seat. In the nearby field was a small farmhouse with a silo in the distance. I stared at the house and wondered how unethical it would be to check out houses for food. Even though the DRI probably took every scrap long ago.

A beep rang out, making us all jump.

Our heads spun toward the minimart where Texas Harry was swinging an arm over his head like a helicopter. Numbers popped up on the tank screen.

"Yes!" I cried. Rylen and Devon got their pumps going. Remy and I hugged each other as the sound of rushing gasoline filled the vehicle.

But after a few moments the pumps shut off with a wheezing sound.

"Damn it," Tater said. "Only a quarter tank."

My heart sank with dread at the thought of having to stop again soon.

Nobody said anything as everyone piled back in the SUV and minivan, and took off back down the road.

I stared from the window. Hunger began to gnaw at me. We would find food. I had to stay hopeful.

We got back on the side road, which soon turned from pavement to gravel. The bumpiness kept me on edge. On one side of us were patchy trees; the other side was rocky flatness stretching into picturesque mountains of striated browns, tans, and reds. In the near distance, running parallel to the mountains, was a main highway. Every so often there were abandoned cars off to the side that had probably run out of gasoline.

The sky above was a soft, hazy blue with grayish clouds that made me shiver. A winter sky, and we were moving north. It would only get colder. I freaking hated the cold.

I looked around at our clothing. Tater and Rylen both wore jeans, boots, and T-shirts. Remy had leggings and a light sweater over a tank top, and I had skinny jeans with a flimsy, poor excuse for a sweatshirt. We were both in sneakers. Our clothes were okay for a south Nevada winter, but not a northern Utah winter. I really wished we had boots with thick socks, and sweatshirts with coats and earmuffs and—

"Fuck, veer off!" Tater shouted.

I grabbed Remy's arm and the oh-shit handle as Rylen abruptly turned into the trees. The SUV bumped and rattled. Up ahead, Devon was doing the same thing in the minivan. We went as far as we could until the trees became too thick to pass. Then we turned our faces to the windows, all of us breathing hard as we strained to see. I could barely make out the mountains and main road now, until a caravan of yellow busses came into view on the distant highway, followed by three white vans and a black sedan.

My pulse pounded in my throat as I imagined townspeople on those busses, just as my parents and Abuela had been, thinking they were being brought somewhere safe, only to be murdered. Suddenly I could hear the screams from last night, people from my town standing at the gates of the camp, screaming and screaming. It was so real that I gasped as my vision cleared, jumping in panic.

Tater saw and stared at me, but I shook my head, mouthing, "I'm okay."

We'd all been holding our breath, trying to will ourselves

and our vehicles to be invisible, until Remy let out an anguished, barely audible, *"Oh, my gosh.* Those people!"

"There's nothing we can do," Tater said. He sounded numb.

My eyes burned and I swallowed hard. I wanted to stop those busses, to save them from their fate. We were ill-prepared to do that, and it left me feeling helpless. After several silent minutes passed, we reversed back on to the road. Remy and I never let go of one another.

We weren't driving much longer when Devon pulled aside again, this time less recklessly. There was a car on the side of the road, halfway into the trees.

"Flat tire," Ry whispered.

"I'll check it out," Tater said. "You guys stay here."

We watched as Tater and New York Josh approached, guns out. Within a minute, they had the doors and trunk open. Tater grabbed something out of it and turned. He held up an unopened big bag of wavy potato chips.

Remy and I accidentally let out yells of joy before covering our mouths. Rylen chuckled at our excitement, and then whispered, "Score," as Josh held up a gallon of water. We all climbed out of our vehicles. My body was too excited about salty goodness to care about the biting chill on my arms. I took the chips from Tater and opened it as I stood in front of our SUV. I rationed it into ten piles on the hood of the car.

Together, we practically pounced. There were smiles and moans all around as we crunched and laughed and licked the oil from our palms and fingers. Except Tater, who ignored his pile and stared off at the mountains.

"Eat," I whispered, nudging him.

"I don't want—"

"Damn it, Tater," I hissed. "Eat the stupid chips!"

"I don't want them!" His shout caused everyone to stop and turn. Again, his jaw set and he glared around at our group. Then he stomped to the car and got in the driver's seat, slamming the door shut.

"So . . ." Mark said. "Does this mean he doesn't want his chips?"

"Have them," I said. Each of the guys happily grabbed one from Tater's pile, and it hurt my heart to see his portion dwindle away until not a crumb was left on the hood of our car. We passed around a water bottle until everyone had had a few gulps. I took the last of it to the driver's side and opened the door.

"Drink this, or so help me." He snatched it from my hand and tipped it back. I heard his stomach give a massive growl, and I fought a rush of tears.

"Tater," I whispered.

"I'm fine." But he wouldn't look at me. "Just ready to be there." When he reached for the door handle, I let him close it.

"Hey," I heard Josh say to the group. "If they abandoned this car 'cause of the tire, I bet it still has gas." He walked to the van and began pulling things out.

I didn't know anything about siphoning gas, so it was fascinating to see Josh work. He stuck a long hose down into the abandoned car's tank, then pushed a short black tube in next to it. He put the other end of the long hose into a red gas canister on the ground. He blew hard into the short tube, and we all cheered a second later as gas began to flow through the long one. It seemed to go on forever, which made me giddy. Between the chips, water, and gasoline, everyone was cheering, clapping each other on the backs.

When I saw a rare grin grace Rylen's face, I threw my arms around his shoulders in a spontaneous hug. The second he stiffened, I became self-conscious and nearly backed off. But then I felt his arms slip around my waist, his hands splayed across my back. He pulled me to him and everything was right in that moment when the side of his face pressed into my neck.

"Let's fill up and get the hell outta here," Tex said.

I exhaled and let my arms fall to my sides as Rylen did the same. He moved away without looking at me. Remy was watching, biting her lower lip. She gave me a small, sad smile. Even moments of happiness were fleeting and awkward, dripping with guilt and loss.

If I had my cell phone I would have texted Remy: FML. It felt like ages ago that we had technology, when it'd really only been a month. I let Remy pull me by the fingertips back into the car. We were silent as a beautiful *glugging* sound came from the gas tank.

"What do you think the date is?" I asked.

Remy shook her head. She opened her door and called out to the nearest guy, Officer Sean. "Do any of you know the date?"

He looked down at his watch and his eyes widened. "Damn. It's December twenty-sixth."

Remy gasped and it felt like I'd belly flopped hard into a pool, like my skin was stinging and the breath had been knocked out of me.

They'd killed our family on Christmas.

Rylen walked over, crossing his arms as he examined our faces. "What's wrong?"

"Christmas was yesterday." I struggled to get the words out. He blinked and his eyes narrowed, as if what he'd heard couldn't possibly be true. The fact that a day so important in our old lives, an event we counted down for and focused so much of our energy on, could bypass us without a blip in any of our minds was so shocking I felt literally spooked. And to have something so wretched happen on that joyous date.

Remy pressed the back of her hand to her mouth. It felt as if the universe had turned on us. And how had we lost track of time? Holidays—those special moments with loved ones were the essence of who we were—we couldn't lose that.

"What?" Tater was there now, and Rylen mumbled something to him.

Tater's hand went into his curly, unruly hair and he grimaced. The look of loss on his face struck me like a blow as he met my eyes. Our Christmas traditions. Our family. It's like we expected all of that to be put on hold while we figured out the mess of the world, and then we could go back to being normal. But things would never be normal again. We would never have a family Christmas again. No more American-Mexican hodgepodge of stuffing a turkey and rolling tamales. Sugar cookies and flan.

But would we ever celebrate again? Or would Christmas forever become the day of the bomb? If it hadn't been clear before, it certainly was now. Our enemy did not cherish the things we cherished. They were not like us. And they clearly wanted to strip us of everything we held dear.

"They've taken everything," Remy whispered.

"Not everything," I told her. "We won't let them."

SIX

WE DROVE FOR A good long while with Remy and I taking turns keeping watch out the back window for any followers. We were on a back road in the middle of nowhere in desert land, so we should have felt safe, but the desertedness felt eerie. The longer we drove, the less I trusted the aloneness. A sense of sadness and fear had draped itself over us, like being tangled in a hot blanket during a nightmare, unable to disengage.

My stomach ached with hunger, and I caught Remy rubbing hers at one point. Had there really been a time in our lives when we could help ourselves to food at any given time? Our old lives seemed like a distant fairytale now.

When the sun dipped low on the horizon, we found the thickest copse of trees possible, also partly hidden from the main road by a hill. We climbed out and it was freaking cold. Like, see-your-breath cold. The guys were stretching their legs as they pulled on beanie caps and rubbed their hands together.

Remy and I took a short walk away from the guys to relieve

ourselves. When Remy came out from behind the tree, she was wincing.

"What's wrong?"

"I hardly peed, and it burned."

Shit. I hoped she wasn't getting a urinary tract infection. "It could be dehydration. Let's get you some water." I would have to keep any eye on her.

When we approached the guys, the ten of us stood there looking around at each other expectantly.

"We have enough food for one more meal," I said flatly. "Should we have it tonight or tomorrow?"

Everyone's bleak faces matched how I felt.

"We had breakfast today," said Sean. "And a snack. I can wait until morning if you all can."

We all nodded, though I'd bet their stomachs were hurting as badly as mine.

"I thought this was the desert," Matt said. "It's cold as shit."

"We're not in the Middle East, dumbass," Mark said, giving him a shove. "Desert means dry, not hot."

And it was definitely dry. I would do just about anything to plunge my grungy body into a lake, or be rained on. I scratched my itchy neck at my hairline and was startled to feel crustiness there. A bout of nausea rolled over me at the sight of the dried blood on my fingers, under my nails. My breaths came out in spurts as I rubbed my fingers on my jeans, digging my nails in.

"What's wrong?" Rylen asked me.

I shook my head. *Don't freak, Amber.* "We should at least drink some water," I managed to say. They agreed.

We all took our portions, but I only drank half of mine. When nobody was looking, I gave the rest to Remy.

"No, you drink it." She shifted from one leg to another, trying to stay warm.

"Remy, don't mess with me." I shoved it at her and she

huffed before taking it and chugging the rest.

"Do we have any trash bags?" she asked.

"Yeah, I think so, why?"

"I know how to try and get some water. I learned it in one of my bio classes."

I recalled her going on a lot of field trips to the outskirts of Vegas desert land with her science classes. It would be epically awesome if she could do this. I dug through the back of the SUV and found a roll of bags with a rubber band around it.

"I hope I can remember the details," she said. "What I remember most is the hot teaching assistant. One of those outdoorsy hipster guys with long hair." She sighed and shrugged when I snorted.

"You can do it," I told her. "What else do you need?"

The guys had watched, enthralled and filled with hope as Remy worked. The next morning, their hope turned to impressed cheer to find the bags filled partway with water from condensation that dripped down to the bottom.

After we'd all drunk a few gulps, I was feeling momentarily content until Remy came back from a bathroom break looking pale. I immediately stood and felt her forehead. She was too warm.

"It hurts worse today," she whispered. *Shit, shit, shit.*

"I want you to drink as much water as you can," I told her. "And wash yourself well."

"I just did," she said. "I mean, as well as I could. I used the last of the handiwipes I had in my purse. I'm out of clean underwear though. I really need to be able to wash clothes." We both frowned, because that was a problem. It was hard to stay clean without any water.

"The sooner we can get to Dugway, the better," I muttered.

"Let's just hope it's okay there," she said. "And it's not a trick."

Those words hung between us. Remy shivered and hugged herself. She watched as I fixed the last of our food. Sean helped me pass it out. We all ate too quickly, and a terrifying sense of urgency overcame me. We were officially out of food.

When we finished, sweat shone lightly on Remy's forehead.

"You should get water and go lay down in the car until it's time to go."

"I can help clean—"

"No, please, Rem. I need you to rest."

She looked toward the guys. "I don't want them to know. It's gross." She scuffed her heel into the dirt.

"I'll tell them you're not feeling well. They don't need to know the details. And you're not gross." Or, rather, we were *all* gross. "Take some ibuprofen in the car." I nudged her arm and gave her a gentle shove to send her on her way, then I joined the guys.

Tater looked at me as he rolled the tent, and then he looked around for Remy.

"What's wrong with her?" he asked.

"She's not feeling well," I said. "I sent her to go lay down. I want her to take it easy."

All of the guys' foreheads furrowed with worry.

"She's sick?" Texas Harry asked.

"I think she has a low grade fever. Maybe a bug. I'll keep an eye on her."

"What do we do if she gets worse?" Matt asked. "What if she needs antibiotics?"

"Sometimes infections can run their course and be flushed out by the immune system without meds. We'll have to wait and see." I knew better than anyone that untreated UTIs could make a person violently ill. I prayed it wouldn't come to that.

Tater shoved his tent into his bag and stood, heaving it up under his arm. "Let's get moving."

Everyone picked up armloads of things to pack away. Most everything went in the back of our vehicle since their van was filled with, well, *them*. Once Tater piled stuff inside, he opened the back door. I thought he was opening it for me, but he leaned in and brushed the hair back from Remy's forehead. She reached up and put her hand on his. Then Tater was climbing in and lifting Remy's head to his lap. I blinked back my shock.

"She's burning up and shivering," he said, rubbing a hand down her arm. He looked over his shoulder and called out to Rylen. "C'mon, man, let's go."

I guess I was sitting up front.

I went around, nearly colliding with Rylen at the back of the car. He gave my disgusting ponytail a quick tug in passing, and then we were climbing in.

"Welcome to the front seat," he said in a low voice. Rylen cranked the heat to high and a shiver overcame me as the warmth hit my numb cheeks. We buckled and he began carefully navigating his way back out of the thick trees.

I turned and looked at Remy. Her cheeks and eyelids were colorless, but I was glad to see she was falling asleep. The crease between Tater's eyes would not go away.

"She'll be okay," I promised him. He continued smoothing back her hair.

When I turned to face front again I found Ry watching me, eyebrow raised, as if asking if I were okay too. I gave him a small nod, though I really wanted to lay my head down in his lap like Remy was doing with Tater. Lately I felt exhausted just from the overwhelming amount of alertness required of us.

When the vehicle was heated, we turned the heat all the way down to conserve gas. I put my feet up on the dash and let my eyes peer around, through the trees on one side, and along the dusty hills on the other.

"How close are we?" I asked.

"Two hundred miles," Ry said. "Maybe less."

That wasn't so bad. We could make that. I felt a fraction lighter, able to take a deep cleansing breath and let it out slowly.

I took stealthy peeks at Rylen in my peripheral vision as he drove. He seemed lost in thought, but not happy thoughts. His jaw was set, and his forearms flexed as his hands gripped the steering wheel. I probably stared too long at those forearms and his rugged, strong hands, but I couldn't help it. I still couldn't believe those hands had never touched his wife, Livia. As jealous as I'd been, I now felt sad for them. I guess it was easy to feel that way in retrospect, now that she was gone. But gone or not, he still felt off-limits. I wondered how long it would take before I was allowed to think he was sexy without feeling guilty.

I straightened my eyes to peer forward through the windshield. After a while I looked back and saw Tater's head leaned back, his eyes closed. The sight of him and Remy both sleeping made me relax a little. They'd both tossed and turned last night in the tent. I glanced at Rylen's lost expression.

"I asked the other guys about their families," I said carefully. "How about you? With your mom?"

His jaw rocked from side to side. He reached up and tugged his earlobe. "After Thanksgiving, I drove out with Liv to check on her and introduce them." His mom was an alcoholic who'd moved in with her sister two towns over when Ry's dad kicked her out. "She kept going on and on about how the welfare office was closed and she couldn't get her check. She hardly heard me when I introduced Liv. And . . ." He made a nervous sound and tapped the steering wheel. "She thought Liv was you. She kept calling her 'the neighbor girl.' We didn't stay long."

My gut churned. "She wasn't happy when she thought you married me, was she?"

He huffed. "Doesn't matter. She doesn't know what she was saying. I left her some food I'd brought, and some money. I never saw her after that."

I swallowed down the sick feeling.

We drove the next two hours in silence. My brother had woken after an hour, but Remy slept on. Before, we would have blasted music, and God knows Tater would have run his mouth the entire time. But not anymore. Every time I looked back at him, his face was a hard mask of remembrance.

Remy woke sweating, which told me her fever had broken for now. Tater felt her head and frowned at me.

"I feel better," Remy said. She smoothed back her hair, which was damp around her face and frizzy in the back.

I forced a smile and faced forward again. In two more hours the fever would be back. And it would keep coming back between doses, worse and worse.

Rylen eyed me from the side. "Don't suppose we can GPS the nearest pharmacy," he said without humor.

I crossed my arms and bit the pad of my thumb. Then I made the mistake of looking at the gas gauge. We were down to just under a quarter tank. I turned my face to the window and exhaled loudly. No food. No gas. No antibiotics. The direness of our situation crashed down on me and a tremor of panic shot down my spine.

"Hey," Rylen whispered. His warm hand landed on my arm, and the heat of his touch covered my cold anxiety for a moment. "We'll work something out. We'll get there." I put my hand over his, and our fingers reached, twining, holding. He didn't let go. He drove with one hand on the wheel, the other holding mine. It didn't mean anything—I knew it didn't—but it felt so intimate and non-brotherly. I would never hold hands with Tater like this. What did it mean? I was too nervous to look over at Rylen.

We kept driving until the gas light came on and Rylen abruptly let go to flick the headlights at Devon. This shook me from my romantic stupor. There weren't any turnoffs in sight, so we slowly made our way across a sea of dirt toward Route 15, the main road where we could find exits. Tense silence filled the car.

"Last chance for gas," Rylen said. "If we can find some here, we'll be there by tonight. If we can't . . . we're walking."

"Oh, no," Remy whispered. She sat up, and Tater pulled away from her, putting distance between them. It was like now that she was awake and alert he didn't feel like he could touch her.

"No worries." Rylen said.

"How far is it?" she asked.

"I don't know. Maybe thirty miles?"

Tater gave a forced nonchalant shrug. "Like a marathon. People do it all the time."

I met Remy's eyes and felt our matching doubt. We were not marathoners. Especially not in a Utah winter with one of us suffering from an infection.

We bounced our way onto Route 15 and took the next dusty exit, which had a sign for one off-brand gas station. My nerves were shot by the time we pulled up and surveyed the area. The shop was tiny, not an actual shop at all, but a booth where you could walk up to pay. It didn't look like it'd been broken into, which was hopeful. Two old-time pumps sat in front of the booth.

"Stay here," Tater told us as we came to a stop and he jumped out. Cold air rushed in, and I crossed my arms. Rylen opened his door a crack so we could listen, but he stayed behind the wheel.

"Dude," I heard Texas Harry say. "We just barely rolled in. I thought we were gonna have to push the van."

"Us too," Ry said.

"Please," Remy whispered. I turned to see her pressing her clasped hands to her forehead, eyes closed. "Let this work."

Devon broke the glass to the booth. He and Texas Harry pushed their way inside while Tater and Matt looked around the outside. Devon broke into a cheer of laughter. His hand came up holding packets of something.

"Peanuts, baby! Boo-yah!" he sang in his booming voice. "And Gatorade!" But he said it like GA-TO-RADE, each syllable accented with joy.

Remy and I smiled, and my mouth watered.

"Yeah, boy," Texas Harry yelled now. "Corn Nuts and Combos. We done hit someone's mother lode stash!"

Whoever they were was probably taken before they had a chance to go back for it.

"I don't see nothing that looks like a generator, though." Texas Harry stepped out and let Matt in to look around. As he circled the small space, touching things and shaking his head, my excitement began to dissipate.

"Oh, no," Remy whispered. "Amber, I really don't know if I can do this."

"I know," I whispered back, clutched by dread.

After a few more minutes of practically turning the place upside down, Tater sent our vehicle a firm, disappointed look, and shook his head.

Remy made a small sound of disbelief. I looked back at her, trying to stay strong even when I wanted to freak out. I glanced down the barren road with its hills and shrubs and distant mountains that seemed to stretch on forever. No part of me wanted to be out there.

"We can do this," I said, as much for myself as her. "We'll all take care of each other. Maybe the fresh air will be good for us."

I expected her to call my bullshit, but she nodded, her eyes panicked. "Okay."

All at once the guys were back at the vehicles, opening the back ends, getting their packs together. This was really happening. I got out with Remy, trying to be strong for both of us. Of all the things we'd been through since Thanksgiving, this scared the crap out of me most because of our lack of resources. If we had food, water, gloves, hats, and freaking snowsuits I might have felt more positive about a thirty-mile trek.

I took a deep breath and shook out my arms. We had no choice. We had to keep going, and this was the only way.

Tater and Rylen opened their bags.

"We need to bundle up," Rylen said. "As many layers as we can put on—especially you two."

Remy and I took out all of our shirts, about three each, and pulled them on.

"Hey," Tater called out to the guys at the van. "If any of you got extra clothes for the girls, toss 'em over."

Rylen took out the remaining trash bags and told us to put them on our legs under our socks and shoes so our feet wouldn't get wet if it rained or snowed. The plastic was crinkly and uncomfortable, but we did as told.

New York Josh came over with a pair of warm looking Army gloves, and handed them to Remy.

"You'll need these," she said to him.

"Nah, I'm used to cold. Plus, I got a decent jacket and sweatshirt. I'll be a'ight."

She gave him a small smile. "Thank you so much."

He nodded and jogged off. I caught Tater eyeing the scene, but he nodded down to the gloves. "Put 'em on, Rem." She did, and he handed her a pair of his fitted sweats to pull on over her leggings, which were lumpy from the plastic bags. She rolled them three times at the waist.

Tall Mark gave me a long-sleeved camo shirt. I put it on over my thin sweatshirt. I let his shirt hang past my fingertips. Remy and I doubled up on socks and I put two pairs over my hands.

"Here you go." Sean handed me a navy blue sweatshirt with ARMY in yellow—a real sweatshirt—thick with a hood.

I looked to make sure he was wearing a coat before I took it and thanked him profusely. I cinched the hood of the sweatshirt so only a round part of my face was showing.

"Pep." I looked down at Ry, who was digging through his bag. "Those jeans are too thin." He held up a gray pair of his physical training, PT, sweats, and I took them gratefully, resisting the urge to see if they smelled like him. I pulled them on and rolled them at the waist, then tucked the bottoms as much as I could into my sneakers. That completed my clown look, and I felt as warm as I was going to get.

Mark grinned when he saw me, and I had an urge to laugh hysterically. I must have looked ridiculous. But I wasn't alone. Some of the guys had track pants tied around their heads and necks to keep them warm.

The next step was to pack as much stuff as possible into our duffle bags and backpacks. The guys were super efficient at this. My bag was already filled with essentials: bathroom stuff, over-the-counter meds and first aid kit, plus my extra undies. Devon came over and shoved two Gatorade bottles into my netted side pouches. Then he gave me a wink and I threw him a thumbs-up as I pulled the heavy pack onto my back and adjusted the straps.

Remy and I faced each other. What I wouldn't have given for a camera phone at that moment. She had someone's cotton shirt around her ears and neck like a scarf. Her backpack was the same size as mine, and I think they'd put all of the snacks and a sleeping bag in hers.

The guys' duffles were filled to the max. Not a single thing was being left behind except an empty propane canister. Tater shut the back end and stared at the car for a minute before giving it a salute. I kissed my fingertips and touched the window.

Bye, Daddy's car.

"Let's go," Tater said hoarsely. I turned with my head down before I could think too much about it.

Remy and I linked arms. "You feel okay?" I asked her.

She nodded.

"Let me know if you feel the fever coming back." She nodded again. Her lack of verbalization showed how nervous she was.

I looked up and found Rylen watching me questioningly. I gave him a nod and as much of a smile as I could muster. His returning nod and stare made me flush with heat as I thought about holding his hand in the car.

"Heidi-ho, y'all," Texas Harry said. "We're off to see the wizard." With that, he set off, and we followed.

SEVEN

"ONE MILE," SHORT MATT said after ten minutes passed.

"Two miles," he said after twenty-two minutes tramping through the dirt.

"What the hell, man?" Tater said. "You got a FitBit or some shit?"

"Yeah." He held up his wrist to show a black band, and everyone laughed. "Doc recommended it when I gained a few pounds last year." He patted his belly, which didn't have much fat on it these days.

By mile three I was actually starting to feel hot, except for my nose and cheeks which were numb with cold. And by mile four my legs were starting to turn to jelly. Remy began to slow next to me. She kept her head down.

"You okay?" I whispered.

It took her a few seconds to answer, and then it was through shivering, panting breaths. "I don't . . . want . . . to stop." I grasped her arm to stop her and tore the socks from my hand.

Her face burned my hand. I gritted my teeth against a curse.

"Guys," I called out. "One sec." Everyone stopped and turned to surround us as I dug out the ibuprofen and opened a bottle of Gatorade.

She took the meds with a shaking hand and looked up with bags under her eyes. "I'm sorry, guys."

"Her fever is back," I explained.

"I can keep going," she said weakly. And I knew she would try, but it would not end up well. Tater peered at her. His eyes went to Officer Sean, the only guy without a huge duffle. He'd been carrying the camping stove and lantern, along with his small tent in a backpack.

"Can you carry my pack?" Tater asked.

"Of course," Sean said without hesitation.

Remy watched with confusion as all of the guys began re-distributing weight, and then her eyes got big when Tater approached her.

"What's going on?" she asked.

"You'll ride on my back."

Her eyes shot to me and I nodded.

"No way, Jacob, I'll break your back."

He rolled his eyes. "This is no time to be girly. Give your pack to Amber."

She didn't move, so I reached out and took the strap, pulling it off her. I pushed my arms through so that I carried it on my chest. Ugh. I felt like I weighed a thousand pounds. I let out a deep, shuddering breath. *You can do this.*

"Please, guys." Her pleas were pitiful, and I knew she was embarrassed.

"It's okay," I whispered. "Just 'till your fever breaks and you feel good enough to walk again."

She swallowed and blinked back tears. Tater backed up to her and raised her hands to his shoulders. After a few seconds of hesitation, she jumped. He caught her under the thighs and she wrapped her legs around his waist, linking her ankles in front. Her arms went around his shoulders and crossed in front of his chest. She looked stiff.

"Just relax," Tater said, adjusting her. "You feel better than my pack, trust me." All the guys chuckled.

We started forward again. Eventually Remy relaxed a little and lay her head down on her upper arm, near Tater's ear. Her eyes fluttered every now and then, and her cheeks were flushed from the fever.

I kept my head down to watch for rocks. Matt led the way with his compass. The guys seemed to naturally take on a formation, one in front, then two, three, and then Rylen, me, and Tater in the rear. We left footprints in the reddish brown dirt, which were blown away in swirls of occasional wind, unearthing cracks in the soil. Small cacti and brittle plants shivered when gusts hit them. The layered mountains in the distance taunted us by never getting nearer.

After a while Tater whispered, *"Psst."*

When I looked over he was hunched slightly forward and Remy was dead asleep, looking like she was going to slide off him. Oh, my heart.

"Rem." I squeezed her arm and she jumped, eyes bleary. It only took a second for her to cry out and wrap her arms back around him, hoisting herself up. Tater stood straighter, and with a nod, he kept marching.

Just when I seriously wanted to beg the guys to stop, Texas Harry, smack in the middle, let out a beautiful string of melodic words that flooded me with childhood memories; he was calling out a military cadence. The sound lit a candle inside of me that grew, warm and bright.

This one was to the tune of "Old King Cole was a Merry Old Soul." I recognized it from car trips we used to take. Dad would chant to us while he drove, and we would call the lines back to him. This particular cadence worked like the Twelve Days of Christmas, working its way up the Army ranks with each stanza, and adding to it until it was complete.

Tex's voice rang out in perfect tune, and we called it back to him, marching to the beat. With every word, I was covered in nostalgia. A contented look was on Remy's face as she listened.

Old King Cole was a merry old soul a merry old soul was he, uh-huh . . .

He called for his pipe and he called for his bowl and he called for his Generals three, uh-huh . . .

Somebody start a war, said the Generals . . .

Somebody shine my boots, said the Colonels . . .

Somebody drive my Jeep, said the Majors . . .

I wanna take that hill, said the Captains . . .

What do I do next, said the Looies . . .

Push, push, push, said the Drill Sergeants . . .

Left right left, said the Sergeants . . .

I want a three day pass, said the Corporals . . .

Beer, beer, beer said the Privates . . .

Merry men are we. . . .

But none so fair that they can't compare to the Airborne Infantry, uh-huh!

For a second after the cadence ended, I imagined my daddy laughing, proud. And when I looked up, the sky had darkened, and it was just us walking in the winter desert again. No more smiles. No laughing memories.

On a happy note, a big chunk of time had passed during the cadence. No wonder they did those cadences.

"I can walk now," Remy said.

"Actually," Texas Harry said, turning and peering around. "We should probably stop and find a place to hunker down before it's pitch black out."

All of our eyes went to the small cropping of short trees fifty feet away. They could help block the wind. Not much, but it was better than nothing. Remy climbed down from Tater's back and insisted on taking her bookbag back from me for the remaining fifty feet.

The lower the sun dropped the colder it got. My face hurt and my hands were stiff. I helped Tater and Ry pop our tent. Three tents all together. Sean's was a one person tent, so he was bundling up in there with his thermal sleeping bag. We had him put his right up against ours. The other two were four person tents, but we were putting five people in each.

"I am going to pass the hell out," Matt said through chattering teeth.

"Let's ration the food first," I said.

We opened all of the snacks they'd procured today, and we each ended up with two handfuls. We passed around the Gatorade until it was gone, and we each got half a bottle of water.

Remy and I moaned at the same time when we bit into the pizza-pretzel Combos.

The sound was like a beacon to the men, because every single one of them swung their hungry gazes to us. Even Ry was looking at me, eyebrow raised. Remy and I froze, mid-chew.

"That good, ladies?" Texas Harry asked.

I almost choked and Remy gave a small nod. Note to self: no more moaning in front of these guys. We munched silently until the snacks were gone.

"I'll take first watch," Sean said.

"No more than two hours, Lieutenant," Texas Harry told him. "Then get me up."

"I'll go after you," Tater told them.

We piled into the tent, and Devon came in with us. It was a tight fit, but the body heat was a necessity. Rylen went to the side, and I immediately followed, guilt be damned. Tater was next to me, then Remy and Devon on the other end. I made Remy take one more dose of meds.

Despite the small bit of sustenance, my body was suddenly as weak as pudding. Climbing into the sleeping bag felt so, so good. I had to bite back another moan of ecstasy at the warmth and the opportunity to relax my muscles.

"Aw, hell yeah," Devon said, sliding down.

There was no chatter that night. Complete silence was almost immediately followed by sounds of deep breathing and light snoring. Once it sounded like everyone was asleep, I let my muscles relax.

I wish I could say it was a restful night, but I woke with a scream in my throat sometime in the darkness of night.

"*Mom!*" I sat straight up, my face damp, my heart racing, Mom's anguished face calling my name as she reached for me through the fence of the encampment. I reached next to me for my brother, but he was gone.

"Tater!"

"He's on watch." Rylen's arms were around me, his low voice murmuring soothing words. He pulled me back down and I faced his chest, curling into him until my heart slowed enough to sleep again. But I woke again soon after to give Remy another dose when she was shivering hard enough to wake Devon.

It took longer to fall back asleep that time because all I could think was *Remy's getting worse.* And even with all my medical knowledge, I couldn't help her. Rylen held me tighter, as if he knew the horrible scenarios running through my head, as if he could rub them away with his strong hand on my back.

Eventually I did fall asleep again, only to be woken once

more by a horrible, loud *thwapping* sound overhead. This time, all five of us sat up in a rustle of sleeping bags.

"Chopper!" Rylen whispered.

He ripped open the tent's zipper and we all clamored out into the frozen air, along with the other six guys. I had to squint at everyone's silhouettes. Most of the night's stars were covered over with gray clouds, but our eyes followed the low lights moving across the horizon.

"Apaches," Tater said, pointing the direction the helicopters had gone.

"Did they see us?" Remy asked.

"I don't think so," Tater said. "They were pretty far off and they never shined the lights over here." Our camp was completely dark.

Matt pulled out his compass. "They're going southwest in the direction we came from."

"Nevada," New York Josh said. "I think they're using Nellis as a base." The Air Force base near Area 51. A chill went up my spine that had nothing to do with the freezing air. Of all the bigger, better bases in America, why Nellis?

"Let's try to get a couple more hours of sleep," Texas Harry said. He glanced again to where the choppers went. "If we can."

"I'll take watch," Devon said. "I'm wide awake now."

The other four of us climbed back in the tent. Sleep came slower this time, but I think I got another hour of rest before dawn broke. I lay there in a puddle of despair as a soft light filled the tent. My body was mush. Remy and Tater were still hard asleep, but Rylen shifted next to me. I rolled over and we faced each other. I let his expression of tender concern cover my gloom and fill every crack inside me. He had a way of speaking to me with those eyes, asking questions and comforting me simultaneously. He knew I was weary. He knew I was worried about Remy. He was telling me to keep strong.

I reached up for his hand on my shoulder, and took his fingers in mine again. Our fingers curled around one another's in a way that made me think of arms and legs, reaching, winding, pulling, needing. Our palms touched, and I swear his breathing hitched at the same time as mine. His thumb trailed slowly up and down my own. When he looked at me now, I couldn't read a single thing in his expression. I just knew I wanted to kiss him.

I closed my eyes against a wash of emotion.

Remy let out a small whimper, and Tater sat up behind me. I let go of Ry, turning to sit up and look down at Remy's curled body. I felt her and she was hot, her hair matted to her head.

"Hurts," she whispered. I pulled up the sleeping bag and looked in. She was holding her lower abdomen. My heart gave a pound of fear.

"We need to get her there as quickly as we can," I said.

Tater's face was pinched. "Then let's go."

My head was dizzy, and my limbs didn't want to cooperate in a timely manner. We packed up and stared around at one another like a pack of ravenous wolves. Remy leaned against Tater, and he put an arm around her.

Hunger clawed at my abdomen, throbbing upward with a shooting pain under my ribs and into my esophagus. I'd never known true hunger. True hunger wasn't discomfort. It was pain. And we weren't technically starving yet.

I forced those thoughts aside, because I couldn't afford to panic.

"Listen up," Texas Harry said. "We've got about eighteen miles to go. As y'all can tell, it's cold as a witch's tit. We got some water, thank the good Lord, but no more food. Remy's sick, so we need to get her there ASAP and hope like hell this place is legit and they got meds. Basically, today is gonna blow balls. Mind over matter. We gotta push through."

A chorus of *"Hooah"*s sounded.

"We can do it, guys," Matt said brightly.

New York Josh leveled him with a glare. "You want some pom-poms to go with that cheer?"

Mark snorted, but Matt just shrugged it off. Texas Harry twirled his finger in the air and pointed northward. We were off.

EIGHT

ONLY HOURS INTO THE day I could already say it was the most difficult day of my life. I wanted to give up almost every minute. I have no idea how I pushed past the hunger pains and jelly legs in those first few hours, the absence of energy, the needling stitches in my sides, the numbness in my face, ears, fingers, and toes, the pain shooting up my feet into my legs. One foot in front of the other, over and over and over again, and Rylen's voice in my ear.

Water breaks became the nectar of life. Each word of the cadences were electric shocks that forced my legs to shuffle forward. Hundreds of cadences—some with lyrics that would've made me blush had I been in my right mind. We chanted until we were hoarse.

I used to wear those old blue jeans . . .
Now I'm wearing cammie greens . . .
But it won't be long . . .
Till I get on back home . . .
I used to eat at Micky Ds . . .

Now I'm eating MREs . . .
But it won't be long . . .
Till I get on back home . . .
I used to date a beauty queen . . .
Now I love my M16 . . .
Whoa, whoa, whoa-oh . . .
Whoa-oha-oha-oh.

The guys offered to take turns carrying Remy since she became dead weight at the height of her fever when she could barely hold on, but Tater insisted he had her. His face was crusted with a layer of dry dust. Everyone's was. My lips cracked, and I didn't have enough saliva to wet them.

I knew we were going too slow. The guys spoke low on breaks, but I heard. We wouldn't make it today at this pace.

And then, hell of all hells, it began to snow. I didn't even notice until Remy gasped and weakly held out her gloved hand. I stopped in my tracks and peered up at the blinding, colorless sky. It was like tiny, peaceful little angels fluttering down on us. We didn't get snow in the Vegas area unless we went way up in the mountains. I'd only seen snow as a young child in North Carolina, and it never lasted long. It was so pretty. I wanted to lay on the ground and watch it fall. Watch it cover me.

How long had we been marching? Long enough for me to lay down, right?

"C'mon, Pepper," Rylen gently urged. "We can't stop." He had to tug me forward to get my stiff legs moving again. Pain sang through my limbs.

"Ow . . ." I sucked in a harsh breath. *It hurts, it hurts, it hurts.* I felt wooden. I shouldn't have stopped.

"I know, baby, come on." Rylen took my hand and pulled me forward until my frozen feet took up the rhythm of the pack.

He'd called me baby. Even though he obviously wasn't in

his right mind, it made my heart flutter. We were all delirious.

Then it *really* began to snow.

Texas Harry let out a harsh, humorless laugh up ahead and held his gloved middle finger up to the sky. "Fuck you, too, Mother Nature!"

We all peered around, our faces scrunched in similar disdain at the changing landscape. Everything was turning white.

"Keep marching!" Devon called out. We picked up our pace.

Before long the snow was deep enough to feel like weird crunching underfoot. Then I started kicking it in poofs as I walked, which slowed me down. Good Lord, it was like three inches deep already. Panic clutched my chest.

"Just raise your knees, Pep," Ry said. "Lift your feet a little higher."

I did as he said, but my muscles were like *nope*. I'd been lucky to shuffle myself along this far, as it was. I miraculously kept going. And going.

"Shit," I heard Tater mutter, and looked over to see him barely catching Remy, who cried out as she slid. She was covered in a thick layer of snow where she must have fallen asleep again. Both of them collapsed, breathing hard. Remy's face . . . oh, no.

"She shouldn't be out here in the snow," I whispered. The whole crew had stopped, and for a moment we stood in a circle around them, all of us stricken by the sight of the growing snow and our complete lack of energy.

"Just a little farther," Mark finally said. "I see a valley between two rocky hills up ahead, and there are trees. We can camp there."

"Dude, we can't camp yet," Tater said, pushing to his feet. "It's hours until night." He bent and pulled Remy to her feet. She leaned against him, tremoring.

"Maybe a longer rest is what we need," Matt said.

"What we need is to fucking get there!"

Rylen put a hand on Tater's shoulder, but he pulled away, saying, "Come on. Help her back up."

"I can't," Remy said weakly. "I c-can't hold on."

Tater's face was a mask of brutal frustration and distress. "You have to, Rem. Come on."

Wind began to whip the snow sideways, throwing it at us in heaping scoops. I couldn't feel my feet anymore. Rylen helped Remy onto Tater's back and he held her legs tightly, leaning forward and grunting with the effort to tramp through the thickening snow.

I kept my head down to shield my face as we made our way farther into the blizzard. What would happen if it didn't stop anytime soon? How deep would it get? I could barely lift my legs. What if a foot or more of snow came down?

Don't panic, don't panic, don't panic.

"Holy shit." Mark's voice made us all stop and look up. He was peering ahead through his binoculars. I squinted at the dark splotch between hills as he spoke low. "There's a cabin in those trees."

Excitement sprang to life inside of me, followed quickly by fright. What if someone was there? Someone unfriendly, or DRI?

"Guns out, y'all," Tex said. "That cabin's ours tonight. Let's get Remy some shelter."

Yes. I stuck my socked hands to the front waist of my jeans where I'd tucked Grandma's pistol. As one, we moved ahead cautiously. I watched the guys ahead and took their hand signals about when to move to the side, when to crouch. Soon, we were in a patch of trees, looking at the cabin, which appeared deserted. My heart pounded as Tex and Devon skirted closer, then split off to go around the building and meet in the back. I blinked against the falling chunks of snow. The guys came back minutes later, both grinning.

"Empty, from what we can see through the windows. But keep your guns out. Let's check the door."

We moved quietly, all crouched, even Remy, who was breathing hard and shaking uncontrollably. All ten of us lined against the front of the log building while Tex stood beside the door, gun at his shoulder, and knocked. My heart pounded. He tried the door. Locked.

Then he shot the wood beside the doorknob and kicked it.

Remy and I both jumped as the noise echoed through the valley. Tex moved in sideways, gun out.

"This room's clear," he called.

One-by-one we filed in. I didn't realize how biting the wind was until we were suddenly out of it. The room felt super warm. Tex flipped a light switch, but nothing came on. No power.

A single, plaid couch was against the wall. Tater led Remy to it, and lay her down as the others checked the bathroom and one bedroom.

"Blankets," Sean said, looking through a small closet next to the kitchenette area. He tossed one to Tater, who opened it and lay it over Remy's curled form. Her chattering teeth could be heard across the room.

"No food." Matt scoured the empty pantry. It looked like it only had paper plates, napkins, and toothpicks scattering the shelves.

I shoved my gun back into my waist and took the socks off my hands, going to the sink. My hands were frozen and stiff as I tried the faucet. No water. But the two-burner stove was gas. I tried the knob, which clicked, and then flamed.

"Guys! They must be on propane!"

"Nice," Rylen said.

I opened cabinets and drawers to find dishes and utensils.

"We've got some meds and vitamins in the bathroom

cabinet," Mark called. *Ooh*! I stood to see, when Devon's steely, careful voice made us all freeze.

"Hold up." He was standing in the corner crouched by a gas fireplace with fake logs, his hands outstretched. "It's hot."

Oh, shit. Someone was just here. Suddenly our whole group was alert, guns out.

Devon kicked back a small rug and scuffed the toe of his boot on a thick line on the floor between boards. He motioned to it and put a finger to his lips.

Some sort of cellar?

I held Grandma's gun tightly and sidestepped across the room to stand before Remy as Rylen and Tater moved beside me and the others went forward.

Devon slowly bent and put his fingers in the crack enough to grab the edge, but when he pulled it didn't budge.

"Yo," he said. "Who down there? Open up."

What the hell, Devon? Was he crazy? We waited in tense silence for six seconds before a polished male voice responded, quavering with terror.

"Get out of my home or I will . . . ignite this bomb!"

Devon's eyebrows came together. "Hey, what kinda bomb you got, man?"

The man in the cellar hesitated before saying, "A big one! And I will blow you the fuck up. Now get the hell out! My partner is coming back any second and he is fucking *huge*! He will kick your ass!"

Oh, this poor guy was terrified, and his threats were pitiful. Officer Sean moved forward and sank to a knee before the trap door.

"My name is Sean. Listen, we're not here to hurt you, or to take anything. We'll even help you in any way we can. We've been walking for two days and one of the girls with us is really sick. Can we stay here, just one night?"

The man was quiet for a long time. "How do I know you're telling the truth?"

"You don't," Sean said. "We've all got guns and we could have shot this door open by now if we wanted to. I guess sometimes you just have to trust."

The guy snorted sarcastically. "Kind of like how you shot my front door open?"

Tex pulled a face and Sean sighed. "Yeah, sorry about that. We were desperate."

We waited, remaining very still. Finally a latch clicked and the hatch creaked open a couple inches. Beautiful brown eyes with dark lashes peered out and stared up at Sean.

"Hey," Sean said.

The guy stared a long time. "Hey," he whispered back. He looked mid-twenties. As he pushed it open farther his entire attractive face was revealed. His hair was black and wavy, well-kept, unlike Tater's mess, and he had a five o'clock shadow that contrasted the rest of his baby face.

Sean stared openly for a moment, then blinked. "What's your name?"

Devon and Texas Harry shifted closer, and the guy gasped in fear, going back down a step. Both soldiers put their hands up.

"We ain't gonna hurt you," Tex said. "Just being nosy 'bout what you got down there."

"We're not going to take anything," Sean reiterated, glancing up at Tex, who glowered at the beratement. "What's your name?" he asked again.

"J.D. And there's really nothing down here but ramen-fuck-ing-noodles that I might die if I have to eat again."

Every single one of us straightened. My mouth watered. J.D.'s eyes widened as he looked around at our faces.

"Oh, my God. You guys are starving."

"We're . . . really hungry," Sean said carefully.

"Dude," Mark pushed to the front. "If you have enough packs, that would be so awesome. We're just staying one night. We've gotta be out of here first thing in the morning."

He studied each of our dirty faces. "What will you give me?" Then his eyes landed on the handgun at Sean's side.

"Do you have a weapon here?" Sean asked. J.D. shook his head. "I'll give you this one and a round of ammo if you let us all have some food.

Tex scoffed. "Your gun for some fucking ten cent noodles?"

Sean eyed him and Texas Harry let out another low sigh. "Whatever man. Your gun."

"Deal," J.D. said softly.

"Um, hi J.D." I stepped forward. "I'm Amber. My friend over there is the sick one."

He grimaced as he glanced at his couch. "What's wrong with her?"

"Nothing contagious. But do you mind if I see what you have in the medicine cabinet?"

He shrugged. "There's nothing much, but go ahead." He went down into the cellar and came back up with ten packages of ramen, then closed the cellar door and slid the rug back over it. I went into the bathroom and opened the mirror cabinet. My heart leapt when I found vitamins and cranberry pills with some other herbal remedies. What were the chances? I ran back into the living room area, beaming, and collided with Ry.

"Antibiotics?" he asked.

"No, but cranberry!"

His forehead scrunched in confusion.

"Cranberry pills are good for your urinary tract," I whispered. "It helps keep new bacteria from growing." I chewed my lip. "Don't tell her I told you."

He nodded. "What can I do to help?"

"Let's melt some snow and get the water boiling."

We worked quickly readying water to drink and use for ramen. Rylen worked by my side, our arms brushing now and then in the cramped space. When the soup began to boil, Rylen whispered, "God, that smells good." He leaned forward enough for the steam to hit his scruffy face, and he closed his eyes. I stared, jealous of the damned steam. When he opened his eyes I quickly looked away and chugged more water. My stomach was about to burst, and for a second I felt sick from drinking so much so fast.

The guys were loud and boisterous, all except Tater, who sat by Remy's feet staring off into space. She slept soundly through it all. Someone had turned on the fireplace, which sent a cozy warm glow over the room. The small space heated quickly, and my bones finally began to feel thawed. Sean and J.D. stood in a corner talking. I watched their curious eyes on one another, and nearly smiled to myself.

I brought a bowl and glass of water to Remy, along with a handful of pills. She sat up, wincing, when I nudged her awake. I showed her the pills.

"Two for your fever, and two cranberry pills. Take them with your dinner, and try to eat all of it." She nodded and her eyes rounded when she saw the soup. She lifted shaking hands to take it.

Soon we all had heaping, steaming bowls. J.D. and Sean sat at the tiny table together. The rest of us sat on the floor. We were too happy to care. For five minutes it was completely silent except the sounds of eating. When we finished we continued to sit there, but the silence turned expectant.

"So," Texas Harry said. "What's your story, J.D.? What are you doing alone out here in the middle of nowhere?"

The guy blushed a little and rubbed his arms. "This is my partner's parents' cabin. We came up here together from Arizona when . . ." He rubbed harder, holding himself tighter.

"When his parents were taken away. We were all supposed to go—everyone in the city—but my partner, Thomas, was freaked out about some things he'd heard. So, we came out here instead. It was crazy. There was a border patrol, and so many cars were trying to leave the state that the border patrol couldn't catch all of us. Thomas had a Rover, so he just went right off the road and took off into the hills."

Before anyone could ask questions, he rushed on, getting emotional. "Thomas left three days ago because we were running low on food. He was going to Salt Lake City. It should have only been a day trip. And the day after he left, a helicopter came down. I got in the cellar, and two people came in. I think they were DRI. They didn't find me, obviously, but when I came back out later they'd taken everything of any value. Every scrap of food and snacks that were left." He swallowed hard. "I don't know why Thomas isn't back yet. H-he's probably hiding somewhere or . . . or he's helping someone. He'll be back soon."

Oh, no. We all looked around at each other, sharing similar expressions.

"No," J.D. said, stubbornly lifting his chin. "Stop looking at each other like that. He's not . . . he's not *anything*. He's fine."

"You should come with us," Remy said softly. Her cheeks were red and chapped.

J.D. shook his head. "I have to stay here and wait for him."

"Listen, man," Matt said. "We understand—all of us had to leave people—but it's not safe for you to be out here alone—"

"I'm not leaving." His voice was firm and final. "If you tell me where you're going, maybe he and I can meet you there. Eventually."

"Can't do that," Tex said.

J.D. exhaled. "Oh well, then." He tried to sound nonchalant, but his expressive face and gestures gave away his worry, and my soul hurt for him.

"I'll stay with you," Sean said. The room stilled.

The guy fidgeted. "You will?"

"Yeah, I will. But you have to swear you'll leave here with me when I say it's time."

J.D. looked down at his thumb nail and chewed his lip. "All right. Fine."

Sean nodded, then peered around the room as if daring us to argue. Nobody did.

A muffle cry sounded from behind Remy's hand, clutched over her mouth.

Tater bolted up straight beside her. "What's wrong?"

"It's just . . ." She sniffled. "So sweet." And wiped her eyes. Tater rolled his eyes when he realized nothing was wrong, and the rest of us tried not to laugh. Sean and J.D. squirmed in their chairs, suddenly very interested in the last of their broth.

I stood and stretched, then brought my bowl to the sink.

"I'll take first watch outside," Rylen said. He started getting his gear back on, tightening his boot strings and wrapping his head. I watched him go and covered my arms against the blast of wintery wind that came in as he exited. Tex, feeling guilty for blasting the door, rigged up a rope to keep it closed.

Since there wasn't a ton of room in the kitchen, I offered to do all of the dishes myself. It wouldn't be hard, considering every bowl and glass was practically licked clean.

The guys and Remy sat around in the living room, sipping water.

Sean and J.D. were quietly talking in the bedroom with the door open. Sean sat on the edge of the bed, while J.D. had scooted up against the headboard, his knees pulled up. I went to mine and Remy's bags and pulled out our dirty undies. Then I put them in a small pot of boiling water.

"What are you cooking now?" Matt asked from his place on the floor.

My face heated. "Nothing. Just cleaning. Laundry."

They looked at me funny, and to my horror, Tex stood.

"Oh, my God, go sit back down." But that only made me grin as he sidled closer to peek in. I laughed and tried to shove him away, but now Mark and Matt were there too.

"Are those sasquatch holders?" Mark asked.

All at once the guys were dying laughing, leaning against counters and falling on the floor.

"What the hell is all this sasquatch shit?" Tater asked.

Remy was staring at me with wide eyes, her lips pressed together like she was trying not to laugh. "It's their stupid word for a girl's crotch," she answered so he'd drop it. "They're cavemen."

Actually, *I* had come up with the stupid word, but nobody corrected her. They were too busy trying to breathe through their laughter. Normally Tater was immature enough to laugh at stuff like that too, but he only glared at them.

I was so glad Rylen was outside. I swatted the guys away from me.

"Don't you have anything better to do than harass me? Go get your sleeping bags out or something." But I had to admit, their laughter had brightened my mood.

By the time I boiled our underwear and was hanging it in the bathroom to dry, Tater had fallen asleep on the couch, lying down with a sleeping Remy in his arms. Texas Harry, Matt, Devon, and Mark were all passed out on a layer of sleeping bags in front of them with their boots still on. It was probably only five o'clock, so it was weird to see everyone sleeping. My own eyes were heavy, and my body felt weighed with weariness.

I knew I should spread my sleeping bag and lay down in front of the fire like the others, but I wasn't ready to sleep yet. I wanted to be outside with Rylen. This was our last night before we'd get to the base, which may or may not have allies waiting for us. Or enemies. I shivered and began wrapping my head with the damp clothing I'd shed earlier when J.D. called out from the room.

"Amber, right? You're going out there?"

"Yeah. Just for a few minutes."

Sean gave me a soft grin, probably knowing why I wanted to be outside. J.D. climbed off the bed and went to a small closet.

"I know it's butt-ass-ugly—it was Thomas's mother's that she kept here—but you're welcome to it." He handed me an oversized women's coat from a hanger with a plaid scarf and wooly gray hat that looked hand knitted. A grateful smile plastered across my face.

"Seriously? Thank you! It's perfect!" He shrugged, having no idea what I would have done for this yesterday and earlier today.

I put it all on and opened the door. I pushed forward against a blast of wind to close the door as quickly as possible.

"Pepper?" Rylen called from ten feet away. "What are you doing? Whose is that?" He pointed the binoculars toward the coat. I raised my tired legs to trudge through half a foot of snow until I was at his side.

"They were Thomas's mom's," I explained.

He nodded. "What was everyone laughing about in there?"

My face warmed despite the cold. "Nothing. They were just being dirty."

"Dirty, huh?" He stared out. "What's Amber Tate's idea of dirty?"

I made an awkward chuffing sound. "I don't know." My face could officially melt all the snow around us. Just the thought of dirty talk with Rylen . . .

"Aw, I embarrassed you." He chuckled. "That's cute."

I elbowed him, but the gesture was muffled by our many layers.

We stood side by side, looking out at the wintery landscape.

The smattering of pines were flaky white, and the hills looked like smooth mounds. Snow hid every jutting rock and imperfection. Flakes drifted down lighter now, and the cloud covering wasn't as thick overhead as it had been hours ago. Some patches of sky had stars peeking out, bright and brilliant.

I marveled. "It's funny how scary the snow was earlier when we were in it, but now that there's a cabin with a fireplace it's . . ."

Rylen peered down at me. "Stunning."

"Yeah," I whispered back. "But do you think it's safe here?"

"I'm not too worried about this place since DRI already checked it out," he said. "Hopefully it's off their radar now." Yet he still peered through the binoculars, turning slowly in all directions.

I stood with him for a long time. Long enough to get cold again. I crossed my arms and took turns bending my knees to try and keep blood flowing. I tried, and failed, to blow smoke rings with my breath. I looked over to see him staring off, binoculars lowered.

"What are you thinking?" I whispered.

Air puffed from his nose and he shook his head. "Doesn't matter."

"Tell me."

He was quiet so long I thought he would refuse, and then: "I wonder if it mattered at all that I got Liv out of her village. Maybe it would have been better for her to have gone with her cousins. Maybe she'd still be alive."

My gut pinched. Of course he was thinking of her. The woman he'd tried to save. The woman he'd hoped to love someday. I wanted to tell him he'd given her a good life here in the U.S., but after learning how unfulfilling their marriage was, I didn't think it would be much comfort.

"I highly doubt she'd still be . . ." I stopped myself, feeling callous. "I mean, those small towns and villages around the world were the worst to suffer from water plagues."

He didn't respond. After a minute he simply raised the binoculars again and kept scouting. He still felt guilty. He probably still blamed himself for not bringing her with us, therefore letting her be taken to that camp and dying with my family. My parents and Abuela cared for her and I knew she liked them, but I understood what Rylen meant. She might have died happier with family members in her homeland, rather than people she'd only known for a few weeks. I wanted to tell him there'd been no way of knowing, and that he'd done nothing wrong, but they were only words.

Time passed and the wind picked up as the clouds thickened overhead again. When my teeth began to chatter, Rylen put one arm around me, pulling me close in front of him, even as he kept watch with the binoculars in his other hand.

I snuggled nearer, pressing us together to garner warmth. His sweatshirt was wet, but I still rested my face against his chest.

"You don't have to stay out here," he murmured.

"I know. But I want to."

"Well, I appreciate the company."

I lifted my face to smile at him just as he pulled the binoculars away to look down at me. We both tightened our grips, jolting to find our faces so close. I felt the warmth of his breath on my nose and cheeks. I knew his mouth would be warm. So warm. When he didn't move away, I slowly went up on my tiptoes and pressed my lips to his cheek, his scruff rough against my softness. I stayed there, my face against his. Oh, my God, what was I doing? This wasn't like holding hands. We were too close. Too intimate. His breaths puffed out faster. My hands moved up to his chest.

"Pepper . . ." I could feel his heart beating fast through his sweatshirt.

I didn't move, didn't speak. His face turned toward me the slightest bit, enough to put our lips even closer, our breaths mingling. Then he cleared his throat and turned his head away. "You should probably go in out of the cold. Get some rest."

All warmth I'd garnered slipped away as I stepped back and wrapped my arms around myself, ashamed and embarrassed. Holy shit. The guy had *just* been talking about his dead wife, and here I was, getting in his face. What was wrong with me?

"Okay," I whispered. He turned from me and rubbed his face. I trudged back into the cabin without having the guts to look at him again.

NINE

"PEPPER," CAME RYLEN'S SOFT voice. "Pep. We gotta go." When I felt his fingers rub my cheek, down to my chin, I opened my eyes. He watched me, crouched close. Sounds of people moving about quietly filled the dim space around us.

Neither of us moved for a minute. I tried to search his eyes to see if he was upset with me for being . . . I don't know . . . forward or whatever last night. But he just sort of gazed at me, like he was wondering something himself.

"Get up, Amber," Tater said gruffly from behind me. That broke the moment. I sat up, back muscles aching, and looked toward where Remy sat at the edge of the couch. One hand clutched her belly, one rubbed her eyes. Judging by the way she hunched into herself, she was feeling like shit.

"I just gave her another dose," Tater said, securing his tightly rolled sleeping bag. "And J.D. said we can take the cranberry pills."

"'Kay," I told him.

"You can use the bathroom," Sean said as I staggered to my feet. "Just bring a glass of water to pour down to make it flush."

It turned out my body needed most of what it took in, because I hardly urinated. I put on clean underwear, two new trash bags on my legs, and warm clothes that had dried in front of the fire. My muscles were extremely stiff and sore, and damn it, I was hungry again. Nobody asked for more ramen, and J.D. didn't offer. I couldn't blame him. A deal was a deal, after all.

I really wanted to boil some water to wash my hair, but there wasn't time now. The guys were itching to get back out there. I pressed Remy's clean sasquatch holders into her hands, along with two new trash bags, and she got up to dress too.

"We've got about a foot out there now," Matt said, looking out the window. "This is gonna suck ass."

"A foot?" I practically yelled. It snowed another six inches over night? My heart began a sickening acceleration at the thought of being out in that.

"We'll be all right," Rylen promised. "Just ten or twelve miles to go."

I gaped. That was a lot!

"Ten miles?" J.D. asked. "There's nothing within ten miles of here except . . . *oh*. I thought it was closed." A light bulb seemed to go off in his head as he imagined the Army base. Rylen gave an apologetic look to the room.

"Have you seen anything going in or out of there?" Texas Harry asked him, now that the cat was out of the bag.

J.D. shook his head. "Nothing. But then again, I've been stuck in here for, like, two weeks, so I haven't seen anything. Not exactly near any major roads."

Texas Harry nodded. "All right. Everyone say their good-byes and gear up."

I didn't expect to get emotional when I hugged Sean good-bye, and J.D. too, but these days you never knew if, or when, you'd see people again. I felt weepy and depressed for numerous reasons as I layered up, eternally grateful for the new winter stuff, though I pulled the warm hat down over Remy's head instead of my own. Geez, only she could make the ugly thing look cute.

J.D. gave Remy and I another two pairs of socks to put on, too. We had to work to shove our feet into the sneakers. *We look like a pack of hobos*, I thought as we gathered together.

The only thing that kept me walking toward the door when they flung it open was knowing we'd had dinner last night, plenty of water this morning, and a good night of sleep. Because every single ounce of what we'd gotten last night was going to be needed today, and then some.

On the plus side, it was no longer snowing and we weren't being battered by brutal winds like yesterday. On the down side, Matt had underestimated. At least fifteen inches of snow covered the ground.

I had to lift my legs high and push down to break through a top crunchy layer of ice that had formed overnight, and it was soft and fluffy underneath. I stared down at it with each step. My sneakers were coated in white, and so heavy. I moved behind the guys so I could walk where they'd trampled already.

Hours of drudgery passed. I couldn't feel my feet or hands, my ears or nose, then my legs or arms. The guys grunted with effort, and nobody called cadences. Cloud cover kept us from being able to keep watch of the sun's movement. I had no idea how long we'd been marching, and though it felt like we'd gone ten miles already, it could only be one. I tried not to think. Not about anything at all. Because even thought took energy that I didn't have.

"Whoa," Tall Mark called from the front. He halted and was

staring ahead with his binoculars. "What the hell is that?" My heart became a hammer in my chest as I stared out, squinting.

Texas Harry snatched the binoculars to take a look. All I could see was a dark line in the distance. Too short to be buildings. Maybe a fence of some sort?

"Solar panels," Texas Harry murmured.

"That many?" Mark asked. "It's like a field of them."

Texas Harry pressed the binoculars into Mark's chest and beamed a red-cheeked grin at the horizon. "We made it, folks."

I knew better than to let out a cheer—we needed to stay quiet—but I fell to my knees, overwhelmed by those beautiful words.

Low chuckles and back slaps floated in the air above me, and I felt Remy fall to my side, linking her arm with mine. We fell back together into the snow and hugged, laughing like maniacs. We were running on sheer glee at that point, because our energy stores were in the negative. I had no idea how we'd made it. All I knew is that I never, ever wanted to walk, march, jog, or run any length of mileage again. Not even for exercise for "fun." Give me a pilates video any day.

"Base is on the other side of those panels," Texas Harry said. "Let's wait 'till the sun drops before we move forward. There's nothing between here and there to cover us."

His words of caution settled over us as the guys sat. We huddled closely, and all of us shivered with tremors of cold and exhaustion. We'd made it here, but we really had no clue what lay beyond. The signal for allies we'd heard on the radio could be legit. Or we could be walking into a trap. Looking around, it would be a good place for a trap. Not a single place to run or hide. The darkness would be our only hope.

Truth was, if this was a trap, it was the end for us. Even if we managed to escape, we had no more food. No more water. And the winter was about to get much worse. Our tents would be no match for the snow drifts and winds.

None of those thoughts needed to be said aloud. Judging by everyone's bleak stares toward the horizon, I wasn't the only person thinking it. This was it.

I licked my dry, cracked lips and tasted blood. I pulled my frozen lip into my mouth to try and moisten it. My whole face felt like it would crack just as my lip had.

The next hour passed in a state of delirium. When it was time to stand, I literally couldn't feel my legs. I sat there, looking up at Rylen pitifully.

"I can't move," I whispered.

It took both Ry and Tater to pull me up and steady me. I wanted to cry, it hurt so bad.

"I can walk," Remy assured Tater when he tried to carry her again. At this, he backed away and her face fell at the sudden distance. I took her socked hand in mine.

The ten of us shuffled forward like undead walkers, leaving trails of dragging feet marks in the pristine snow. Matt stumbled and fell to his hands and knees under the weight of his pack, but Devon and Mark were there to hike him back up by the arms. He gave his face a hard rub and kept going.

As we approached the solar panels, it truly was a remarkable sight. Acres and acres of fields filled with dark, rectangular panels tilted upward to catch sunrays. It was amazing to think of how much energy this could supply.

Past the field of panels I could make out telltale military fencing that ran around the base: tall chain link fencing with barbed wire circling the top. The main road was in sight, along with the gates to the base. This caused us all to slow, even though no people were in sight yet. It appeared deserted except for scattered boulders and rocks. Everyone readied their weapons. I took off my sock-gloves and got grandma's gun ready in my hand. I could barely feel the handle.

We made it past the solar panels and Texas Harry motioned for us to spread out. We'd only taken about five tentative steps forward when Tater let out a loud hiss and seemed to turn into a statue. All heads whipped toward him.

"What's wrong?" Remy whispered.

"Move away from me," he said through clenched teeth.

I had no idea what was wrong, but my heart began to gallop. I grabbed Remy's arm and pulled her back from Tater by a dozen feet.

Rylen began to jog toward him, but Tater growled, still like a statue, and said, "Get. The fuck. Back." He closed his eyes and said, "My foot is on a landmine."

TEN

NO. THE CRUELTY OF it made me nearly scream into the frozen, dark air.

Remy's hand slapped over her mouth, both of us watching in disbelief. I held her tight as Rylen took careful, tentative steps away from Tater. We looked down at Tater's left boot, which was flush to the ground in a hole of snow. If what I knew about landmines was correct, the slightest movement of his foot would set it off.

"Everyone watch the ground!" Texas Harry called down the line. They moved stealthy and quietly back toward us, kicking snow to scan the ground in the small bit of moon and star light.

I couldn't think straight. I wanted to bend over and dry heave until my stomach turned inside out. Words. I had to form words. "W-what can we do?" I asked.

Remy had gone into a stillness that freaked me out. She watched him, like her own movement might affect him.

"Stay still, Jacob," she said. "We'll help you. We'll find a way."

Tater's eyes were still closed, frozen in the exact pose he'd been in when he must have felt the click underfoot. If it weren't for the severe clenching of his jaw, I'd think he looked calm. Tater had always favored Mom in his appearance, but right now his fierce, controlled look was such a Dad expression. I took three deep breaths to thwart my panic.

"Tater, hang on," I said, looking to Texas Harry. "Can't we switch out the weight of his foot with a rock or something?" I had zero idea what I was talking about. It was probably something I'd seen in a movie, but I couldn't let myself believe there was nothing we could do.

"Doesn't work that way," he said. "Best we can do is yank him by a rope and hope he only loses a leg, not his life."

Oh, my God.

Remy sucked in a breath and clasped her hands together under her chin, whispering under her breath. "Please don't take him." Matt dropped his pack and went to her side. "It's okay," she said, when he tried to comfort her. "He'll be okay." She sounded crazed in her confidence. "Right, Amber?"

My thoughts were spinning, and her words forced me to shove away my bout of alarm. Tater was in trouble. *Screw you, universe, you're not getting my brother, too.*

"Right," I said, licking my lips. We had to act. Now. "Who has a rope? Let's do it." I was so afraid he was going to move or pass out and end up dead. Maybe if we could all yank the rope fast enough and hard enough . . .

"I've got one," New York Josh said. And just as he laid down his weapon and started to open his pack, a series of distant *clicks* sounded, and we all stilled.

"Drop your weapons!" shouted a male voice.

We spun and it took a second for my eyes to comprehend. One of the boulders had opened, like it was on a hinge, and a man in full desert camo stood there pointing an assault rifle.

Down the line, all of the rocks and boulders were cracked open with people staring out, guns aimed at us.

"Well, I'll be," Texas Harry whispered as he bent to the ground and settled his gun at his feet, kicking it with a puff of snow. I slowly bent at the waist, hand shaking, and placed my gun down. The others did the same.

"Hands on your heads!" The man yelled, taking a step toward us. We obeyed. All except for my brother, who hadn't moved an inch.

"I said hands on your head!" he yelled again, this time directing it at Tater.

"He can't!" I said in a shaking voice. "He's on a landmine. Please," I pleaded. "Don't make him move."

"It's not a landmine," the man said.

Tater's jaw rocked from side to side, his only movement. "Is that right?" he challenged. "Then why don't you come stand real close while I step off it."

The man pointed his rifle and took a step forward. "Put your fucking hands on your head."

I held my breath as Tater slowly raised his arms and linked them on top of his head without moving the lower half of his body.

"Now, if you all do exactly as I say, this will be quick and painless." The guy sounded as young as we were, and his directions had a militaristic, choppy tone to them. "You have no less than twenty guns aimed at you this very moment. You will not move a muscle as your weapons are taken, and your bodies are examined." *Bodies are examined?* "If one of you moves or attempts to fight, every one of you will be killed on the spot. No hesitation."

When nobody said anything or moved, several of the men Army-crawled out from the cracks of their fake boulders and quickly snatched up the guns at our feet. Then they started pulling up coats and sweatshirts, untucking shirts and looking at the sides of everyone's torsos, beneath their arms.

What they hell were they looking for on our skin?

When the guy got to me I held my breath so long I almost fainted. Just like the others, he yanked my shirts and sweatshirt up, flashed a light on my sides and ran a hand over my upper waist. The heat of his hand on my cold skin made me shiver. He checked my other side and then moved on to Remy.

Then the guys jogged over to the leader and faced him.

"All clear, sir."

He gave them a nod. "At ease." The men moved to stand beside him, their guns hoisted and ready, but no longer pointed at us.

"What brings y'all out here in this fine weather?" the man asked.

"We came to sing Christmas carols," Texas Harry said.

The man almost grinned. "Little late for that. Tell me your business or you can freeze your asses off out here all night."

This time it was Ry who spoke up. "We heard a radio comm for Dugway Proving Ground. So here we are. You working for the DRI, or what?"

Now the guy really did grin. "I'm sure you can understand, but we're a little untrusting these days. You all need to be questioned before you get any answers."

"Will this questioning be indoors?" I asked. "Because that would really be nice."

The guy's eyes landed on me for the first time, and then traveled to Remy, before he gave a nod. "Follow me." DRI or not, I nearly fainted at the thought of warmth.

"Wait," Rylen called. He pointed at Tater. "What the hell is he standing on, if not a landmine?" Oh, crap, Tater! My brother was still like a statue with his hands on his head.

"Ah, that." The guy nodded. "It's like a doorbell." He walked forward and stood two feet in front of Tater. "Step off."

My heart pounded. Even with the guy standing so closely, I worried it might be a trick.

It took ten seconds for Tater to work up the nerve. When Tater jumped forward, flying past the guy like a freaking cartoon character, I couldn't help but laugh with relief, and I wasn't alone. Remy and I both ran to Tater and tackle hugged him. He managed to stay on his feet as we squeezed him.

I breathed through the lump in my throat. Relief made tears press against my eyes. *No more crying.* Instead, I punched Tater's arm weakly. "God, you scared the shit out of me and you weren't even in danger!"

"Good to know you care, *peque.*" *Little sis.* He sounded as weak as I did.

"All right," said the leader. "That's enough. Single file. Hands on your heads. Break rank and you die. Let's move."

Soldiers in camo lined us on each side as we followed him into the gates, closing them behind us, and marched us down stone steps into what looked like a bomb shelter hidden in the ground. Heat hit us almost immediately in the darkness, stinging my face, and I let out a breathy sound at the same time as Remy. We might be walking to our doom, but at least we would die warm.

ELEVEN

WE WALKED STRAIGHT DOWN a dim, narrow hallway. Our gaits were stiff, still frozen, and my extremities hurt as the thawing process began. The sudden quiet and warmth made my entire body tingle. We passed several doors as we were marched along, and then we abruptly stopped. Remy was trembling beside me. I wanted to feel her forehead, but I was afraid to move.

"We require your cooperation at all times. Everyone here is armed, and we do not take chances. You are to be interviewed separately. No talking until you get in your rooms."

I shared worried looks with Tater and Rylen, but they gave me nods. These guys did not feel like DRI. They felt like military—safe. But it was so hard to trust. I didn't want to be separated. As we were pulled along, guys from our group were led into rooms and immediately shut in. I wondered how long this would take. How long until we could earn ourselves food and water. How long until we could find out if they had any meds here? How long until we could pass out?

I whispered to Remy, "Make sure you tell them you're sick."

"No talking!" the guy in front shouted. My insides jumped. How did he hear that?

Within the span of another minute they pulled Remy into a room, and she sent me a tired look over her shoulder. Tater watched grimly as the door shut with a *click* behind her. He was taken into the next room. Then my upper arm was grasped by the soldier behind me, and I was pulled through a door. With one backward glance I caught a serious look from Rylen; a look of strength before the door closed and I was left alone.

The room was tiny, and I was surprised to see it was an exam room. It had a small medical bed with a single chair and cabinet. On the counter under the cabinet were glass jars of cotton balls and swabs. I stepped forward and put my hand on the cabinet door, but a mechanical *whir* sounded behind me. I spun to see a video camera in the corner, and I dropped my hand. Damn it. Curiosity burned from the inside, but I sat in the chair and let out a huff.

My whole body hurt, and sitting there, I could do nothing but feel every ache. I shivered as my frozen parts slowly, painfully, came back to life.

After a while I got too warm, so I stripped off Rylen's dirt-crusted sweatpants. My skinny jeans felt stiff and gross. The plastic underneath stuck to my legs, itching from the salty sweat trapped in the folds. Thankfully there was no mirror in the room, because my face felt dry, cracked, and filthy as I untwined the shirt I'd used as a scarf from around my neck. I stared at the bed with its pristine white paper cover over a blue pleather cushion. So much time passed, that I climbed up on it. More time passed, so I laid down. A groan of comfort escaped me as I let my eyes shut for just a minute.

Just a minute . . .

The *click* of the door opening was like a gunshot in my ears.

I woke from a dead sleep with a scream, nearly falling off the bed in my flailing confusion.

"Whoa," said a man.

I pressed a hand to my chest as I looked up at him. He was in Army BDUs—battle dress uniform—of faded green camo with black boots that could use a shine. But his hair was pristinely cut in a buzz. He looked like he was in his late-thirties. Stern face. Behind him was a much shorter, stockier man, also in BDUs. They threw out some seriously intense vibes.

"What is your name?" the man in front asked.

"Am—" It came out scratchy, so I cleared my throat. "Amber Tate."

He stood in front of me, feet spread, arms crossed. "I'm sure you're tired and hungry, Amber Tate."

"Yes." Oh, God, food . . .

"First, tell me your story."

So I did. I told him about my family, where we were from, my parents' jobs, my job, Tater, Remy, and Rylen. I told him how my grandparents and parents were killed, but I skimmed over the details of our disobedience to the DRI. Just in case. He didn't miss that fact.

"And why weren't you on that bus with your parents?"

I cleared my throat and looked at my cracked hands. "We were, um, at our old high school, so we found this room where we used to go, and we were just talking when they took everyone out . . . they missed us."

Wow, I sounded lame in my half-truth. His stern face said he wasn't buying it.

"Is that right? Seeing as how they told you they wanted to move everyone for your own protection, seems like you would've wanted to be on that bus with your family. To be taken to safety."

I gave a small shrug. "Yeah . . ." I ran my fingernails down my jeans and stared at the lines they made.

"Look at me, Miss Tate. And answer me." I looked up and my mouth went dry when he asked, "Why did you directly disobey the DRI? I require the complete truth from you. If your father was Army, he would've taught you the value of honesty and bravery, am I right?"

Yes. My eyes filled with moisture at the thought of Dad. Would he trust this guy? Would he be honest with him? I wanted to be a good judge of character. I was scared of the DRI, but if these guys were with them, I was going to die anyway. So I pictured Dad and Mom in my mind and I nodded.

"We didn't trust the DRI." My voice shook as the truth tumbled out of me. "We wanted to get our parents away from them too, but we were too late."

The man's stern voice did not soften. "Why didn't you trust them?"

"I don't know. At first, something just felt off. And then their regulations became so inflexible that they were killing everyone who disobeyed. Good people. They killed my grandfather, an old man, right in our living room because he defied them!"

A hot tear slid down my face and I swiped it away angrily.

"What would you say if I told you I was DRI?"

I gritted my teeth and my stomach soured. Was he for real? Was he one of them? If so, I was so screwed that it didn't matter what I said next. So I said what I wanted to, trying not to cry. "I would ask you why. Why you killed my family? Why you bombed entire towns of good, hard working people?" I clamped my teeth against the urge to rail.

He watched me carefully. "And what if my response was that those people, your family, were no longer useful to us?"

Not useful? My healthy, upstanding parents? My Abuela who could cook better than anyone I knew? "Then I would say *fuck you!*" I snarled.

The man didn't even flinch. After a moment of watching me trying to catch my breath, he let out a deep chuckle that became a laugh and a genuine smile. He stuck out his hand. "Welcome to Dugway Proving Ground, Amber Tate. The U.S. Army is glad to have you."

What? My skin turned hot then cold with a flush of fear and anger turning to relief. I put my hand in his and shook my head, letting out a breathy laugh. "You scared me."

"That was the point. For what it's worth, you didn't look scared to me. You're just the kind of person we need around here." He released my hand and clapped my shoulder. "I'm First Sergeant Grandstone, but everyone calls me Dog Balls. This is Puppy Nuts." He hitched a thumb at the guy behind him. They kept straight faces, so I forced myself to do the same.

"Hi, thanks. And I was wondering about my friend, Remy. She's—"

"Sick," said Dog Balls . . . er, First Sergeant. "She's being cared for."

A smile practically broke my face, and I had to press my hands to my cheeks. "Thank you." Could it be true? We were safe and they had meds for Remy? I couldn't stop smiling. Then I blurted, "My dad was a First Sergeant. Top." Top was the nickname, but you sort of had to earn the right to call a First Sergeant that.

He nodded. "I know. Let's get some food into you and give you a tour of the compound while your quarters are being readied." Food? Quarters? Freaking yes! "For now, you can wash up at this sink."

I stared at the sink. My heart pounded. It had been a long time since I used faucet water.

"It's safe," he assured me, then he left me alone.

I turned on the water and hissed when I put my hands under. It was warm. I washed my hands, up my forearms, and then my face and neck, cringing at the pink tinge in the water. I wanted to stick my whole head under, but forced myself to hold off. Instead, I grabbed a jar of petroleum jelly on the counter and rubbed some on my lips. The immediate relief was blissful.

In the hall, Remy stood against the wall, looking exhausted. I ran to her, hugging her tight.

She pulled a Z-pack of antibiotics out of her pocket and we both smiled weakly. Two were missing, so she'd already taken her first dose.

"Everything's going to be okay," she whispered. *For now*, a voice in my head said, but I ignored it.

One by one the guys were led out of their rooms, each breaking into grins. We all looked filthy and depleted next to the other soldiers. When Rylen came out and met my eyes, I couldn't hold back a huge smile, even though it hurt my face. Despite how frightening I must have looked, a light came on behind his dark gray eyes, like a cloud had rolled away from the sun as he soaked in my happiness. Heat spread through me, and I had to look away when Tater approached.

They took us into a sparse meeting room with a long black table and folding chairs. Then they brought in a pitcher of water, glasses, and a tray of sandwiches. We dove at the tray like a pack of wolves on a venison carcass. I'd devoured half of my sandwich before I paused to see what it even was. It looked like a loaf of homemade white bread with tuna salad and spinach. Fresh spinach? Did they grow it here?

My stomach constricted and I pressed a hand to it, feeling dizzy. I had to slow down on the eating and take smaller bites. I sipped my water and met the eyes of the other guys around the table. Exhaustion was clear on everyone's gaunt faces, despite their smiles. We'd been left alone.

"This is legit, right?" I whispered. The guys all quieted and looked at me, then each other.

"I think so," Tater said.

"Yeah," Rylen agreed. The others nodded. Most of them had already finished their sandwiches and waters, and were eyeing the empty tray.

"Now we need to find out what their plan is," Texas Harry said. "Are they just surviving, or do they plan to take action?"

We all nodded. It wasn't enough to simply live anymore.

The door opened and Dog Balls stood there looking serious. He saw that we were done eating and motioned toward the hall. "Right this way."

I guess trust only went so far, because we were flanked by armed soldiers during the tour, and we were told we could get our own weapons back "in a couple days." We had to prove ourselves, and I couldn't blame them for being cautious, though I hated feeling vulnerable.

The tour took over an hour. It would have been much faster but we had a million questions and we were dragging ass.

Dugway was a small Army base that specialized in biological warfare. The solar panel field had been up before the war began—that's what they were calling it: The War—but they were taking full advantage of it for their electricity, which was necessary since the entire compound was underground without nature's light. The aboveground base was now abandoned after the DRI shut it down, like every other base. But the enemy didn't know about the underground compound. Not even most of the soldiers who'd worked at Dugway had known about it.

"So, why is it here?" I'd asked as we passed through the kitchen area. "Why the secrets?"

Dog Balls gave me a sly grin. "Perhaps as a precaution."

Hm. Not exactly an answer. All our guys narrowed their eyes, probably wondering what the full story was there, just like I was. Because judging by the looks of the halls and kitchen decorum, this compound had been around since the nineteen seventies.

I peered around the kitchen area and asked, "Where did you get the spinach?"

He nodded in appreciation at the question. "Aboveground we have a greenhouse. We send people up at night to work it and harvest. Nobody goes aboveground in daylight except a handful of watchmen and scouts." I nodded.

We came to a commons room sort of area, larger than any other room we'd been in, and sunken further into the ground to make the ceiling higher than the halls and small rooms. This room had long rows of cafeteria-style tables and benches on one side, and on the other side were couches and tables. Three guys and a girl playing cards looked up at us as we passed. First Sergeant gave them a nod and promised to introduce us to everyone in the morning.

They watched us as we passed, and we watched them back. Some of them wore their BDU pants with white T-shirts, but one of the guys was in jeans. The girl was in boots, black pants, and a black tank top. She looked tall and slender with icy light blue eyes that didn't miss a thing. Her brown hair was short in back and angled down longer around her face in the front, where it turned blond. Her eyes stayed on Rylen for way longer than necessary. He noticed and gave her a nod of greeting before looking away. Weird.

We stopped at the far edge of the room in front of a large, steel door.

"Now, here's where things got tricky," First Sergeant said. "We've got one hundred twenty-nine people here—one thirty-eight including you all—and there wasn't enough room in the compound to house everyone. As you can imagine, it was tight quarters in here that first week until we knew we had to do something. Thankfully we have some handy troops who were able to dig a tunnel from here out to the Army hotel, about half a mile from here."

Every eyebrow in our group went up, and First Sergeant chuckled. "Yep. It took twelve days. They just finished last week. Now we have full access to the Army hotel, which appears stranded from the outside. All windows and doors have been shut and boarded."

"Wait," Remy said. "We're staying in a hotel?" Her cheeks seemed to get color for the first time in days. First Sergeant gave her a nod and a grin. We all smiled, because the idea of it was pure luxury.

"Now then. Each person is allowed five minutes of shower time per day. You'll find that the lobby of the hotel is where most of the socializing happens. This room is where we eat and break from work. Each person has a daily job. We'll figure out something tomorrow for each of you. I assume none of you is opposed to work."

"No, sir," we chimed. He nodded and turned to the steel door. When he pried it open, an earthy scent blasted us. Inside was a tunnel, literally carved into the dirt, about seven feet high and six feet wide. And it was pitch black.

"Oh, my gosh," Remy whispered.

"That's half a mile long?" Devon asked. "Y'all walk that every day?" His voice sounded wary, but it was his face that gave away his fear. His eyes had gotten huge.

"What's wrong, Big D?" Texas Harry asked. "You don't like tight spots?"

Several guys chuckled, and Devon grinned, shaking his head. "Not when it's half a damn mile long."

First Sergeant handed him a flashlight. "It's secure, Sergeant. Our engineers are solid. Let's go, unless you want to sleep in a chair in here."

Devon looked at the chairs like they might not be a bad option as we began to pile into the dirt hole in the wall. I followed behind Rylen, grasping his shirt. He reached back for my hand and I reached back for Remy's hand. I wasn't normally claustrophobic, but this was a daunting tunnel. All was quiet but the echo of our feet, and Devon's occasional whispers to baby Jesus.

Just when it felt like the tunnel might never end, the flashlight reflected off steel, and First Sergeant was pushing open a door. We spilled out into a basement laundry room that smelled heavenly, like it actually got used on a regular basis.

"Each person gets a day of the week to do laundry, and we recommend combining your clothes with another's to fill up the washers. We will flog anyone's ass who wastes water around here."

Point taken. And I'd never been more happy at the thought of doing laundry in a machine versus a pot.

First Sergeant clicked off his flashlight, and Devon did the same, blanketing us in darkness. "Watch your step. The stairwells use minimum light."

We continued to follow as he walked up a flight of concrete stairs from the basement to the first floor, until we spilled into a dimly lit hotel hall.

"This floor's got the lobby, gym, some meeting areas, and rooms." He stopped in front of a room marked GYM and opened the door. It was medium sized. A man was running on a treadmill while another two lifted weights. My eyes scanned several machines and a space with mats before the door closed again. "For those who work out, you'll be allowed one half scoop of protein powder with water per day that you work out thirty minutes or more. Everything is heavily rationed here."

The guys nodded appreciatively.

Next we followed him to the second floor. "We only have three rooms in a row together. I assume you guys wanted to be nearby, not spread out. One is a king, so I'm giving that to the ladies. We've only got twenty-four women in the compound, now twenty-six, and I expect all my men to treat them with respect."

"Yes, sir," came a chorus from the guys in the rear.

First Sergeant turned, handing Remy two keys. "Get some rest. Breakfast is at eight-hundred." Eight o'clock AM, military time. "Someone will be ready at oh-nine-hundred to talk with each of you about your jobs. Feel better, Missy."

"Thank you," Remy said.

"Sir," New York Josh said, "Is it okay to use our five minutes of shower time tonight?"

First Sergeant chuckled. "We're all hoping you do, Sergeant."

"Hooah," Josh said with a laugh, rubbing his hands together. A tingle of pure joy shot through my body and I felt light enough to fly. I was going to get this dried blood out of my hair!

He gave a key to Tater and New York Josh, and then he left us. The hall was quiet and none of us moved.

"This is weird," I said. Almost too good to be true.

"How 'bout for once you don't worry," Texas Harry joked. I shot him a bird and he laughed.

I went forward and hugged him, letting him rock me back and forth before releasing me. Remy and I went around to each guy, hugging them, thankfulness all around. I noticed Tater pulled away from her quickly and didn't look at her. His hug with me was half-hearted as well. I needed to get him alone and talk with him tomorrow.

I ended with Ry, feeling his cheek rest on the top of my head. "You all right?" he asked. I nodded into his chest. After what we'd been through, this was like a dream. This much goodness couldn't possibly last, but I'd take it and enjoy it for however long we had.

TWELVE

REMY AND I WERE new people the next morning, clean, hydrated, and rested, but my legs. Good God, my legs were so sore. The bed had been heaven, and I could have stayed in it all day if Tater hadn't knocked on the door to wake us.

Remy had woken with a fever during the night, but it was much lower. My cheekbone was still lightly bruised where I'd been hit, but the swelling was gone, and my lips were mostly healed. All in all, we were a mess, but we'd be fine.

The room was unnaturally dark, making it hard to discern the actual time of day. I went to the thick curtains and pulled them back an inch to see sheet metal with wooden boards nailed along the edges. We couldn't see out, not even a sliver, therefore nobody could see in. I was really going to miss sunlight.

It was strange going out into the hall and seeing all our guys with clean shaven faces. Except Tex, who wanted to grow his. Ry's eyes looked extra blue when he ran a hand through his damp hair and gave me a small smile.

"You look good," he said to me. My face heated and before I could answer, Matt came up whistling.

"Who are these hot girls? Do we need to surround you guys with a wall of protection?"

I rolled my eyes and Remy giggled.

"You look like you're feeling better," Matt said to her. His words sounded intimately sincere there in our tight group, like they were alone. Tater crossed his arms and sniffed loudly.

"I feel better. Thank you."

He smiled down at her, and New York Josh cleared his throat. "Cut that shit out before I puke. Let's go."

At that moment, a bunch of doors on our hall opened, and people filed out. They all stopped when they saw us by the stairs. One guy even pulled out his gun and held it at his side. Remy sucked in a breath, and Rylen moved to stand in front of us.

Texas Harry stepped out and held up his hands. "We came during the night. Faced the Spanish Inquisition. Dog Balls gave us keys." He waved his room key for good measure.

The group of guys made their way over, eyeing us with special attention on Remy and I. I guess when there were four men to every woman, that was going to be natural. As long as they kept their hands to themselves, everything would be fine. We did a quick round of introductions—everyone was military except Remy and I—and we made our way down the stairs into the basement to the tunnel. I was going to have a hard time keeping track of all these Sergeants and other ranks.

The tunnel seemed much shorter this time. Maybe because I wasn't as dead on my feet. Speaking of feet, mine were painful with every step, and my muscles felt tight and shrunken. I didn't dare complain, though. I wasn't the only one walking stiffly.

"I wonder how much weight we've lost," I whispered low to Remy when the door was in sight up ahead.

"I know," she whispered back. "I've lost at least a bra size."

"That's a damn shame." Texas Harry's booming voice came from close behind us and we both jumped.

"Geez!" I hissed. "Do you have to overhear every embarrassing conversation we have?"

He chuckled. "Can't help it if I've got good ears."

"Or if you're a nosy perv," Remy said without anger, which made him chuckle harder.

Noise from the communal area spilled into the cave as we got closer. At least fifty faces, people eating and chatting, stopped to look at us as we entered. The scent of coffee wafted against my face and I grabbed Remy's arm.

"Coffee! Oh, my God, Rem! Coffee!"

"Settle down," she said. "You look like a crazy woman."

Rylen laughed, and it was the first real laugh I'd heard from him. He met my eyes and his laughter faded into something like a moment of peace that changed to guilt as he looked away.

"Sorry," he said in a low voice. "Feels wrong, you know? To laugh."

"It's not wrong," I said, but I understood how he felt. Smiles and laughter clashed with the grieving. Hurting hearts did not easily welcome happiness.

A stream of people came out of the tunnel behind us, forcing us forward.

Tater led the way along the outskirts of the sitting area and cafeteria area to the large kitchen where trays were set out beside bowls of oatmeal with raisins, scrambled eggs likely made from powdered rations, and yes . . . a huge coffee urn. I didn't see any cream, but there were packages of sugar with a sign that said *One pack per day per person*.

"Quit pushing," Remy said as I bumped my tray against hers, but she was laughing at me as I finally got to the front and made my coffee. It was light brown, not dark like I used to require it, but I would deal.

We took our trays to an empty round table and each of us groaned and made scrunched faces as we sat. Everything hurt.

"No more marathons for me, guys," I said.

Remy nodded. "In the freezing cold and snow."

"With no food or water," Matt added.

I closed my eyes, smelling my coffee before I took the first sip. Then I let the warmth touch my lips. Slightly sweet. Slightly bitter. Complete perfection.

"Do you seriously have tears in your eyes?" Tall Mark asked.

I opened my eyes and sure enough, they were watering.

"Just like Dad," Tater said softly. We made eye contact, and his face fell. I blinked the moisture away.

"Well, I hope someday I find a girl who loves me as much as you love coffee," Mark said, taking a sip of his and smiling.

"Hate to tell ya, man," Texas Harry said, "But you'll never make a chick feel *that* good."

Mark let out a false guffaw then held his cup up to me across the table. I held mine up too. Then we all raised our cups.

"Cheers new guys," said a husky female voice from behind me. "And girls."

We turned our faces up to the tall, slender girl we'd seen when we came in last night. Her stance and expression were all badass, from the oversized T-shirt knotted in the back, down to the camo pants slung low on her hips. Her blond bangs angled across her face, coming to a point beneath her opposite jaw. She looked straight at Rylen.

"We meet again, airman Fite. Sleep well?" *We meet again?* Wait, they knew each other? Something ugly clenched deep in my belly. Remy cast me a look, like she was curious too.

Ry's expression remained unfazed as he set down his glass of water and nodded. She gave a tight smile. "Good." Then she looked over our group. "I'm First Lieutenant Linette Thompson.

Finish up. I'll be giving you your jobs."

"Sure thing, officer," Texas Harry said. He grinned, but she didn't smile back. She just stood there while we quickly finished our breakfasts, which, by the way, tasted amazing and I wished we'd had time to savor it. I didn't appreciate having this officer breathing down our necks, but the others took it in stride. I guess being in the Army gave people a higher threshold for annoyances. Or taught them to fake it really well.

We took our trays into the kitchen where an older man and woman took them and washed them, using a tag-team effort. Linette turned and looked down at Remy.

"Bio background, right? You're needed in the greenhouse, which is after-dark work. You'll report Monday through Saturday at twenty-one-hundred."

Remy shot me a look of panic, I assumed at the military time.

"Nine at night," I explained, and she relaxed.

Linette looked annoyed by the disruption. "You'll need to learn military time by the end of the day, civvy or not."

I didn't care for her rude tone and apparent disdain for civilians, but Remy quickly nodded and said, "Okay. So, food production, then?"

"Affirmative."

I tried not to roll my eyes. Did she really need to lay it on so thick with the lingo?

She turned to Matt. "You'll be in the Comm room." Matt clicked his feet together and saluted. "At ease. No need to salute in here. Sergeants Depaul, Harris, and Tate?"

New York Josh, Texas Harry, and Tater stepped forward.

"You'll all be trained for perimeter guard duty. You'll rotate between day and night shifts. Sergeant Mahalchick you're on watchman duty." They all nodded. She turned to me, all seriousness. "You'll be with Captain Ward in the med unit.

He's our only doc on the premises. Actually, he's a dentist. Thankfully we don't have many med emergencies." Several of the guys chuckled.

"Airman Fite." Rylen's hands were clasped in front, his feet apart as he watched her. "Based on your background, you're needed for top secret work with Dog Balls."

His expression never changed as he heard this and gave a single nod, but the rest of us got wide eyes. Top secret? It seemed like there should be no more secrets with how things were going these days. What could they possibly be doing? Was it dangerous? Well, that was a useless thought—of course it was dangerous.

"Any questions?" She eyed us. When nobody said anything, she turned and walked away.

"You know her?" I whispered to Rylen.

He shook his head. "She questioned me yesterday."

She was his questioner when we arrived? The thought of them alone in a small room together, her in a power position over him, made me uncomfortable. I crossed my arms over my chest so he couldn't see me making fists. I knew I was being jealous, though there was no reason for it. I needed to stop.

"Whelp," Texas Harry said with a stretch. "See y'all on the flipside." Josh shot us a peace sign, tapping it to his chest. Tater saved his last glance for Remy before they left us. She looked at me, confused. He'd been hot and cold with her for days.

"You know where to go?" Rylen asked me.

I did. "I remember passing the med room in the main hall yesterday."

"All right then."

He started to walk away, and I quickly said, "Ry . . . be careful."

"Always am." He rewarded me with a soft look before going.

Remy grasped my arm and whispered, "Can you teach me

the time thing before you leave?"

"Yeah," I said. "It's basically a twenty-four hour system instead of twelve and twelve. For morning hours you turn them into hundreds instead of saying o'clock. Like, one in the morning is oh-one-hundred. Then, instead of starting back over after noon, you keep counting past twelve. So 1:00 PM is thirteen hundred. 2:00 is fourteen hundred. If it's 3:30 you say fifteen-thirty, and so on." I had no idea if I was making sense. I'd never had to explain it to anyone before.

"Oh." She looked relieved. "That's not so hard."

I nodded. "You okay?"

She was still a little paler than normal with bags under her eyes. I knew her energy had to be low. The infection was still in her system. When I peeked over her shoulder I noticed that three whole tables of guys were watching us. I let out a small sigh.

"I'll be fine," she said. "Don't worry about me. Have fun with the dentist."

"Rest when you can," I said. "And don't feel like you have to play nice with any of these guys if they start to hassle you."

She turned to see who I was talking about and quickly whipped her head back to me with huge eyes, hissing, "They're all staring!"

"I know," I said. "Please, just ignore them. Be a bitch if you have to."

I walked with her back to the kitchen so she could introduce herself to the people in charge of food production, and then I headed to the med clinic. It was two doors down from the room where I'd been questioned, but this room was bigger and had more cabinets.

A thirty-something man with an Army buzz and a white lab coat over jeans peered at me through round spectacles. He wasn't big, but he looked soft in the middle, like he hadn't done

PT—physical training—in too long.

"Miss Tate?"

"Yes, Amber Tate." I stuck out my hand and we shook.

"Captain Jerry Ward." He sighed and looked around. "It's not too busy around here, but it'll be nice not to have to be on call twenty-four-seven."

"What kind of stuff do you see?" I asked.

"Occasional sprains and strains when the guys horseplay. We had one broken arm, which was a joy, let me tell you." He looked grim. "Never had to reset a bone before. Hope I never have to again." I tried not to smile. Bones were awesome. I'd seen plenty reset.

"I have experience with that kind of stuff." I gave him a bit of my background information and his shoulders seemed to relax with relief as I spoke. It had to be stressful to be expected to do things you'd never been trained to do.

"Most of the women here are on birth control," he said. "And all our meds are kept locked up. We have a limited supply." He pointed to a single cabinet with a padlock. "This place is sanitized regularly, but if some sort of bug were to come through here, we'd be wiped out. I'm hoping they'll send a mission team next month to raid pharmacies between here and Salt Lake City."

If they weren't raided already, I thought.

He showed me where all of the supplies were and where he kept track of all of his visits. They weren't bothering with electronic records.

"How's the girl you came in with yesterday?" he asked. "Miss Haines?"

"Yes, Remy Haines. She's much better, but she should probably still be in bed." After yesterday's hike, we should have *all* still been in bed.

He sighed. "No rest for the weary anymore."

We sat there quietly for a while. It was strange to have down-time while at work. But as sore as I was, I shouldn't complain about a chance to just sit.

"Were you stationed here at Dugway when everything happened?" I asked.

His head bobbed as his eyes went somewhere far off. "Yes. There, um, had been some issues on base in the months prior, things that in retrospect should have had us all on guard, but we assumed human error."

"Like what?" I asked.

"Dugway is, *was*, a chemical and biological testing facility. There were rumors of samples going missing, being misplaced during placement transfers. And then we heard the rumors were false, that it was simple miscalculation and poor record keeping. But those rare strands ended up in water sources all over the country." He looked at me, and I felt the weight of his words as he continued.

"I got lucky. On the day all officers had been called in, First Sergeant was at my office getting his teeth cleaned. We were ordered to come straight to the Officer Unit. It was the day before D.C. was bombed. As a dentist I'm not privy to the intel of other officers, but First Sergeant worked alongside officers doing top secret clearance. You should have seen his eyes when I got that call, like it was something he'd been waiting for but hoped would never come. His face was enough to make me ignore orders and go with him, and we snagged a couple other officers on our way underground, but it was chaos. Comm shut down that day after the announcement. We couldn't even call our families.

My stomach dropped. I looked at the ring on his finger. "Your wife?"

He swallowed hard. "If I'd known, I wouldn't have come be-lowground with Top. I would have gone straight home instead.

Because those officers never made it back from that call. None of us knows where they took them or what happened. After two days belowground, some of us were panicking for our families, as you can imagine, so they let us out at dark for recon. The entire base was deserted. Every vial of chemical warfare was missing. All of the family housing had been evacuated. My wife and two sons, gone." His eyes were wet, and so were mine. "I don't know if they were taken, or if they left to find safety somewhere else, but none of us down here got to say good-bye to our families."

My throat constricted. After what I'd seen aboveground, I knew the likely fate of his family. I rubbed my palms down my jeans, trying to pull myself together.

I thought about the missing deadly strands prior to the attacks. "So, we were infiltrated by DRI long before this happened?"

He pressed his lips together. "How much has First Sergeant told you?"

"Nothing," I admitted.

He drew in a long breath and let it out slowly. "Then I suppose I shouldn't say anything more."

Frustration rose up. "We're all in this together, we should all know what's going on."

His face remained strained. "It's . . . complicated. It's a lot to take in."

I stood to face him. "I can handle it."

His eyes fluttered away from mine. "You'll find out the details soon enough. All I can say is yes. Yes, the DRI infiltrated the U.S. military long before the attacks happened. And nothing is what is seems, Miss Tate."

His eyes were spooked when he looked back at me, sending an icy finger trailing down my spine. What kind of intel could put that kind of haunted look into a man's eyes? Suddenly, I wasn't in such a hurry to find out after all.

THIRTEEN

WE WERE ALL TIRED at dinner, stuffing spaghetti into our mouths. I could hardly appreciate how good it was because my body revolted against the idea of not being vertical. I was about to fall asleep in my food like a baby in a high chair.

Remy was the most upright one at the table. I was happy to hear they'd sent her back to the room after breakfast to rest until her shift tonight. And apparently for her job she only had to work nine to midnight. She was told to help where she saw a need during the day, cleaning and whatnot.

For the first time in many days, I felt fully satisfied, like my body finally had the sustenance it needed for normal survival. Gratitude rushed through me. I never wanted to take my meals for granted again. I heaved a sigh and sat back heavily.

Rylen had been zoned out all through dinner. I wondered what he saw in his over-working mind at that moment.

"Hey, Rem," Matt said. "Want me to walk you to your shift tonight? I can hang out here 'till you're done and walk you back." He pointed to the hangout space with loveseats and chairs. Remy began to smile until Tater cut in, his voice harsh.

"I'm taking her."

Remy's eyebrows came together. "You are? Why? So you can make a point of ignoring me more than you already do?"

Matt and the rest of us looked down at our plates or to the side, anywhere but at them.

"Never mind then," Tater said, standing and grabbing his tray.

Her face pulled with guilt as he strode away. "Nobody *needs* to walk me. It's safe here."

"Well," Matt said with a shrug. "I'll be out here anyway, so just holler if you need me. My shift is at one o'clock."

She fiddled with her fork. "Oh-one-hundred?"

He held out his fist, and she bumped it. Tension still filled the table in Tater's absence. I wanted to follow him and talk to him, but he was already gone. I looked at Rylen, whose lips were pressed in a tight line.

"Do you think he's okay?" I whispered.

He shook his head. Yeah, dumb question. Negativity practically radiated off him all the time now. Remy scooted closer to me.

"I'm sorry," she said. "I shouldn't have said that to him, but it's frustrating. One minute he's acting like he cares, and the next minute it's like he's a complete stranger and wants nothing to do with me."

"I know," I told her. "He just needs time, I guess." But I wondered if time would even help. It killed me to think Tater might always be like this now, his emotions in upheaval, scared to get too close to Remy, but not wanting anyone else to get close either.

As Mark chatted up Remy, I glanced at Rylen beside me. He was lost in thought again.

"How was your day?" I asked.

"Fine," he responded robotically. "You?"

"Probably not as interesting as yours," I said.

His eyes cleared as he looked at me with probing questions, like he wondered what I knew. That look from him sent a stab of nervousness through me. I could only guess he'd learned something today that he couldn't get off his mind. What the hell was going on in this place? Nervousness rose up again, and I was too afraid to ask, even in quiet confidence. Right now I was in a state of ignorance. I knew once I found out what this big secret was, there would be no going back from it. The logical part of me wanted to know *everything*, but the emotional part wondered how much I could handle.

A blast of weariness made me slump in the seat. I could have closed my eyes, curled up, and slept right there in that noisy room.

"Come on," Rylen said to me. "I'm heading back." He cocked his head toward the side of the room with the tunnel, and I nodded gratefully.

"You want to come to the room?" I asked Remy.

She looked up at me with slightly pink cheeks. "I think I'll just stay here and hang out until my shift. Get to know people and stuff. I don't really want to go back down that tunnel until I have to."

"Okay. Night." She grabbed my dangling pinky with her own and gave it swing before turning back to Matt and Mark.

I gave all the guys a wave and followed Rylen past the common area to the tunnel. My legs were super stiff by the time we got to the hotel. I would have taken some pain meds if I wasn't restricting the ibuprofen stash to emergencies. I figured one more good night of sleep and I'd be normalish again.

"I want to see if Tater's in your room," I said.

Rylen opened his door, and sure enough, Tater was laid

back on the bed, his legs dangling from the edge. Rylen spread a hand to welcome me in.

"I can wait out here," he whispered. I handed him my key instead, and he nodded, leaving us.

I went in and Tater turned his eyes toward me without getting up.

"If you're here to yell at me—"

"I'm not," I assured him. I climbed on the bed beside him, curling up and placing my head on his chest.

In half a second his chest heaved up and he pressed his palms to his face. My own eyes burned for the pain he felt. I pulled him up and his arm went around me. I held him around the waist as he cried.

"Tater—"

"We're all going to die," he said, pulling back and roughly rubbing his face.

"Well, no shit." Usually my sarcasm could make him laugh, but not today.

"They're going to kill you. And Remy. Rylen. Eventually, they're going to—"

"*Stop.*" I grabbed his arm. "You can't do that. You can't think like that. It's not healthy, Tater. They've taken too much already; don't let them take your hope, too."

"You really have hope?" he asked skeptically.

I chewed my lip. "I have you guys, and you all give me hope. This place, these people, that gives me hope. It's not much, but it's something."

He shook his head. His face was so barren, like he'd fallen into a pit and I couldn't reach him.

"When is your next shift?" I asked.

"The morning."

I took his hand. "Promise me you'll try to get some sleep."

Without a word, he rolled to his side on the bed, staring

across the room blankly. My heart ached inside my ribcage. I pulled off his shoes and peeled off his socks. He just . . . let me. Then I kissed his head and whispered, "I love you so much."

He closed his eyes and said nothing.

I was still trembling inside when I got to my room. Ry sat on the edge of the bed. I gave him a sad shake of my head. "He's laying down. He's depressed."

He watched as I yanked off my shoes and fell face first onto the bed.

"I'll let you rest," he whispered. I felt the bed move as he stood. Suddenly the room felt really empty. How long had it been since I was alone? The feeling sort of freaked me out. Ry had the door halfway closed behind himself when I sat up and called, "Wait."

He stuck his head back in. "Yeah?"

"What are you doing now?" I asked.

"I was just going to read."

"Oh." *Don't be needy. You'll be fine in here alone.* "Okay."

"Do you . . . want me to stay?"

"If you want. I mean, I'm just going to lay down, but if you're just going to be sitting and reading anyway—"

"All right," he said gently. "Let me grab my book and check on Tater."

A flutter of happiness shot through my nervous system. Rylen was back minutes later with a huge hardback missing a cover. Something about airplane mechanics was written on the spine.

"Do you think Tater's okay to be by himself?" I asked, suddenly feeling bad for taking him away.

"Devon was just coming up, so he'll be there. And Tater's eyes were shut."

"Okay," I said. I vowed to myself to check on my brother and talk to him every day.

I went in the bathroom to change into a nightshirt and brush my hair and teeth. I'd showered both last night and this morning, so I couldn't do it again yet.

When I came back into the room Rylen was sitting on top of the covers on Remy's side, his long legs stretched out and crossed at the ankles. He was already deep into that book on his lap. He looked up and caught me staring.

"Oh, uh . . ." He glanced at the desk and chair. "I can sit over there." He started to get up.

"No! No, it's fine." I climbed into bed and slipped into the sheets, making an accidental sound of pleasure. Oh, man, my muscles were screaming with release. A full belly, a soft bed, warmth, and this man by my side. I mean, he wasn't *my* man, but he was still here, so I'd take it.

I glanced up at him drowsily from where I was snuggled down like a kangaroo in a pouch. His eyes searched my face for what felt like forever before he spoke.

"You can sleep," he said softly. "I'll be here."

He didn't have to tell me twice.

New Year's Eve came. Remy and I sat together and watched the festivities in the Lobby—mostly just dancing and mingling—without partaking in it ourselves. It was strange to see Remy on the sidelines at a party. She'd been quiet the past week, mostly chatting with the guys in her off time. But she was far from her old self. She kept a small smile on her face as she talked to them, but her body language showed she was closed off: arms crossed, keeping distance, never touching, even casually. Now and then I'd see her and Tater make eye contact, only for him to look away with a stiff coldness.

I'd tried to talk to him every day, but he wasn't always having it. He didn't open up to me again, and didn't show any emotion as he'd done that night in his room. Rylen promised he'd keep an eye on him too.

Remy and I sat side by side on a loveseat against the far wall, looking out at the hundred-plus bodies crammed in the room, young men and women of various ages and races, all with military ties. It was so much louder than usual. There wasn't much partying that went on in the bunker, that was for certain. And even now there were a ton of watch guards on duty outside. A sense of safety blanketed this place, but I think we all knew it was too good to be true. I was on my guard constantly, waiting for the moment when the DRI would find us.

Try to relax and have fun, I told myself. I sat back and exhaled.

Of course I knew where Rylen was in the room at any given time. My internal radar sensed him and followed his movement like a bonafide stalker. He sent glances my way now and then, as if checking on me. My stomach dipped each time I found his warm eyes on me, and then he'd go back to his conversations. The guys were good at meeting people. Remy and I? Not so much. And most of the women had their groups that they stuck with. Except Linette. She seemed to be friends with all of the guys. She was one of those girls who knew sports facts and loved to hunt. She made me look like a girly girl. I hated that I felt a little jealous of how she could command the attention of an entire room, and I especially despised the way she talked down to Remy.

Right now Remy was staring off, chewing her thumb nail. She used to get manicures every two weeks, and now she'd chewed them to nubs. Her hair was full of bright bounce again, but she'd lost a good bit of the voluptuousness that she'd always proudly displayed.

"Hey, Rem?" I said.

"Hm?" She still stared off.

"Want to go talk to anyone or dance?" I didn't feel like

dancing, but I'd do it for her.

"No, I'm okay." She gave me a small smile.

"What are you thinking about?"

"Actually . . ." Remy pushed her hair behind her ears, casting her eyes downward. "There's this group that meets after dinner on Mondays and Thursdays—a grief group—I was wondering if you'd go with me?"

Every ounce of guts inside of me sank like lead to the floor. I could not think of anything worse. I'd seen that group huddled together in one of the meeting rooms, all of them looking serious about something, but I hadn't known what was going on. Yeah, I had a lot of shit in my head these days, but my method of coping had always been to keep it to myself, or occasionally confide in Mom.

Now my only choice was to stuff those feelings down deep inside of me. They were mine. My problem. No amount of talking would make them go away. And the thought of hearing everyone else's stories made me sick to my stomach. Maybe that made me a bitch, but I just wasn't good at it. Sharing and comforting. My entire job as a paramedic had centered around being with people in the most traumatic moments of their lives, and I had a way of stuffing each story deep inside of myself afterward, down into the darkness where I couldn't see it or feel it anymore.

Remy shook her head when I didn't answer. "Never mind, it's okay."

"No, I'll go with you." *Damn it.* "I'm just—you know I'm not good at that stuff. I don't know if I'll be able to talk, but I'll be there to support you."

The grateful look she gave me made me feel like the hugest jerk for not wanting to go.

"Ladies." We both turned our heads up to the voice.

"Hi, First Sergeant," I said. Remy and I both stood.

"Happy New Year," Remy told him.

He pretended to tip an invisible hat to her. My dad would have liked this guy.

"First Sergeant," I said. "I've been wondering. When do you think we'll be able to, you know . . ." My nerves suddenly skyrocketed. "Learn more about what's going on here, and what the plan is."

Remy's eyebrows went up, but First Sergeant didn't look at all surprised by my question. He linked his hands behind his back and pursed his lips in thought.

"This place is run on a need-to-know basis. Much of our intel is highly classified, and disturbing to the point that more than one soldier has lost his mind after learning everything there is to know. Not everyone can handle it."

My heart thudded and Remy's eyes now rounded with horror. My God . . . what in the actual hell was going on? I was dying to know, but also terrified. I wanted to think I could handle it, but had it really made people go insane?

"We have to know eventually," I said. I wasn't feeling brave, but the lack of knowledge made me feel vulnerable and I hated that sensation.

"True, Miss Tate. And time is of the essence." The gravity in his voice turned my stomach. "Soon. Okay?"

I swallowed and nodded.

He started to go, but turned back and said, "Oh, and ladies? Call me Top."

I grinned. He walked away and Remy was trembling as she looked at me.

"Top? Isn't that what people called your dad?"

"Yeah." My heart expanded.

"What do you think he's talking about?" she asked. "What could it be? I know we're at war. Everyone knows that. Why wouldn't a soldier be able to handle that? What more is there?

Do you think maybe the DRI is some religious cult that does disgusting things or something? I mean . . . besides bombings." Her voice dropped.

"I have no idea," I said. And I really didn't. My mind was whirling a million miles an hour trying to figure out who we were fighting that had the power to do this kind of worldwide damage. I used to think it was dumb luck, that the enemy caught us all off guard and we never had time to defend ourselves before millions were wiped out. But who *were* the enemy? All of the DRI I'd met seemed like normal-looking people who could've been from nearly anywhere, though their personalities were severely lacking.

Now that I thought about it, I couldn't quite place what race most of them were. All of the DRI had attractive attributes, as far as fit bodies and symmetric faces, nice, thick hair. But thinking about their facial features—they weren't quite white or Hispanic or black or Asian. Their eyes weren't quite round or slanted. Their skin was olive toned or creamy tanned. Their lips were perfectly full, their noses somewhere between narrow and wide. What a weird coincidence that not a single one of the ones I'd met had distinctive nationality traits.

"What's wrong?" Remy asked. I must have been scrunching my face.

I shook my head. "I don't know."

My attention was spear-headed at the sight of Linette passing us with a cigarette in her fingers, walking that sure, sultry walk of hers, straight to Rylen and Tater. My jaw clenched. Remy followed my gaze and groaned. Linette and the guys chatted comfortably. I, however, watched in complete discomfort. I needed to stop letting her get to me. Jealousy was the worst feeling. I hated it.

"Should we go over there?" I asked.

"No," Remy whispered sadly. "Tater needs some positive

attention right now, even if it's from her. And you don't have to worry about Rylen. His mind is always on bigger things."

Yeah, I told myself. Bigger things. Okay. No problem.

"And do you really not care that she's talking to Tater?" I asked.

"Me and Jacob talked last night after my shift." She watched him as she said it. "We're both too messed up right now to have anything. We'll just keep hurting each other."

"You can have *something*," I said. "It doesn't have to be romantic."

"Yeah," she replied. "But I have a hard time being just friends with a guy when I like him."

"So, you like him." I nudged her and she nudged me back.

"You know I do. And I can't handle the emotions right now."

I nodded.

A loud voice from the other side of the room shouted, making me jump, but after a second I realized he was counting down.

"*Fourteen . . . thirteen . . . twelve . . .*" And everyone joined in. I hadn't realized it was almost midnight already.

My first instinct was to move to our friends across the room, but Linette was literally hip-to-hip with Rylen as she counted down, punching the air with each number. He stood with one hand in his pocket, the other holding his cup of water, not smiling or counting, but *not moving away from her*. His eyes scanned the room and found me.

I felt myself freeze as the air stuck in my lungs and I stared.

"*Two . . . one! Happy New Year!*"

In seeming slow motion, Linette turned to Ry, her cigarette raised, and kissed him right on the lips. It was only a second, not even long enough for tongue or anything big, but it was enough to make me press my hand to my stomach as the worst case of green monster in history tore through my body, shredding me in a fury.

Rylen's eyes focused on her with surprise, but she just gave him a sly smile before slinking over to Tater and hugging him. Rylen found my eyes again through the crowd, my heart pounding, pounding, pounding.

I couldn't do this again. I couldn't. I wouldn't.

"Did she really just kiss him?" Remy asked.

As Linette made her way around my group of guys, hugging them, sometimes pecking them on the lips, and then clobbering Tall Mark when he grabbed her ass, I moved toward them, possessiveness rearing its wild head.

"Amber . . ." Remy's voice held warning. "What are you doing?" She followed behind me as I sewed a path through the crowd. By the time I got to the other side, Linette had moved to another group, greeting them just as happily.

I tapped her shoulder and she turned to me, her head pulling back in surprise. I must have looked unfriendly, because she snubbed out her cigarette and crossed her arms.

"Can I help you, Tate?" She had to raise her voice in the super loud room.

"Yeah," I told her. "Stay away from Rylen." Oh, my God. I couldn't believe I'd just said that.

Her eyes narrowed to fighting slits. I felt Remy behind me, her hand clutching the fabric of the back of my shirt, like she was prepared to pull me away.

"Who? Airman Fite? And why should I do that? Oh, right. You're like his sister or something. Well, he's a big boy. No need to protect him."

"I'm *not* his sister," I snarled. "His wife died one week ago. He's still grieving!"

She slanted her face closer to mine. "I know his story better than you think I do. He spilled his guts when I questioned him. He needed to get it all out, and I let him." She swished her long bangs out of her eyes and focused on me with precision. "None of us is guaranteed a full life anymore. Every one of us is mourning someone, and we don't have years to get over it. Sometimes the best way to heal is to move on. Now, if you'll excuse me."

She turned her back to my face and I stepped away, almost knocking Remy over. She pulled me away.

"I can't believe you just did that," Remy hissed. "You just totally gave her ammunition against you, you know that, right?" She faced me, crossing her arms. "Now she's going to hate you and go after Rylen with all she's got. You need to hurry and go after him yourself!"

My jaw fell open.

"I meant what I said!" I told her. "It's disrespectful to 'go after' him right now. She doesn't know him like I do. If he hooks up with someone this soon after Livia's death, he *will* feel guilty. That's how he works."

"Well, Linette is not going to stop, regardless of how he works. So either you have to trust that he will make the right decision and turn her down, which no guy I know would do, or you have to step in and claim him once and for all."

I swallowed hard as moisture filled my face. "He told her . . ." I took a deep breath that rattled my chest. "He told her I'm like a sister."

It would always be the thing that held me back. The thorn in my side. That fear of rejection—of ruining the sweet relationship we had by trying for something more if there was a possibility he didn't see me the way I saw him.

"There you guys are!" Matt grabbed Remy and picked her up off her feet, spinning her and making her squeal. "Happy New Year!"

I felt a hand on my shoulder and turned to see Texas Harry's bearded smile. I hugged him, and passed out hugs to all the other guys, ending with my brother. His hug was weak. I cleared my throat and let him go. He was glaring at Remy and Matt as they talked.

"How's it going at work?" I asked. "Out there at night?"

He shrugged. "Fine, I guess. Not much to see but snow." Yeah, he wasn't interested in talking. He kept glancing at Remy.

"You can talk to her," I said.

"She's busy. And it's better if we don't."

"Why? It's okay to care, Tater—"

"No," he cut me off. "It's not." His jaw set. Stubborn ass.

I looked around for Rylen, who was nowhere.

"Where's Ry?" I asked.

"Tired, I guess. Gotta work early, so he went back to the room." I followed Tater's eyes to where he was watching Remy approach us.

I looked at the far wall, and sure enough Rylen was disappearing through the lobby door. A knife of disappointment planted itself in my navel. He'd left without a good-night or a New Year greeting. I couldn't help but think the kiss had something to do with it. It probably rattled him. My entire body itched to go.

"Happy New Year, Jacob," Remy said softly.

"Yeah," he said. Tater scratched the back of his head. When he didn't reach to hug her, the two of them stood there awkwardly, both looking . . . sad.

"I'm gonna go back to the room," I said.

Remy sighed. "I think I'll go too."

"Night." Tater turned away from us.

Remy followed me through the crowd. When we got up to our floor, she inclined her chin toward the guys' room. Rylen would be in there alone.

My heart, which had begun to accelerate, was racing now. I shook out my hands and walked slowly to his door. Remy gave me a good-luck smile and disappeared into our room. I let out five nervous breaths before working up the nerve to knock.

It took half a minute for Rylen to open the door. He was in boxers. That's it. And it did nothing to slow my heart or breathing. I tore my eyes up from his waistline, over the pepper tattoo on his pec, and to his face.

"Hey, Pep." He shifted to the side. "You okay? Let me just . . . uh . . ." He glanced behind him and the absolute worst thought struck me.

"Are you alone?" I whispered.

"Yeah." He cocked his head at the fear in my voice. "I'm just gonna grab some pants. Come on in." Oh, thank God.

I put my hand on the door but gave him a second to go inside. When I went in, he was stepping into track pants. I leaned against the wall, more nervous than I'd ever been, as he sat on the edge of the bed, legs wide, and gazed up at me.

"What's up?" he asked. He sounded tired.

Say it. Say something. "I know it's not my place to say this, but . . . I think you should be careful of Linette."

He grasped the back of his neck and stared at the floor. "Nothing is going on with us—"

"I know." I rubbed my face. Every word I'd planned to say sprinted out of my mind and left me standing there completely empty headed. Awkward, expectant silence stretched between us.

"I don't think she understands or respects where you're at, and what you need."

He looked at me then, with such suffering in his gaze, and asked, "Where am I, Pepper? What do I need?"

The anguish there made me nearly slide to the floor. I closed my eyes against the wave of emotions and forced myself to speak.

"I think you're hurting and you need time."

His eyes dropped to the floor again, silent. Was I wrong? Was Linette right, that he needed her affections to help him heal?

No, damn it! I could not stand the thought of her ever touching him again like she'd done tonight. I was going to comfort him my own damn self. I took shaky steps forward until I stood between his knees. I saw his shoulders hitch with an intake of air, but he didn't raise his head. I moved forward until his forehead was pressing against my stomach. Then I slid my hands around the back of his head and held him there.

Before I could be self-conscious or wonder if I was forcing affection on him, his arms went around my back and pulled me closer, his face pressing against my abdomen. I felt his warm breaths through the cotton of my shirt as we held one another in the most tender moment I'd ever experienced with him. I knew in the way he pressed into me, pulling me tighter, his fingers rubbing into my skin through the shirt, that this was exactly what he needed.

I held him, and held him longer, and felt him, and though it might not have been sexual to him, it was the most sensual moment of my life. My entire body went taut and heated at the feel of his hands on my back. His face pressed to me. My hands in his hair.

Footsteps and voices coming up the hall shattered the delicate moment. I moved away from him at the sound of the door unlocking with a click. New York Josh was talking loudly about the Yankee's baseball record; apparently Tater had tried to bust his balls. They both stopped and shut up when they saw us—Rylen still sitting on the edge of the bed, and me now standing a couple feet away.

Josh hitched a thumb over his shoulder. "You need us to find another room?"

"What?" Rylen said. "Man, shut the fuck up."

"All right." Josh winked at me. "My bad."

Tater looked between the two of us.

"I was just leaving," I said. "Good night." I gave them an awkward wave and shot a glance at Rylen as I turned to leave. His elbows rested on his knees, watching me go, the heat of his gaze steaming me from the inside out.

FOURTEEN

MY PALMS WERE SWEATING when Remy and I joined the circle and took seats in metal folding chairs. *Please, please, please let this be over quickly, and don't make me talk.*

Eleven of us sat around the circle, five women and six men, including the Army chaplain leading the grief group. He smiled pleasantly. "Most of us know each other, but I like to start with everyone introducing themselves."

Cue internal groaning.

When it got to Remy she said, "I'm Remy Haines, twenty-one, from just north of Las Vegas. I was in my final year of college, majoring in biology when the war started. My dad was a pastor. My mom was in real estate. I wanted to be a middle-school teacher."

Everyone nodded appreciatively and then chuckled when the chaplain said, "Ah, brave girl."

And then it was my turn. "Um, hi, I'm Amber Tate. From the same town as Remy—we're best friends from high school.

I'm a paramedic. And, um, I'm not really here to share, to be honest. I'm here to support Remy."

The chaplain watched me with deep eyes that seemed to prod at my emotions and say, *"I know you're hurting."* I swallowed and looked away, gripping the sides of the chair I sat in. This hour was going to suck.

As people began telling their stories, most of them crying or getting teary-eyed, I had to build the familiar shield around my heart that I used to build for my job. It didn't always work. Some stories were able to climb that barrier or somehow slip through cracks, and it made me physically ill. I tried not to listen now to the pain in people's voices, thick with emotion. I tried not to process their words . . .

"My wife was visiting her hometown in Washington. We never got in touch, and I don't know if she's still alive . . ."

"I watched my four-year-old son and six-year-old daughter die from something in the water. Their tiny bodies were bloated with sores—I tried everything to keep them comfortable, but they cried and cried . . ."

"My husband ran outside during a curfew when he saw DRI dragging our neighbor out of his home. I watched through the window as they shot him four times. My husband, and then the neighbor. I screamed into a pillow. I screamed until I didn't have a voice anymore . . ."

Remy freely cried with the others as the stories were told. I continued to grip the sides of the chair, leaning slightly forward, my head down so I didn't have to see the anguished faces. I struggled to breathe evenly, my jaw clenching so hard my head pounded.

When it got to Remy and her story poured out, I let myself go completely numb, because her story wasn't just her own. Her story intertwined with mine. And I didn't want to relive it. I had to keep it in the past, far away from me, where it couldn't slice me open. I let her words become a distant *whomping* in my head. By the end of her testimony, I was rocking forward and backward, chanting *No, no, no, no, no* in my mind.

I startled when a gentle voice said, "Amber?" The chaplain. I kept my head down and shook it. "This is a safe place to speak, Amber." I shook it harder. He left me alone, but Remy's soft hand pried mine off the seat and we linked our fingers together. I couldn't look at her, but I held tight.

When he dismissed us, I shot out of that chair like a bullet and didn't stop until I was far enough away that nobody would bother chasing me to try and small talk. I paced by a loveseat in the lobby until Remy was done saying good-bye to the others, and then I moved straight to the door, speed-walking. I was a quarter of the way down the hall when Remy grasped my hand from behind and pulled me to a stop.

I turned and our arms went straight around one another. We hugged and I breathed in the clean smell of her hair.

"I'm sorry, Remy. I just can't—"

"I know," she said. "It's okay."

When we both calmed down enough, we let go and continued the rest of the way to our room.

I was deep asleep when I heard a shout from the next room, followed by running feet and swift knocks at our door. I was already shoving my legs out of the bed, sprinting to rip the door open. Rylen stood there, shirtless and breathless.

"Tater," is all he said, and we both ran, Remy close behind.

Tater was on the floor of their room, breathing hard through groans, his hands gripping the curls at the top of his head. Panic attack? I fell to his side, suddenly aware with all the eyes on me that I was only wearing a T-shirt and panties. I shoved that thought aside and focused on my brother.

"Careful," Josh murmured. "He clocked the shit out of me."

Keeping a small distance, I called Tater's name and put a gentle hand on his forearm. He jumped and swung out his arm, but I leaned back, ready for it. His eyes were slits, like he was still half sleeping.

"Tater, it's me. It's Amber." And then throwing all caution to the wind, I wrapped him in my arms, holding him despite his thrashing and repeating, "Shh, Tater, *esta bien*. You're okay. I'm here, *guero*."

"Amb?" It came out as a sob and he clutched his arms around me. "You were dead. H-he shot you."

"It was just a dream," I murmured. "I'm safe. I'm right here."

He was breathing hard and I felt his heart racing in his chest. I pulled back and looked at his eyes. "Take a deep breath," I told him. He closed his eyes and obeyed. His entire demeanor changed, calming, and he opened his eyes again. When he focused on me, I gave him a small smile of encouragement, but on the inside, I was wrecked. He gave me a weary nod.

"Just a dream," he whispered.

It had been more than a dream. It was PTSD. I was certain now. All the pieces fell together.

We stood on shaky legs, and I tugged my shirt down.

"Sorry," Tater said to everyone, running a nervous hand through his hair.

Josh waved it off. "You can kiss my shiner in the morning."

Tater huffed an embarrassed sound through his nose.

I turned to go. Remy had been behind me, watching in worried silence. She nodded and left. Rylen held the door.

"Thank you," he whispered when I got to him.

"I'm glad you got me," I whispered back.

I left, feeling my thighs on display, and promising myself that from now on I would sleep with bottoms on. Just in case.

FIFTEEN

REMY AND I LIKED to hit the gym mid-morning when most of the people in the compound were leaving for their day shift or resting after breakfast from being on the night shift. Problem was, our group of guys figured out our schedule and liked to join us. We'd come to the conclusion that they enjoyed our company and couldn't keep away. Truth be told, after all we'd been through, we were kind of attached. I felt more comfortable with them near me, and I think they felt the same.

So, I ran on the treadmill with Remy on the stair-climber beside me. After ten minutes of getting our heart rates up, we would drop to the floor for squats, lunges, sit-ups and push-ups. But for now we watched as the guys worked. Tex spotted Devon at the weight bench. He could probably press mine and Remy's weight combined. Tater, Josh, Mark, Matt, and Rylen were doing a race that I fully enjoyed watching: one hundred jumping jacks, twenty-five pushups, fifty squats, and fifty sit-ups.

Seeing as how we faced them, I could watch with no fear of

repercussion. The guys were shirtless, except Matt, who was still self-conscious of his physique, though he looked fine to me. Rylen, Tater, and Josh all sported six packs these days, but poor Mark had a hard time putting weight onto his thin, tall frame.

I watched Rylen unabashedly, sweat running down my neck. I tried, and failed, not to look at his crotch during jumping jacks, but holy wow. I couldn't peek at Remy because she always made me laugh. Let's just say none of the guys packed jock straps for the trip. I watched as Rylen dropped into a perfect plank for his pushups, moving up and down as if he weighed nothing, and never losing form as his arms worked: forearms, biceps, and triceps on full display. Squats were especially fun—bulging thighs and muscular butts. By that point they were sweating nicely. And the grunts always sounded really dirty to me. I would never admit to a soul how much I enjoyed gym time.

"That was only forty-nine squats, Matt, you cheater!" Remy called.

"Aw, damn it!" He jumped back up from where he'd fallen on the mat, did one more squat with a grimace, and fell back down to do sit-ups. The other guys were trying not to laugh as they curled up and down as fast as they could.

Tater splayed outward with a groan a split second before Rylen with Josh close behind. Mark finished two seconds later, and Matt was a full ten seconds behind.

"Jacob wins!" Remy called.

I clapped, trying not to lose my concentration on the treadmill.

The guys stood, breathing hard and sweating. Rylen looked over, and I swear his eyes superglued themselves to my bouncing chest. Not as bouncy as Remy's, but still. He didn't stare very long, but it was long enough to make my nipples tighten and my core flush with heat. I swallowed hard and hit the Stop button. His smoky gaze flashed up to my face and he turned away, grabbing a towel and rubbing it roughly over his face and neck. I glanced at Remy to see if she'd noticed, but she was too busy watching Tater run a hand through his dark, damp waves.

My heart rate was way higher than it needed to be as Remy and I went to the other side of the mat and began our lunges. *He's a guy,* I thought as my thigh muscles and calves burned. *A lonely guy who glanced at your boobs. It could've been anyone's boobs. It just happened to be yours.*

Yeah, but Remy's are more impressive, and he wasn't looking at hers.

"What's wrong?" Remy asked through panting breaths.

Oh, shit, she'd moved on to squats and I was just standing there.

"Nothing." I joined her in squatting, holding my hands out.

I nearly fell on my ass when the gym door burst open. Top let out a huge sigh as he took us in.

"There you all are."

Every one of us jumped to attention, alert.

"What's up, Top?" Tex asked.

"The two men you told us about—J.D. Frazer and Lieutenant Wilcott?"

My heart leapt in my chest and we all moved forward.

"They're here?" Devon asked.

"Yes. Can I get one of you to verify their identity?"

"I'll go," Rylen said.

"Me too," said Devon.

Screw that. We were all going.

Our entire sweaty crew ran down the halls and tunnel, bursting into the common room and to the entry hall. When we found Sean and J.D. in the meeting room, it was like a family reunion. Hugs and laughter, like we'd known each other forever, not just a few days.

"Guess that's an affirmative," Top said. "I'll give you all

some time." He closed the door behind himself.

Seeing the tired, shrunken, shivering bodies of Sean and J.D. made me recall the day we'd arrived. J.D. wrapped his arms around himself and peered around.

"What made you come?" Rylen asked. "Did something happen?"

"Ran out of ramen," Sean said. He sent a nervous look to J.D., who did not chuckle along with the others.

"No word from your partner?" I guessed.

J.D. swallowed hard. "We could have given it another day, or at least left a note."

Sean's jaw clenched, but he said nothing. I had a feeling it had been a fight to get him out of that cabin.

"Well, you're as safe as you're going to get here," Remy said. "And there's food."

Both of their eyes lit up at this.

J.D. peered around at us, his eyes catching on all of the six packs on display. "Why are you all so sweaty?"

"We were at the gym," Remy said with a laugh.

His arms tightened. "This place gives me the creeps. I have a feeling it's not homo friendly."

"Nobody's gonna mess with you," Tex said with absolute authority.

J.D. gave him a bashful, grateful smile. "Okay."

Josh laughed. "These bastards will be glad you're not more dudes they have to compete with for the handful of females."

J.D. snorted, but he seemed to loosen up a tiny bit.

"I'll get you guys something to eat," Remy said. When she opened the door, Top came in.

"You should all go, except Miss Tate." He looked at me. "I'll need you to take their vitals after they've been questioned."

J.D. blanched and reached for Sean's hand.

"It's all right," Sean assured him.

We filed from the room. I turned toward the exam room and felt fingers take hold of mine. I spun to Rylen, who held my hand.

He gave me a small smile. "This is good, right?"

Him holding my hand? My mouth bobbed open and closed.

"Them making it here?" he clarified.

"Oh, yes. It's awesome."

He squeezed my hand before releasing me and heading down the hall. I stared at his tapered waist. The tribal tattoos that spiked down the backs of his arms. His perfectly toned calves under the nylon shorts. Why did he have to be so hot? And confusing?

I went into the exam room, but didn't have to wait long for J.D. to enter. They'd already partially debriefed him before Top came to get us. J.D.'s vitals were all normal, but he was underweight and still cold.

"Did Remy feed you?"

"Yes. Thank you."

"No problem. Few days of food and some warm showers and you'll be feeling more like yourself. They'll want to find a job for you. What did you do before?"

"Modeling. Some commercials."

Oh. Well, crap.

"And I was a hairdresser."

My eyes lit up. "They totally need someone here to give cuts. There's a barber set that gets passed around, but half the guys have butchered hair when they try to do it themselves, so they end up shaving it short. It wouldn't be glamorous work, but it would be helpful."

"Sure. I'll do whatever." He swallowed hard. "I asked them if Thomas had shown up here, but he hasn't. I don't know where he could be. He's smart. Very capable. Not gullible like me; he's the one who knew there was a problem with the DRI.

He saved us."

He was still trying to talk himself into believing Thomas was safe somewhere, but I knew better. I was certain J.D. would also come to that conclusion in his own time.

"It's not safe out there for anyone," I said. "I'm so sorry, J.D. I can't imagine how awful it is not to know."

He closed his eyes. "Sometimes I can't handle it. I close my eyes and pretend I'm home reading Riley Hart and sipping a Manhattan. And then Sean comes along and makes me insane, trying to keep it real and toughen me up. He's a bear, you know."

I smiled. "He comes across very kind and gentle to me. And cute."

J.D. opened his eyes just to roll them at me. "I'd never date a ginger. Too bossy. Even one who's sort of auburn-ish, not that orangey-red."

"These are strange times," I told him. "Never say never."

SIXTEEN

WEEKS PASSED IN A blur of work, gym, eating just enough to sustain us, and sleeping. An unspoken tension settled over everyone in the New Year. We had no idea what the DRI were up to, that I knew of, and the waiting stirred up a sense of unrest. I was antsy with the slowness of my job and being stuck underground, so I volunteered to help with other things.

"You're welcome to help with cleaning," Top told me after dinner one night. I must have glared because he chuckled. "What did you have in mind, Miss Tate?"

I craved fresh air and sunlight, but I knew sunshine was out of the question. "Maybe I could help on night watch? Up in the tower with Sergeant Mahalchick?"

"It's freezing aboveground, you know."

Oh, yeah. Freaking winter. Remy said it was evil out there. She got to be in the outdoors for the two seconds it took to run from the bunker doors to the greenhouse during her shifts. It was funny to see her dressed in all black with her hair shoved in a black beanie like a bank robber or something.

I shrugged like it wouldn't bother me. Like I was Elsa.

He chewed the inside of his lip and exhaled. "Even the watchers have to be armed and ready to defend, if necessary."

"I know how to shoot, sir. I work well under pressure. Ask my brother."

He thought a moment longer. "I'll see if I can work you into a rotation for training, but you'll still need to be on call for med emergencies."

"Of course," I said. "Thank you!" Day. Made.

Four days later I was bundled up so well I was sweating as I followed Mark to the meeting point at the bunker entrance we originally came in. It was ten at night. The biggest, heaviest gun I'd ever held was slung over my shoulder. I'd spent the last three days learning how to use it. Mark and I met in the hall with two other guys in winter gear who nodded at us, and didn't seem surprised by my presence. I followed them up the concrete steps at the end of the hall with Mark behind me, and I felt nervous when the door sentry lifted open the hatch to the outdoors.

A crunching sound came as the guys marched out. Ice had formed in places where snow had been trampled down and refrozen. I paused as I stared out at the white blanket covering everything. It appeared serene and peaceful. Mark gave me a gentle nudge from behind and I moved forward. The effort it took to lift my legs with each step reminded me of our trek to the base, and I was glad we didn't have to go far.

I followed them to the watch tower where we climbed the stairs. My face was cold, but the rest of me stayed warm. The watch tower was dark and old, slightly creaky. I marveled when I faced the long window and saw everything. The hotel outside of the base, which appeared completely dark and deserted, the greenhouse inside the base, the never-ending acres of solar panels, the nearby bumps where "rocks" sat with soldiers hiding within—all softened by layers of snow. The moon and starlight shone off the surface like white glass that stretched as far as the eye could see.

I wanted to say something about how pretty it was, but the others seemed used to it, so I admired in silence. They showed me the ropes: the walkie-talkies, the button to push to send an alert to Top, and the major alert button that would sound an alarm to the entire bunker. And then we each took a side of the square room and stationed ourselves to look out with binoculars. It took all my self-control not to stare up at the sky, which I hadn't seen in so long. I missed it. Instead, I kept a steady watch on the horizon where the dark sky met the land. After ten minutes I was thoroughly bored, which shamed me because it was an important job. It was only the fear that DRI could come into sight at any moment that kept my eyes focused.

And focused.

And still focused.

After four hours I started to shiver a little. There was no heat in the tower.

"Amber, right?" said one of the guys.

I blinked and swung my head, but he was staring intently out his window through his binoculars, so I turned back to my own and refocused. "Yeah?"

"Got your eye on any of the guys here?"

Mark snorted and my face flushed with heat. Actually, I'd met most everyone in the bunker by now, and several soldiers had tried to hit on me, but obviously I wasn't having that.

"Noneya," I said, making all three of them laugh.

And now that the silence had been broken, an easy banter began, with each of us intently watching our zones. It helped pass the time and settle my jitters. Being out here was cool, but it was impossible not to feel exposed and vulnerable. Just the thought of a fighter jet whizzing over that horizon toward us gave me the chills.

"How about your friend, Remy?" the other guy asked.

"She's sort of taking a break from everything," I told him.

"Why?" he asked.

I really didn't want to talk about it. After the grief counseling sessions I'd attended, I avoided talking serious at any cost.

"She lost her parents on Christmas, and . . . you know. She needs time. Next subject."

"Damn," he whispered. "Sucks."

That killed the convo for a while. Finally we saw movement at the bunker entrance; the next shift of watchers were coming out. I breathed a sigh of relief, but kept my eyes on the horizon until the next group entered the room to relieve us.

I gulped down as much fresh, cold air as I could and watched the stars as I tramped through the crunching snow, back into the depths of our safe haven.

SEVENTEEN

THE FOUR OF US watchers came out of the long hall into the common room, all of us stripping off the top layers of our uniforms. We were laughing about something when a far door opened—the door where secret things happened and nobody was allowed to enter—and my stomach flipped at the sight of Rylen and Linette walking out together, heads close in conversation.

What were they doing at four in the morning? I thought Rylen only worked the day shift. Seeing as we were the only people in the room, they stopped and saw us right away. Linette wore a nice expression until her eyes landed on me and hardened.

Back at ya.

When Ry saw me he completely froze, and his face went through the strangest series of emotions: surprise, fear, nervousness, and then he seemed to shake from his reverie and plaster a stoic look in the place of the dire ones. Seriously, what had they been doing? I was shaking and it had nothing to do with the cold clinging to me.

The guys greeted Rylen and Linette, then headed toward the tunnel. Linette gave Rylen a good-bye nod and seemed to communicate something heavy through her eyes. He inclined his head in return, and she left us, not looking at me again.

Rylen's jaw rocked side-to-side as he waited for Linette to be gone. Then he looked at me and I felt myself rock back on my heels from the heaviness of his gaze.

"What's going on?" I asked. I couldn't keep the fear from my voice.

He swallowed. His mouth didn't open to speak. He blinked and peered around as if trying to make sense of his surroundings. I stepped toward him.

"Rylen, what's wrong? You're scaring me. Is it . . . is it Linette?"

"No." His voice sounded dry, and I watched as he swallowed again. "Just work stuff." Then it hit me.

"They told you things, didn't they? Intel?"

When he stared at me without responding, I knew I was right. His freaked out expression made me feel woozy.

"What is it? Tell me."

"I can't," he whispered. And suddenly he moved forward and I was in his arms, and he was hugging me so solidly I could barely breathe. I had never seen Rylen this freaked out. It scared me.

"Tonight." Even that single word sounded like he struggled to get it out.

"You'll tell me tonight?"

Rylen pulled back, ran a hand over his hair. "Everyone who doesn't know will learn tonight." I wanted to push for more, but something held me back. Perhaps the fact that he was too out of sorts to talk, or that I was terrified to hear whatever had shaken him this hard. For whatever reason, I didn't question him further. I just led us to the tunnel, turned on my flashlight, and got us to our rooms. He waited for me to get inside mine before going in his.

Remy snored lightly and snuggled up to me, but I couldn't fall asleep. I could only toss and turn as my blood buzzed with fear of the unknown.

Rylen came to get me from the med room at the end of my half-day evening shift. He said nothing, and our steps were heavy as he led me to the forbidden door. Our group of eleven stood there waiting, along with about twenty others. The quiet tension as we waited for First Sergeant to get us was unnerving. Remy stood so close, our arms were fused. I think we all knew that whatever news we were about to learn would change us forever.

"Here comes Dog Balls," Tater said in a hushed tone.

We turned to face Top as he approached from the tunnel with Linette and Puppy Nuts by his side. He said nothing as he opened the door and ushered us in, down a narrow hall.

We filed into a large room that reminded me of a college classroom: rows of long, thin tables with a screen at the front of the room. I sat with Remy on one side and Rylen on the other. Once everyone was seated, First Sergeant came to the front. Puppy Nuts and Linette stood to the side. She leaned against a desk with her arms crossed.

First Sergeant cleared his throat and began. "Thank you all for your patience. I know you've all been curious about what we're facing, and I wanted to gather as much information as possible before we debriefed the entire staff. We now know as much as we possibly can, and I don't want to hold off another day on educating you about what we're up against.

"This war did not begin on Thanksgiving. Plans for the

attacks on Thanksgiving began over a hundred years ago." The hairs on my arms stood at attention as a chill swept over me. A hundred years? He began to pace back and forth as he spoke, his hands behind his back.

"Though our communications with worldwide entities has been sparse the past six weeks, what we'd gathered is that the situation is the same across the globe. Every major country's government and military were infiltrated. And while we've been studying this enemy for over one hundred years now, we were unaware of their power and outreach. Their numbers. They blended in and eluded us." He paused. "We severely underestimated them, and we failed."

Texas Harry shook his head and asked, "Who, sir?" Who are they?"

First Sergeant seemed to steel himself, and it looked like he'd begun to sweat at his hairline. "They're called the Baelese. From a place called Bael."

My mind scoured through old geography lessons, but I couldn't place it.

"Sir," said New York Josh. "There's no country by that name."

"It's not a country." Top appeared pale now, and even Linette shifted uncomfortably as he said the next words. "It's a planet."

EIGHTEEN

MURMURS, EVEN LAUGHTER, ROSE up in the room.

Remy whispered, "What? That's not funny."

I looked at Rylen. He remained very still, his eyes deadly serious. My heart gave a resounding pound that turned into a *whomping* in my head.

"Aliens, sir?" Texas Harry said with half amusement.

First Sergeant did not crack a smile. He just stared Texas Harry down, as if daring him to take it as a joke.

"Wait," said Tater. "You're fucking serious? Excuse my language, sir, but you're for real?"

"This is not a laughing matter." His face was so grave. As were the faces of Puppy Nuts and Linette. "You'd all do well to adjust your minds as quickly as possible to this new reality. The Baelese race has wiped out nearly the entire human population, and they plan to use the remaining humans as slaves."

"What the fuck?" J.D. let out a high-pitched whisper behind me, and I turned to see Sean moved closer to him, though his own face had gone pale enough to hide his freckles.

I looked at Remy with a hand pressed over her mouth and she began to shake violently as her eyes slid to mine.

"It's okay," I whispered stupidly. Of course it wasn't okay. But the assuredness of my voice made her nod, like she was clinging to the mantra. *It's okay, it's okay . . .*

Tater looked past her to me, and our eyes locked in a moment of mutual holy-shitness. He rubbed a hand roughly down his face. Whispered curses of disbelief rose up like a morbid chorus around us, echoing in my still-*whomping* ears.

Oh, my God. I grabbed the side edges of my seat and tried to control my breathing. This had to be a nightmare. I glanced at Rylen again and when he looked back I remembered the haunting he'd experienced last night, how shaken he'd been. And I knew from the steady look in his eyes that this was all true. Every unbelievable word.

"There has to be a mistake, right?" Remy whispered. The mantra must have stopped working, because her breaths were loud now, like she might hyperventilate. I took her hand and we squeezed hard.

"Sir, how do we *know* this?" asked a man in the back.

"Let me tell you all we've learned, and then I'll explain how we learned it."

Top gave Linette a nod and she typed something into a computer next to her. The screen lit up with a map of the universe.

"Bael," he explained, "is the equivalent of Earth in a bordering galaxy, but much smaller." He pointed to a tiny cluster of light. "The Canis Major Dwarf Galaxy, like ours, has one sun, but their galaxy is ancient in comparison to ours. Their sun is in the process of expanding from a yellow dwarf to a red giant, meaning rising temperatures that will make their planet uninhabitable. It will eventually engulf their planet's orbit, and so they seek a new home."

The entire room gaped, frozen, with rapt attention as each horrifying word was spoken.

"The Baelese are exceedingly intelligent creatures, and Bael is much like Earth in its temperatures and air properties. Their symbiotic relationship between plant and animal mirrors ours, taking in oxygen, giving off carbon dioxide, and vice versa. Their race is highly evolved, having been around millennias longer than ours. We've learned that, in their known history, they suffered a meteor shower that wiped out most of their population. The way they came back from it was to unite all survivors under one government, learning one language, which eventually led to one race. We believe that is their plan for Earth."

I felt like a giant had reached inside me and was crushing my intestines and lungs with a tight fist. Top's words were scientific. Logical. And yet my mind severely rebelled against it. Not a single person spoke or moved.

"The superior technologies and communications of Bael are unprecedented. They were able to track and find the nearest planet compatible to their beings, and scout us long before we'd invented motor vehicles or begun probing the first layers of our atmosphere. They left their planet in stages, dying and reproducing en route. They abducted a handful of humans in order to study our ways as they continued to orbit our planet and plan. One quarter of their population arrived here on Earth over a hundred years ago in a series of four landings. We believe another batch arrived in rural Nevada shortly before Thanksgiving."

Dear God, it *was* true. "Yes," I whispered, then put my free, trembling hand over my mouth. I remembered the woman whose stress I'd treated at her house—the case that was taken over by FBI—she hadn't been insane. They'd really landed in her field. Was it possible that so much of what we thought was crazy alien lore was true?

The people around me stared at me, but I couldn't speak.

"More will come this summer," Top said. "And the rest will arrive every year or two for the next fifty years."

"This is fucking crazy," someone whispered with terror from behind me.

My sentiments exactly. Because even if we could somehow miraculously overcome the ones who were here, we were being steadily invaded. It would be an ongoing war. Mine and Remy's interlocked hands shook with tremors, and her breathing was still audibly loud and fast.

On her other side, Tater muttered, "No. Fuck that." He pushed his seat back and bent his head forward as he grasped the table, like he might pass out. Remy put her hand on his back. Several people stood and began to pace behind us, grabbing their heads, trying to make sense of the insensible.

Top never stopped to coddle us. "As far as our intelligence, two spacecraft from Bael have been secured during this one hundred years. The one from 1947 in Roswell was originally kept at Nellis Air Force Base, but seeing as how Area 51 became public knowledge and fascination, the entire enterprise was quietly moved up here to Dugway. Much of it was a mystery that our brightest scientists and engineers could not figure out. It wasn't until the landing in Nevada two months ago that FBI were able to capture one of their males and we began to finally get answers. Unfortunately, by the time we figured out how to make him talk, it was too late. The bombs were dropped."

They captured one? My brain was going to explode. This man who I respected, who was not prone to jokes, was standing before us talking about UFOs and aliens in that matter-of-fact tone. Aliens! *Aliens are real!* My brain. My brain. Oh, my God, I felt light headed. I so badly wanted to reject all of this information.

A shuffle of quick footsteps in the back had us all turning to see one of the guys running for the door, followed by his retching sounds in the hall. Remy squeezed my hand and I pulled her chair closer to me. I caught Tater's gaze over her shoulder and he looked as lost and sick as I felt.

When the guy shuffled back in, pallid and sweaty, Top continued.

"Physical attributes of the Baelese. At one time they were much like humans, but over time their bodies evolved to be more efficient. Most of them are born with three or four arms." Yes! The woman who'd witnessed the landing said this! First Sergeant surged forward, ignoring our gasps and whispers. "That is why we checked each of you when you arrived. Apparently the Baelese who infiltrated human ranks surgically removed their extra arms, though the scarring is so minimal it's barely noticeable. Moving on. Their hair is thick and wiry. By wiry I mean you can literally shape it in your hands, smooth it down, curl it around your finger. It's weird as hell."

Remy and I shot each other shocked looks. No wonder all of the DRI women's hair always looked immaculate!

"Their skin is stronger and thicker than ours. At the cellular level, they have a type of cell wall, similar to plants here on Earth, and it makes them less susceptible to infection or minor injuries."

The medical enthusiast in me was fascinated and wished for a microscopic slideshow.

"On a cultural level, they are a matriarchal society. Their females are highly logical and driven for survival. They're the masterminds and the males are the muscle, not to mention the sperm donors. And this is where it gets really interesting."

When Linette smirked I knew we were in for something weird.

"Baelese woman are born with only five to fifteen eggs,

total. Unlike the rest of their biological makeup, their eggs do *not* have cell walls. They are extremely fragile in comparison to human eggs. For this reason, the Bael people are not able to perform any sort of 'test tube' conceptions, surrogacies, or in-vitro procedures. Also unlike humans, they cannot conceive at any given time of year. Their women are fertile only once every eighteen months. During that time, their society basically shuts down normal operation in a desperate attempt to continue the race. As far as we can tell, it is their one true downfall. And it gets better."

Remy and I leaned forward.

"They only, and I mean *only*, perform reproductive acts during this mating season." A few of the men scoffed, and First Sergeant nodded, continuing. "Because for the Baelese men, the hormones that are excreted in their bodies during this time, have a drug-like effect on them, and it is addictive."

Linette bounced her eyebrows up and down once without smiling or otherwise moving. Outright chuckles of disbelief filled the air now, and I found myself smiling at the outlandish ridiculousness of it. But Top remained dead-serious.

"I wouldn't believe it if I hadn't seen it for myself," he said.

Um . . . what? Remy sent me an *Ew!* glance. Rylen leaned back, arms crossed. He'd heard all of this already, I realized. His shell-shocked expression this morning and lack of shock now made perfect sense.

Top gave Linette a nod and she pushed another button. Dear God, what were they about to show? I braced myself.

A video began of a man with DRI appearance tied to a chair in a nondescript, dimmed room. Remy gasped and grabbed my hand. I looked closer and I could make out a third hand pinned to his side, then a fourth. A shiver raked my spine as I watched four hands wiggle to find comfort in their restraints.

"This is the Baelese man we apprehended soon after his

vessel landed in Nevada. We questioned him for two weeks and he wouldn't say a word. At first we believed he couldn't understand us."

I sucked in a breath when the video showed a hand striking out against the man's face, then the other side of his head. They were beating him. He let his head swing from one side to the other, blood dripping from his mouth, but he never spoke. As the video time-lapsed I squinted at the violence, and Remy turned her head to the side, looking away. Even as our enemy, it was hard to watch.

"So we decided to try another tactic."

The sound, which had been off before, came on with a crackle, and Linette entered the video. I went very still as I watched her stalk around him. He looked nearly dead. Honestly, if he weren't being held upright with ropes he would have been a puddle on the ground. His head hung down.

"All right now," Linette's sultry voice was a soothing purr on the video. "It's just you and I. I'm not going to hurt you." She walked behind him and placed a hand on his shoulder, trailing it across his upper back as she slowly paced, and then up into his hair. When she brought her hand up, his hair spiked straight up like it was wet.

I leaned forward more in my chair, mesmerized in a morbid way. Linette pulled a chair in front of him and ran her hand through his hair again, making a soothing sound. She was careful of his cuts and the places where blood had congealed on his head and face.

"Maybe you don't understand my words, but you understand my touch, right?"

She ran her hands slowly across his shoulders and down the outsides of his top arms, over the ropes that pressed deep into his skin. Heat crept up my neck and into my face. Remy started biting her thumbnail as she stared. It was quiet in the room, and uncomfortably intimate.

The video showed the man eventually raise his face enough to make eye contact. She gave him a grateful smile and encouraged him to relax. Still he said nothing. Her hands made it down to his wrists and she moved back, resting her palms on the tops of his strong knees. His breathing hitched as he watched her.

"I'm not going to hurt you," she told him again. And her hands moved up to his thighs. Up. Bingo. He jolted and she murmured, "Tell me your name."

In a choked voice, he said, "Marmot."

"Oh, my gosh," Remy whispered.

The video cut off and everyone stirred. The prisoner could totally understand her.

Top eyed us. "Turns out, he was fluent in English, Spanish, French, Portuguese, Russian, and German, though his dialects were a bit rusty and old-fashioned from studying intel received in the late eighteen hundreds. With a little help from First Lieutenant Thompson," he motioned to Linette, "he spilled his guts."

In my peripheral vision I could see Remy gawking with her mouth in a little round "O." Tater put a knuckle to his lips.

"Wait," Short Matt said. "Sir, are you saying . . ." Matt looked at Linette and she raised her eyebrows. He shook his head. "Never mind."

"Yes, Sergeant," Linette said in that husky, I-take-shit-from-nobody voice. "I seduced an alien for intel. Is there something you'd like to say about that?"

I fully expected him to shut up, but to my surprise he blurted, "What was it like?"

When everyone laughed, he said, "No, I mean, I'm not trying to be perverted, I just mean . . . are they, like, the same as us?"

"Anatomically," I clarified for him. Rylen shot me a look and

I shrugged, blushing. "Just helping him find the word." Again, the scientific part of my mind was darkly fascinated.

"Yes and no," Linette said. She looked at First Sergeant as if asking permission to continue, and he waved a hand as if she may as well go on. Linette took a soldier's stance, feet spread, eyes watchful and full of no nonsense.

"Their testicles are internal." This simple sentence caused a hushed guffaw to rise up. "Will you all grow the fuck up?" Her shout hushed everyone and she continued. "Their testicles are on the inside. Everything else is . . . similar enough. That's why we have to check all the males who enter the compound." She glanced around the room and her eyes landed on Rylen, then back to Top as if she were finished.

Holy freaking shit of all shits. She had *checked* him? As in, Linette saw Ry's junk? I turned to him, my eyes bulging. I know he could feel me looking, but he stared straight ahead, his arms crossed. He reached up and tugged his ear lobe. I scoffed and faced front again, crossing my own arms and grinding my teeth together.

"Any more questions?" Top stared hard at the room.

"How about the females?" Tall Mark asked. "Are they similar to human females?"

Top nodded to Linette to respond. "Biologically very similar, from what the subject told us, except the fact that they have zero urge for sex outside of mating season. We learned that sex outside of mating time is legally forbidden because it makes the men worthless. They're not permitted to have homosexual relationships or to masturbate." Sputters of shock filled the room. "And there's no hiding it. If a man in Bael has somehow activated his sexual hormones, it's like he's been hitting lines of coke or shooting up. He's out of it. Eyes rolling back, incoherent for up to two days afterward. Those who become addicted and can't get their acts together are not tolerated."

I shook my head. They sounded like a miserable race, and for a second I felt bad for them. Until I remembered they were the people who'd taken over our planet and killed my family.

"Do they kill them?" Tater asked.

"Worse," Top said. "They basically deactivate their personalities. For a thousand years they've been using an uninvasive procedure to control those who show signs of rebellion. Tiny, mechanical worms that they insert in a person's nose or ear. It makes its way to the brain and essentially imbeds like a clawed hook into the anterior portion of the frontal lobe. That part of the brain controls planning, problem-solving, organizing, behavior, emotions. Basically personality. Without that function they are robotic, receiving and acting on commands."

The hair on my arms went straight up and I had to rub them down. "Sir," I asked, "Have they been using those on humans?"

"To be honest," he responded, "our Baelese prisoner is under the impression that the Bael who took over had run out of the worms, and the two ships that landed this century were out as well. But his own ship had plenty, along with the scientists to make more. So they have them now, and I'm betting they're trying them on humans as we speak."

Nausea rolled through me. All I could do was shake my head. This was how they could make slaves of us.

"Continue with what you were saying, First Lieutenant," Top said to Linette. I tried to shake off the creeping sensation and focus.

"Okay. Ah, their gestation times for pregnancies are shorter, around six months, and during their evolution they phased out breastfeeding. The babies are mostly cared for by the younger generations of women using a type of bottle for the first several months until they can eat solids. So, basically they start going into their mating season from the ages of thirty to forty, and the girls and young men from seventeen to mating age generally care for the children. Child rearing in Bael is a communal process. Their collective civilization centers on the whole, rather than the individual. They don't have traditional family units as we know them." She looked back at First Sergeant and stepped back in front of the desk, signaling she was done.

"We have one last bit of information," First Sergeant said. "And it's important. Probably the largest obstacle we've faced, and will continue to face, when it comes to this enemy."

Worse than their superior knowledge, super bodies, freaky worms, and complete lack of compassion for individuals? I felt myself frowning as he prepared to drop this next bomb on us.

"These beings possess a mental capability that humans do not possess. They have a second brain the size of a marble in their frontal lobe area that is able to radiate mental energy outward on ultraviolet wavelengths within close range, say ten to fifteen feet." Cold sweat beaded across my skin. "This is a device for the amplification of brain waves. In this way, they are able to silently communicate with one another . . . not in words, but in moods and intentions. They're also able to push their own desired moods and intentions into another's mind."

What. The. Hell.

My hands went clammy, and if I were standing I would have passed out.

"Holy shit," Tater said. "I think they used that on me." He looked at Remy, me, and Rylen. "When Grandpa . . ." His eyes unfocused. "I had this weird urge not to get in the way."

"Yes," I whispered. Strange pieces began to fall into place— all the times I'd wanted to argue with the DRI women, but found myself feeling suddenly compliant. They'd been *in my head*. It was a violation of the worst kind. I wrapped my arms around myself, feeling disgusted, my mind spinning like a funnel around all of the memories.

First Sergeant looked at our pinched faces. "We have many

instances of soldiers here experiencing similar things during their interactions with DRI. But from what we've gathered the waves can be muffled by the use of earplugs. We have to process the waves as a sound, like . . ." He shrugged. "Like a dog whistle."

We were like dogs to them. It was all making so much sense.

"Other questions?" First Sergeant asked.

I raised my hand. I had so many. "Were all of the DRI . . . aliens?" The word felt weird in my mouth—a word that used to be something we laughed about and was now a horrifying actuality.

"From what we know, yes. And they used humans as Disaster Relief Personnel to do their dirty work, mostly people who were in dire straits and could be bribed to work for food."

"What happened to him?" a woman in the back blurted. "The, uh, *Baelese* guy you captured?"

"He is still alive, still confined and under guard."

"Where?" she asked. "Here?"

"That I cannot say."

He was here. I knew it. An alien was probably somewhere in this compound with us. A creature who could mentally manipulate us. Aliens had been in my house, at my job, and I'd looked them in the eyes, talked to them like people, even though they'd given me the creeps.

"This is a lot to take in," First Sergeant said. "And though this is a different kind of enemy, we will fight it. We are not alone, though I cannot divulge who or where our allies are. When the time comes, we will take our home back. We've been tirelessly working on plans to do just that, and I want you all to be involved." He moved to stand behind the desk and leaned his fists on the top as he looked at us. "In the time between now and this summer when their next vessels arrive, it is pivotal that we take them down. We will have to be precise.

Expedient. Soundless. We have very little time to plan, and I need every single one of you. We are the past and present, and we are the future. It's up to us."

The room was absolutely still as his words fell on us. I felt my heart pound with belief. We could do it. We *had* to.

"Go," Top said. "We'll debrief again soon. Hooah."

"*Hooah*," we all murmured.

We were silent as we shuffled out of that room, back down the hall. And as we entered the common area where people sat and chatted, I understood the look on Rylen's face when I'd seen him come out with Linette after learning the truth. Nothing felt the same. Everything that used to appear normal was now blurred. Looking around at Remy, Tater, Rylen, and all the guys I'd come to count as friends—we were all smudged around the edges. Changed. Lost. Like gravity had lifted and we couldn't quite get our feet to plant on solid ground again.

The world and everything we'd taken at face value wasn't what we thought it was. I understood how the information had made some turn to madness, because I felt very small and fragile at that moment. Like we were all standing on landmines.

NINETEEN

EACH DAY I WOKE hoping the unsettled, floating feeling would subside, but it never did. Remy had taken to crying out in the night, and her eyes unfocused throughout the day. I had a constant stomach ache, and I hated that I couldn't keep track of Rylen with our crazy schedules. I worked off and on with medical duties in the day and watch duties at night.

A month passed after learning of the aliens from Bael. A month with otherworldly strange vibes hanging over us, keeping us edgy.

At breakfast, Matt handed Remy and I paper roses from across the table.

"Aw," said Remy, smiling down at hers. "You made this?" He nodded at her.

"Thank you," I told him. The smile felt strange on my lips.

"You know today is Valentine's Day, right?" he asked.

"Is it really?" J.D. asked. "God, I always hated V-day."

"Me too," Mark said. "Blowing a whole paycheck just to

try and get laid."

"Didn't work, did it?" Tex asked, winking. "Gotta act like you don't give a shit."

"Aw, that's not true!" Remy threw her napkin at him across the table.

"Isn't it, though?" Texas Harry had a full, scraggly beard now, and it suited him. Nobody here cared if anyone shaved or kept their hair short, though many still did out of habit and respect for "old" ways.

A bizarre sensation of reminiscence filled me as everyone laughed—a longing for our old world—and I quickly shook it off. Those kinds of feelings and thoughts only hurt my psyche. Still, I kept staring at the rose, intricately folded and detailed.

"Aren't you just a romantic," Josh joked.

Matt shrugged. "Us short guys have to work extra hard."

Everyone chuckled again, and it was a nice, warming sound. I looked over at Rylen just as he looked at me, and our gazes caught, making my breath halt and my chest ache. I missed him. He wasn't even at breakfast most days.

The others must have been thinking the same thing, because Josh said, "Dude, what the hell do they have you doing back there every day?" He inclined his head toward the door in the corner. The door that gave me shivers every time I passed it.

"This and that." Rylen finished his coffee.

Texas Harry leaned in and whispered, "You met him yet?" We all knew who the *him* was, and we turned to Rylen, waiting. He'd gotten a haircut and shaved, looking fresh-faced and handsome despite the gray crescents under his eyes.

"Only seen him through glass." He leaned back in his chair and crossed his arms.

"Please tell me you get to watch him being interrogated," Texas Harry said with a dirty grin. My stomach turned.

"Ew." Remy looked at Rylen with question in her eyes.

"He's pretty much already told them everything he knows," Ry said, and I noticed that wasn't an answer. "He was intercepted before he got to see their operation on Earth. They had minimal communications on the vessel with their people here because their comm gear was partially damaged when they entered the Milky Way. We know they have a leader they call the Bahntan, and their leaders are always female."

Weird. So weird. Hearing these things made me feel like I was at a Star Wars convention, and I had to remind myself this was not play. This was very real.

Matt finished up first and left the table. I nearly groaned out loud when I saw Linette heading our way with a coffee in hand. She kicked Matt's chair closer to Rylen and sat down right next to him, not looking at any of the rest of us.

"You joining us on the run or not?" she asked him, sipping her coffee as she watched him over the brim. My permanently unsettled stomach felt like a hole was burning through it as she eyed him.

Rylen let out a breath and ran a hand over his head. "Yeah, I'm in."

I did *not* like the sound of that.

"Run?" Texas Harry asked.

Linette turned to him. "We're taking a single convoy to the outskirts of Salt Lake City for resources tomorrow. Got room for one more. You interested?"

"Hell yeah," Tex said.

Oh, my God. Rylen was leaving the compound? He was going out there? I bit my tongue against the urge to beg him to stay. I couldn't be the clingy, paranoid, non-girlfriend, sisterly person.

"All right," she told him. "I'll let Dog Balls know." Now she turned to Rylen, leaned closer, and began to murmur. He listened and nodded. The other guys stood and stretched. Remy rested her hand on my knee under the table. Linette must have felt me staring—I couldn't help myself—and she turned to me.

"Can I help you with something?"

I let out a laugh. "You're two feet away, at our breakfast table, whispering. Rude much?" Rylen swung his head toward me, as if surprised by my tone. He moved a fraction away from her.

Linette glared and I stood, grabbing my tray. Remy got up with me.

"Amber," Rylen said.

"I'll see you later," I told him.

I was seething as I dropped my tray in the kitchen.

"Why do you let her get to you?" Remy whispered to me.

"Hey," Texas Harry said from behind us. I turned to him and he nodded toward where Rylen and Linette were still sitting close, talking. "They're just talking work shit, but you ought to stake your claim before it's too late." His eyebrows rose and fell meaningfully, and my jaw clenched. He walked away, leaving me with Remy, who propped a hand on her hip and smugly said nothing. I gave my head a hard shake.

"Seriously, Amber?" she hissed. "The world's been taken over by freaking aliens and you're still scared to tell him you love him?" Her words were filled with a frustration bordering on anger.

I deflated as the ridiculousness of my fear registered. For a second, as it was all put into perspective, my personal fears were miniscule. In the scheme of things, I had no time to waste and nothing to lose. Except Ry . . .

"*Fine*," I whispered. But even that word sent a shock of trepidation through me.

She gave me a hard peck on the cheek and muttered, "You're such a brat," before walking away. *Not a brat*, I thought to myself. *A coward.*

I was not happy about the resource run. If Linette and Rylen were so integral to whatever behind-the-scenes things were going on, it seemed to me they should have sent other soldiers. It was clear that what Linette wanted, she got, and she was a thrill seeker. My jealousy of her knew no bounds.

I caught Rylen that night as he was bringing his clothes up from the laundry room. I was on my way down with mine. I may or may not have known he was doing his at that exact moment.

"Hey," I said. We stood on the landing between flights of the stairwell, both of us holding our laundry in our arms, flashlights blazing. We didn't have much. Just a couple basic outfits that we wore over and over.

"Hey, Pep. You okay?"

I hesitated. "I wish you weren't going on that run in the morning."

He paused to process this. "Don't worry about me."

My feet shifted. "Aren't you nervous?"

"Nah. I'm actually looking forward to getting out of here for a day. Feeling kind of cooped up, you know?"

"Yeah," I whispered. My heart picked up speed. I'd been planning all day what to say. I was going to ask him if we could hang out when he got back, just the two of us. But what came out instead was, "Be careful of Linette, okay?"

He gave a shrug. "She's harmless. Just a little wild, but she knows what she's doing out there. She's led all the runs."

"No, I don't mean about the run." I hiked up my drooping pile. "I don't think she, uh, respects the fact that you're in mourning . . ."

His eyes narrowed on mine until I got nervous and dropped my gaze.

"I don't get that feeling from her," he said. "She's friendly to everyone, not just me. And most of the time she's obsessing about work. Look, I know you don't like her, and I know she's rough, but she's good people."

He had no idea she had eyes for him. And for once I was glad of his cluelessness. But how would he react if, or when, she made an official move? He hadn't been with a woman in, well, months at least.

As if reading my mind, he said, "I'm not looking for that anyway." But he sounded . . . frustrated.

My jaw tightened. I wished he would have said he wasn't looking for that *from her*. How was I supposed to tell him how I felt, knowing he wasn't looking for that *at all*? I wanted to respect this, but I knew damn well Linette wouldn't.

His jaw clenched as he readjusted his stance, "And what if I was looking for that, Pepper? I'm not a saint. Would that make me so fucking terrible? Because someday—"

The door below us opened and voices echoed up the stairs. My heart was hammering and my knees freaking wobbled. Was he saying he wanted to start hooking up with girls soon? With Linette, maybe?

I held my clothes tightly as Rylen and I moved aside to let people pass. As luck would have it, Linette was in the rear of that group. Ugh, my stomach. She slugged Rylen in the arm and watched him with sultry eyes as she passed. Throwing up was a definite possibility.

"Get some rest, Airman. Big day tomorrow."

He lifted his chin in response. She flicked her eyes to me for a second and continued up.

Yeah, see, the thing about Linette was that I reluctantly admired her. I'd always thought of myself as a girl who could hang with the big dogs, but she took it to a whole other level. If she wasn't after Rylen, I'd try to make nice. But as it was, I was currently swallowing bile due to her, so no thank you on making nice.

"All right," Rylen said when we were alone again. He let out a long breath. "Just . . . forget I said that."

Not a chance. "I don't expect you to never move on. It's *her*, in particular, that I don't—crap, I don't know what I'm saying."

"You want to pick who I'm with someday?" he asked. I couldn't get a reading on his tone. His intensity was making me nervous, like he was angry or his frustration had escalated. Rylen had never been this way with me before. He moved up to the same step as me, looking down, searching my face. "'Cause what if the woman I want is not who *you'd* choose for me? What if you don't want what I want?"

My eyes burned and I swallowed moisture away. I picked through the confusion of his words and chose my own carefully. "Of course I don't think I get to pick for you, Ry. I know I have no say-so in your decisions, *believe me.*"

"What does that mean?" he asked.

"Nothing." I shook my head, my face hot. "I need to go to bed." I turned to go up, away from this conversation and the direction it had turned.

"Aren't you doing laundry?"

My face flamed. "I'll wait 'till morning." *Stupid, stupid, stupid.*

We took the stairs up and then paused in the hallway between our rooms. I had no idea what had transpired between us in the stairwell. I just knew I felt dejected.

"I'm sorry," he said. "I shouldn't have said any of that. I have a lot on my mind. It's no excuse, I know."

As embarrassed as I was, I didn't want to leave things like this, not when he was going on a dangerous mission tomorrow.

"We haven't talked in so long." I swallowed, looked down at the carpet and then back up. *Say it, Amber.* "I miss you."

He stared at the wall and I swear his muscles all relaxed as his face took on a tired expression. "I miss you too. I know our schedules have been nuts since we got here. We should all hang out when I get back tomorrow night."

All? Oh. Of course.

"What?" he asked. My face must have fallen.

"Nothing." I forced a small smile and held my dirty laundry tighter. "We should definitely hang out tomorrow when you get back. Be careful, okay? No crazy heroics."

"I'll do my best." He leaned forward and kissed my forehead, then watched me as I let myself into my room, feeling less excited than when I left it.

TWENTY

FRAYED NERVES HAD ME on edge. The convoy could only be out during sun hours because they'd be spotted too easily at night if they had to use lights. So I paced the med room all day. Now and then I stopped and tried to study. I'd taken to reading some of the dentist's medical books to teach myself things I didn't know. My training was mostly in basic emergency treatment, stabilizing people until they could get to a specialist. I usually poured over the books in my free time, but today I couldn't concentrate.

I kept looking at the clock. The convoy was due back by seventeen hundred. It was fifteen hundred now. Two more hours. A light knock on the door had me jumping as I turned.

"Just me," said Remy. "Want some company?"

"Yes." I sighed. She was just what I needed. "How's it going in the greenhouse?"

"Good. The romaine lettuce is sprouting and the next cherry tomato plant is about to ripen. We have salads in our future! Plus a ton of zucchini buds. I'm already getting together recipes.

Zucchini muffins will be awesome for breakfast."

I had to smile at her veggie enthusiasm. I wanted to tell her about my failed attempt to get Rylen to agree to alone time, but saying it out loud would leave a bitter taste in my mouth.

"So," she said. "I know the grief meetings aren't really your thing, but I've talked to Tater and he's agreed to join me."

My eyebrows shot up. "Really?"

"Yeah. I had to ask him, like, ten times. He probably agreed just to shut me up, but I think he needs it as much as me."

I nodded, feeling my chest tighten. She was right. Tater was struggling hard. He'd always worn his emotions on his sleeve and had a difficult time controlling his anger. Between watching our grandparents and parents killed, then killing a man himself, he was not himself anymore. Rylen said he had to drag him to the gym on most days.

"So, you guys are talking? Are the two of you . . . ?"

"No." She hopped up on the patient bed, rustling the paper. "I still like him and care about him, but we just can't. It's weird. Sometimes he's waiting for me when I get off shift, and we walk to our rooms together in silence. We hang out, but we don't talk. I think just being with someone you knew before helps. It's comforting. A lot of the people here don't have that."

My hands suddenly became very interesting. We were so lucky to still have each other, and I did feel guilty about all the lonely soldiers here while I was busy keeping to myself. I wasn't good at . . . people. Thank God for the Remys of the world—people who would stop and hug someone they saw crying—people who went to grief groups and actually supported others.

"Thank you for being there for him," I said.

Before she could answer, we were jarred by a buzz that I knew to be the "doorbell," and then we were on our feet at the sound of shouts coming down the entrance tunnel of the compound. My stomach swooped.

"Medic! Man down!"

My heart and innards twisted and dropped as I nearly tripped over my feet running into the hall. I pushed my personal fears aside and sudden clarity overcame me, like old days. I saw the scene clearly. A man, his boots dangling down as four others carried him. My eyes scanned the faces and saw Rylen as one of the carriers, his hands under the man's arms from behind—relief physically crashed over me and I grabbed the wall. Further scanning told me the patient was bearded.

Shit. Texas Harry. The clothing over his entire arm and torso were covered in blood.

"Oh, my gosh!" Remy said.

"Go get the dentist," I told her. "Captain Ward." I would need help.

I rushed forward to run along beside them. I didn't even have to ask for information.

"Shot in the shoulder," Linette said. "Fucking civvy bandits."

"He's lost a lot of blood," Rylen said. "We kept pressure on it this whole past hour, but he lost consciousness." I could see they'd tried to wind a bandage around the wound, but it was in an awkward area. I had to get it cleaned ASAP.

I sprinted back to the med room ahead of them and began grabbing the things I'd need: scissors, alcohol, sterilized bandages, IV needle and fluid bag.

They brought him in and hoisted his heavy body onto the table with grunts. His cheeks, normally tinted pink, were colorless like plastic. I got to work cutting off his clothing while I shouted orders.

"Ry, find his file and see what his blood type is." I pointed the scissors to the filing cabinet. "Linette, can you cut the rest of his shirt off while I get his IV ready?" She didn't immediately come forward and I looked to see her grimacing at his bloody form like she was about to puke. Great. "Never mind. Go sit in the hall," I told her. She rushed out. I didn't have time to marvel in the fact that Linette had a weakness.

"He's A positive," Rylen said.

Thankfully the dentist ran in at that moment and I thrust the scissors at him. He began to cut away the material while I got the IV line ready.

"Rem, see if anyone in the kitchen or common area is A positive. We need blood donors." She ran from the room.

After the shirt was cut, Rylen helped me yank the entire thing off his torso. His shoulder was a gory mess. I swabbed the crook of his good arm with alcohol and got the IV in him, fluids and antibiotics running. I gave his pulse a quick check. It was slow. Way too slow. I tried to keep my emotions at bay, but Tex's joking smile filled my mind and I nearly choked on a wail. I pushed it back down.

"Come on, big guy." I patted his cheek. "We've got you. Hang with us."

Captain Ward had begun cleaning the wound, and he frowned. "Bone particle."

"Get it all out," I told him.

"I've never done this."

We switched places so I could clean the wound. The bullet went clean through, but it hit bone and made a disgusting mess of things. If we could get the worst of it cleaned and closed, the muscle and bone would heal themselves over time.

"We have to get his body heat up," I said. They threw blankets over him and found a beanie hat to pull over his head and ears.

Devon and a petite woman I recognized as Linette's roommate, Shavonta, stopped in the doorway. "You need A-positive?" Devon's hand went to the top of his head, and his voice wavered. "Ah shit, Harris?"

I looked at the dentist. "Can you take blood?" He nodded and took Devon and Shavonta to the next room.

"Make it quick!" I called after them.

"What can I do?" Remy asked.

I shook my head. He really needed blood and to have his wound closed. Sewing skin was not my specialty. "Stand by his head and talk to him. Rub his chest and his other arm. We need to try to get him alert. Keep checking his pulse."

I shuffled past Ry and grabbed a sewing kit from the drawer. Poor Texas Harry was going to have a killer scar when I was finished with him. I was halfway done with the front wound when the dentist came back in with bags of blood.

"Can you take over the sewing?" I begged.

Captain Ward moved to my place and I quickly began prepping Tex for the blood infusion.

"Come on, Big Tex," Remy murmured. Her steady hands ran over his face, down his neck and to his chest, massaging the stronger muscles. "We've got you. Stay with us." She checked his pulse and moved her fingers around, pressing into his neck harder, frowning. "I can't feel anything!"

Shit! "Don't panic."

The blood was moving into him now. I reached for his pulse. Nothing. I turned and grabbed the defibrillator off the wall with a hard yank.

"Back!" I ordered. Everyone flew away from him with their hands up. I stepped onto the stool and placed the handheld paddles over their correct areas, then pressed with all my might. Texas Harry's body jolted under my hands and I heard him suck in a short breath. *Yes!*

I tossed the hand paddles to Rylen, who stored them away again while I felt for a pulse. It was back, slow, but steady. I felt my own thundering heart slowing back to normal speed.

Remy kissed his cheek and said, "Quit trying to scare us,

you big grizzly." Her voice was choked with emotion.

Within five minutes of fluids, blood, and closing wounds, I said, "I think he's stabilizing. He won't be able to do much for the next two months, though."

"He's going to be all right," Rylen said behind me. I turned and saw that he wasn't talking to any of us. Linette stood in the doorway with her arms crossed as she looked at Texas Harry. It was the first time I'd ever seen her look vulnerable. She gave a terse nod and walked away.

Rylen let out a deep breath and ran a hand over his head.

"Can you let everyone else know?" I asked him. "No visitors tonight."

He turned to go and I grabbed his arm, making him look at me. This could have so easily been him who was shot and dying. "I'm glad you're back safe. Thanks for your help."

He gave me a solemn nod and left. Remy watched with a small smile. We stayed with Texas Harry, holding his hand and talking to him while Captain Ward finished sewing him closed.

"Thank you," I told him when he finished. He looked wiped out, so I sent him on his way until his shift.

Remy pulled Texas Harry's hat off so she could smooth back his hair, finger-combing it. Then she took a damp cloth and cleaned the blood splatter from his neck, beard, and face. "Wakey, wakey," she said softly. "Time to open your eyes."

"What'll you give me if I do?" he asked in a weak, scratchy voice.

My face split in a smile and Remy laughed. She kissed him right on the mouth for five seconds and pulled away, beaming.

His eyes cracked open. "That's it?"

"Don't be greedy," Remy chided.

His eyes closed again. "Tell me the damage."

I ran through all of his injuries and the plan for healing, which hinged on him resting the arm and wearing a sling. He groaned about that.

"Don't be stubborn," I told him, "Or you'll ruin your arm and joint permanently. Right now, the most important thing is for you to rest. And I have a little something to help you with that."

I shot morphine into his drip line, and then pulled up the side rails of the bed. Captain Ward was on night duty, so he'd get to keep an eye on him. The bed was a bloody mess, but I didn't want to move him until he was more stable. I hoped Texas Harry had a high threshold for pain because there wasn't a lot of morphine or other pain meds.

Remy waited with me until the dentist came back for his shift. When we got to the common room, everyone was having dinner. They all looked over at the doorway, and cheering began, everyone clapping and whistling. What was going on? I looked around, and then people started laughing and pointing at me.

"They're cheering for you," Remy said.

"What?"

My face got hot when I realized they really were looking at me. Remy took a step away from me and I wanted to yank her back and hide behind her. I gave a small wave and rushed toward the kitchen with Remy giggling behind me at my awkwardness.

"You saved someone's life, Amb," she told me. My face was still on fire when I took a tray.

"I just did my job," I muttered. I wondered how many lives I'd saved in the past. I'd been thanked profusely by crying people, but this was different. It filled me with warmth, like I was more needed and important than ever before. I started to imagine what Mom and Dad would think, and if they'd been watching from wherever they were now, but I had to blink that thought away when I could hardly make out the rice casserole dish in front of me through the tears.

I pulled myself together and said, "You go first," to Remy.

I walked close behind her, using her as a shield as we moved quickly to our table and I slid into the seat beside Tater.

"Dude," he said. "I was sleeping—I didn't even know what went down until I got here for dinner. Go, sis." He held out a fist and I bumped it.

"God, I can't believe he almost died," J.D. said. He pushed his food around his plate with the fork. "He seems so . . . indestructible. He's lucky you're an expert."

"I had lots of help," I said, hoping to take the spotlight off myself. I looked beside Tater to Rylen. "What happened out there today?"

He sat back and exhaled. "It started off great. We found a drug store that the owner had boarded up. The place was pristine. Untouched. We filled the van."

"Drugs?" I asked. The thought of meds got me all excited, and he must have known because he gave me a grin.

"Oh, yeah. We raided every last thing. Everything at the drugstore was solid. It wasn't 'til we stopped at a gas station that everything went to shit. Bunch of men attacked. No training, just standing there shooting us up. Sad, really. They were skinny as hell. Harris gunned down two from his window before he was shot."

We were quiet momentarily, until I asked, "What did you get from the drug store?"

"It was a mom and pop shop, so they didn't have a ton of each item, but they had one or two of almost everything. Medicine. Toiletries. *Candy*."

Remy and I sat up straighter. Every guy at the table laughed at our sudden postured attention.

"Merry late Christmas," Rylen said. He slid two slightly smooshed chocolate peanut butter trees across the table.

We snatched them up like prized treasure and held them to our chests. The candy had probably been put on the shelves in

November when Christmas stocking stuffers were starting to be sold, but I didn't care if they were months old. I was already dreaming of eating it in the privacy of my own room, taking tiny nibbles and savoring every single morsel as I moaned to my heart's content.

I started to put it in my pocket when Ry said, "You're not gonna eat it?"

"I'm going to eat it later," I said, feeling kind of bad about denying them the joy of seeing my orgasmic enjoyment.

"Me too." Remy put hers in her pocket.

"You two are going to make out with that candy in your room, aren't you?" Josh asked as he grinned and nodded.

Remy turned super pink as Mark pretended to kiss something in his hand and then rub it all over his chest as his eyes rolled back.

"Shut up," Remy said. "You all like to watch us a little too closely."

"We gotta get our kicks somehow," Matt told her.

"Yeah, well," I said. "You'll just have to use your imaginations."

The guys booed us, but there was laughter around the table.

"All right," Rylen said. "For real, though. We're all hanging out tonight. Everyone at the compound. We're having a party in the hotel lobby."

"A party-party?" Remy asked.

"Yep," Matt answered. "I got the sound system up and running last night. No more little boom box."

He bee-bopped with his mouth and it was surprisingly good. Rylen caught my smile and watched me, causing a tingle to spring up my spine. It wasn't the one-on-one hang out I'd been hoping for, but it would do.

"And what Ry failed to mention," Josh said, "Is that the drugstore-owner-dude had boxes of liquor in his office. *Cases*.

Brother was storing up."

"Is that really a good idea?" Remy asked. "For everyone to drink?"

"Not everyone," Matt said. "The night shift suckers will be out there working."

"Like me," Mark mumbled. "I can hang 'til midnight, but I can't drink. You all have one for me."

Remy frowned and Tater softened his demeanor. "We cleared it with Top. He said one night, one celebration, then back to work."

"What if it gets too loud?" Remy asked. "This place isn't soundproof."

"There's nobody out here to hear us," Matt told her. "If anyone comes near, the watchers will spot them and word will be sent for us to shut the hell up. No worries." He winked, and she chewed her lip.

We all peered around the table. It was frightening to think about being invaded while our numbers were inebriated. We'd have no chance at survival. But if it were a normal night, with no imminent danger, it could be just the release everyone needed.

I nudged Remy. "It'll be fun."

She looked at me like, *Who are you and what have you done with my boring bestie?* I shrugged. I'd been so uptight since we got here. And after everything today with Texas Harry, I felt the rare desire to have a drink. And maybe that one drink would give me a little liquid courage.

"If anyone needs a haircut before the party, I'm in business," J.D. said. "Room 325." He pointed his fork at Tater. "Nobody here will let me do any fun styles, but your hair is amazing. I could do something hot with it. Give you a leg up on the other guys for the few single females here." J.D. waggled his eyebrows, and I swear I saw Remy's lip curl up in a quick snarl.

"Nah, I'm good," Tater told him.

J.D. shrugged. "Suit yourself." Sean watched him carefully and glanced around the table whenever J.D. spoke, as if gauging everyone's reaction to him. But his protectiveness was unnecessary.

"Come on." Remy stood and glanced at me. "Let's get ready and eat our Christmas presents. Thanks again, Rylen."

He inclined his head with a grin, but saved his last glance for me before Remy pulled me away.

TWENTY-ONE

I LOVED BEING IN the lobby with its high roof and cabinesque feel. The windows and doors had all been shaded with the same metal as our rooms, but it still had a wide-open sensation that made me breathe deeply.

The room was already filled with people milling about and sitting in the soft chairs around the unlit, oversized rock fireplace that rose to the ceiling where wooden beams lined. Tater and the other guys stood in one of the corners, but Rylen wasn't with them. I looked around. He wasn't here yet. Most everyone held cups, and I noticed a makeshift bar had been set up at the old check-in desk. Devon and Shavonta were behind the counter, laughing about something.

"They're cute together," Remy said. Yeah, they were. She was short and curvy to his tall and muscled.

We approached and Shavonta took out two cups. I stared at the line of liquor bottles and cans of sodas. Sodas!

"Are you really allowed to use all of that?" I asked.

Devon nodded and Shavonta said, "Top said all this is

considered non-essential, so no need to ration. He expects it to be all gone tonight." She winked at me.

"So, I can have a Coke?" Remy asked.

"Yeah, girl," Devon told her. "Whatchu want in it?"

"Ice if you have it." She smiled, and both of them laughed.

"Just ice?" Shavonta asked.

"You're not going to have a drink with me?" I asked. "Just one?" Wow, it was like we'd switched roles.

Remy gave a shy shake of her head. "Just a Coke." The drinking thing probably went hand-in-hand with the no-hooking-up thing.

"Well, I'll have a rum and Coke," I offered.

"Yeah, baby." Devon chuckled and held out his fist for me to bump.

Shavonta handed us our drinks and Remy and I clinked the plastic together before sipping.

"Oh, my gosh, so sweet!" Remy winced. "I can't believe I used to drink this!"

I took a sip, and she was right. It was like syrup followed by a severe burn. I coughed and gave Shavonta a bug-eyed glance, which made her bend over laughing.

"You can handle it," she said, waving us off. "Go have fun."

I would have to take this one slowly.

We made our way over to the guys, who loudly held up their cups at our approach.

"Where's the music?" I asked Matt.

"Dog Balls wants to speak first and then we'll turn it on." His cheeks were mottled with pink as he smiled. I wondered how many drinks he'd had already.

Mark came between Remy and I and put his arms around us, pulling us to him. I could smell the bourbon from his half-full cup.

"I thought you weren't drinking," I said.

"Got someone to switch shifts with me. Sucka!" He took a swig. "How were your peanut butter delights, ladies?"

Remy and I both moaned at the memory, making the guys laugh. Mark tapped his cup to mine and we drank.

For the first time in a long time I felt . . . light. Not completely unburdened—there would always be a lingering sensation of loss and danger—but it wasn't as heavy on me at this moment, and I let myself bask in it. If only Texas Harry could be here. And Rylen. Where was he? I looked around again. I wanted to ask the others, but I didn't want to be obvious.

"Look," Remy said. I followed her gaze to where Sean and J.D. stood talking in the corner. They looked like they were arguing. Sean reached out and ran a finger along J.D.'s hand, making the other guy stop talking long enough to peer at him through those dark lashes. Then J.D. slapped Sean's shoulder and crossed his arms.

Remy giggled. "He's playing hard to get."

"He still thinks Thomas will show up any day," I said.

I knew the two of them were sharing a room with two beds. Nobody here got a room to themselves. But it didn't look like they'd taken the plunge yet.

Halfway through my drink I felt the warmth of a buzz creep through me, stretching like a yawning feline from my core to my limbs. It was a glorious feeling with just one drawback . . . it loosened my lips.

"Where's Rylen?" I blurted to the group.

"He's finishing up a meeting with First Lieutenant," my brother answered.

Linette. Of course. "Can't she give him one freaking night off?"

Tater eyed me. "Why you so bitchy to her?"

"Me?!" I sputtered.

"Yeah, every time you see her you give her that damn death glare."

I had no comeback for that. Except that she treated me the same way, but I couldn't say that because Tater would probably quote Mom: *Two wrongs don't make a right.* Ugh. I took another drink.

"There they are." Matt nodded over his drink. "I can get the music ready now." He jogged off. I turned to see Top coming in with Linette and Rylen behind him. But they were *still* talking. In fact, they moved to stand along the wall and continue their conversation. I had to remind myself that we were at war, and they were probably talking strategy and important things. I needed to chill.

I took another drink.

"Hooah!" First Sergeant's voice rang through the room, echoing all around us. Every head turned and repeated the greeting, even Remy and I, giving him our attention.

"Glad you all could make it," he said. "This will be a one-time thing, so I want you to take advantage of the break. God knows, we've got a lot of shit in our future. So, partake of the drinks until they're gone." He motioned to the bar. "And enjoy the sound system fixed by our comm boys. If we hear the sirens sound, you'd better sober the fuck up real fast." Chuckles rose. "Oh, and one more thing . . ." His eyes searched the room and landed on our group, then honed in on me. *Uh-oh.* "Amber Tate. Get your ass over here and take a shot with me. This gal saved one of our men who was shot on the run today."

Someone shoved me from behind as the room lifted a cheer. I made my way to him, wishing there was a way to deny this honor without seeming rude. Two shots of brown liquid were passed from the bar to the First Sergeant and he handed one to me.

"I heard you were amazing under pressure," he said. "And we're damn lucky to have you."

"Thank you," I said.

He raised his glass and I did the same, holding my breath and hoping I wouldn't gag it up in front of everyone. It went down smooth for one second, and then a fiery burn rose up my throat. I chased it down with the last of my rum and Coke. My eyes watered and Top chuckled.

"Gotta love Jack." He gave me a pat on the back and raised a thumb to Matt, who fiddled with some buttons on a wall panel. Seconds later Biggie Smalls filled the air with a thumping beat. Another cheer rose. I turned to make my way back to Remy when someone took me by the elbow. It was one of the other guys who'd been on the run yesterday. He held two shots and gave one to me.

"I didn't think he'd make it," he said over the music. "I thought for sure he was gone. That was a miracle you preformed."

"No—"

He raised the shot and held it up until I did the same. Oh, what the hell. Three drinks, and that would be it. No more. I threw it back and grimaced. The guy grabbed me in a bear hug and then released me, walking away.

"Well," said Remy, appearing at my side.

I grabbed her Coke and took a swig to wash down the strong flavor of whiskey.

"No more for me," I said. I tried to hand her drink back, but Remy was chewing her lip and staring over my shoulder. I spun, blinking at the dizzy spell it caused. And then my eyes cleared and I saw Rylen and Linette now sitting together on a loveseat. He sat, staring down at a drink in his hands, his legs spread, nodding at something she was saying. But it was Linette's body language that made my skin crawl.

She was turned toward him, one elbow on the back of the seat, one leg tucked under herself and the other leg crossed, touching his knee.

"She's going for him, Amber."

"They're probably just talking about the run," I said defensively. "He told me he's not ready for anything." But my heart raced erratically. I couldn't lose him again. I couldn't live with another regret like that. And even if they hooked up, and it was meaningless, I would still throw up every day forever.

The music suddenly changed from hip-hop to a Cuban Salsa tune that had me raising my head. I found Tater making a beeline for me. He grabbed my hand and pulled me to the open area in the middle of the room. Tater wanted to dance? I couldn't believe it! I put my drink down and gave him my full attention.

In that moment, my worries about Rylen fell away as the music swirled all around me, the tune grabbing me by the hips and lifting my chin with its seductive finger. This was the sound of my childhood, my family, my life.

Tater grabbed my hand and spun me in a double spin. I resisted the urge to throw back my head, keeping my body tight and posture perfect as Mom had taught me. A crowd gathered around us, and everyone began clapping. Tater stole the show, as always. He could whip his limbs precisely and swivel his hips to perfection, like something off a dance show. But with the alcohol loosening me up, I gave him a run for his money, even making him laugh with my bolder-than-usual moves.

Dad always said we were Mom's best pupils. To see Tater like this again filled me with hope and gratefulness. In that hidden room, in the middle of the forsaken wintry desert, in the midst of a war against extra-fucking-terrestrials, I felt a moment of joy.

It was our best dance ever. Mom and Abuela would have been proud, and Dad would have been highly entertained. At the end, we hugged while everyone cheered, and I glanced over to see Rylen watching from across the room, a small smile on his lips and heat in his cloudy eyes. Linette nudged his arm. Once. Then twice, until he blinked and held up a pointer finger to say "Give me a minute."

I glanced up at Tater as the song changed back to hip-hop, and it was like the candle inside of him suddenly snuffed out.

"Hey." I grabbed his arm. "Thanks. That was fun."

"Yeah." But his voice was sullen again, and he left me to go stand by the wall. My heart sank. I looked toward Rylen and my heart sank deeper when I saw he had given his attention back to chatty Linette.

The three drinks were like fire in my system now, everything inside of me blazing with life. This was supposed to be our night to hang out, and Linette knew exactly what she was doing. Remy was right—she was going for it. And so was I.

Matt grabbed Remy, pulling her onto the dance floor where others began to pile on, shaking hips and lifting arms, letting loose in a way none of us had for many months. The air filled with excitement.

I made my way through the crowd, saying hi to New York Josh and a few other guys who stood nearby, and then stopping to stand between Rylen's feet.

"Hey, look," Linette said. "It's your little sister."

My claws came out.

"I'm *not* his sister." I felt ashamed for rising to her taunt, but the three drinks had crushed my filter. I looked at Rylen, whose eyes were lit with . . . something. He leaned forward, making Linette scoot out of his way.

"You okay?" he asked, peering up at me. There was something in his voice. I couldn't place it. I wanted to believe it was hope. Hope that I would spirit him away from her.

"Dance with me?" I said. My heart gave a hard thump.

His shoulders fell a little. "You know I don't dance."

Linette's body shook with a laugh. *Ignore her.*

"I know," I said. I reached down and took his hand, which he held firmly. I tried to tug, but he had a hard grip. What was in his eyes now? Embarrassment? I couldn't read him and it was driving me nuts.

He began saying, "Can't we just—" when Josh was suddenly at my side, nudging me with his elbow.

"This chump ain't gonna dance with you? Come on, girl. I got this."

Rylen's jaw locked and his face hardened as Josh led me away. But halfway to the dance floor a country song came on and Josh said, "Aw, hell no." He led me to the bar instead.

My buzzing blood was prickling my senses. I didn't know how to feel, or what exactly had happened back there, but I felt the sting of rejection. Again.

"Two Jacks," Josh told Devon.

"And another rum and Coke," I said. I knew I shouldn't. I *knew*, but rebellion was upon me, and I was too weak in my current state to control it. If Rylen was going to choose to sit with her all night, or whatever was going on between them, I wanted to be numb. I didn't want to hurt.

Josh handed me a shot. "Bottoms up." We both took it and I barely winced that time. I chased it with a sip of cold, sweet, bubbly rum and Coke.

"You know," Josh told me. "Fite ain't the only guy here." He held out his palms, like *just saying.*

"I know." I chewed the inside of my lip and stared down at my drink.

He was right, of course, but Rylen had always been the only guy for me. No matter how attractive Josh and the other guys were, or how much I enjoyed their company, my heart called out for Rylen's. Even now, I could feel his presence from half the room away, and if he left I would feel the loss.

I was halfway through my drink when the country song ended and something harder came on with a wicked rock beat. Josh grabbed my hand and led me out. Before his body pressed to mine, my gaze snagged with Rylen's. He wore that same hard expression as he watched us, leaning forward, his hands dangling in a clasp. Josh's hands firmly took my waist and pulled my hips to his.

"Who you dancing with, Amber?" he asked in a gravelly voice, his accent thicker after a few drinks. "Me or him?"

I ripped my eyes away from Rylen and focused on Josh. In that moment, the full force of my alcohol intake hit me, and I leaned all my weight on him. How many had I had? An angry sort of righteousness rose up, telling me *fuck it—you deserve to be drunk and pissed off all you want.* So I paused and chugged the rest of my drink before tossing the cup to the nearest table.

I let the music lead me, arms up, body swaying, pressing against Josh's toned soldier body. He had the moves of a guy who'd spent plenty of nights clubbing. I knew if I let him, he would take good care of me. But I couldn't help it; I took another glance toward Rylen. Linette had his face in her hand, as if forcing him to look at her, and she was saying something, looking into his eyes. He closed his eyes and took her wrist, pulling her hand down from his face. But he didn't scoot away from where her leg was pressed against his. It was like a war raged inside of him.

I spun my body and pressed my ass against Josh's front, raising my arm to drape across the back of his neck.

"You trying to kill me?" he said in a low voice into my ear as we moved in sync.

I turned back around and wound both my arms around his neck, but he kept his face slightly turned aside. His body was totally into this, but I could see on his face he was holding back.

I rubbed the back of his head and watched as his eyes closed, clearly enjoying my touch. For a moment everything blurred and I forgot where I was and who I was with.

Suddenly a warm, strong hand was on my shoulder, giving me a tug away from the warm, masculine body of Josh. I felt like I peeled away from him in slow motion to see Rylen's livid face looking down at me.

"'Bout time, asshole," Josh muttered, walking away. Rylen let the remark go.

"I think you're done," he said to me. "I'll take you to your room."

I scoffed. "Really, Dad? And, wow, I thought you and Linette were superglued together. Hope it didn't hurt too bad when you tore yourself away."

His jaw rocked. "We were talking."

"And touching," I reminded him. "She was touching you."

He stepped closer. "What's it to you, Pepper?"

His words were a slap to the face. I opened my mouth to say who-knows-what, when I heard Remy's loud voice carry through the music. She was arguing with Linette.

"Oh, no." I pushed away from Rylen and was horrified when I tried to go forward and instead veered to the left, falling into a table before righting myself and moving in the correct direction. I bumped every person and piece of furniture along the way, wondering when it got so damn crowded in here.

"Oh, look," said Linette as I made my stumbling approach. "Here she is now."

Remy's cheeks were dark pink against her blond hair.

"What's going on?" I asked. Or, that's what I meant to say, but it came out sounding gummy. Linette laughed and Remy sort of cringed.

"God, how many did you have?" Linette asked. "Save some for the rest of us. Although, it is nice to see that you're not so perfect after all."

"Neither of us think we're perfect," Remy said. "Stop saying that!"

"Right." Linette swung her chin to get hair out of her eyes. "The beauty queen and the over-achiever, pretending to be oblivious of every man sniffing around their virginal crotches."

Remy's mouth opened in a gasp and I said, "We're not even virgins. Stop judging and worry about your own damn self."

Remy looked at me funny, and panic hit me square in the chest. What had I just said? This conversation had veered very wrong at some point. I'm thinking it was the point when I opened my mouth.

"Wait." Remy's attention was fully on me now. "*We're* not . . . ?" She glanced at Linette and said, "Never mind."

"Oh. My. God." Linette said, a half-smile playing on her smug face. "Did *you*—" she pointed to Remy, "—think *she* was a virgin?" She pointed to me. "But you're not? Wow, Tate, that's low. Best friend fail."

Remy's face. My stomach. I'd never told her. I'd never told *anyone* about that awful night with Ken.

"Shut up," I told Linette, moving to get in her face.

"That's enough, Lin." Rylen's voice boomed right behind me as he grasped my waist to keep me from getting to her. Linette's eyes rose to him, hardening.

"Stop babying her, Fite."

"It's none of your fucking business," he said.

Linette put her hands up and huffed a laugh through her nose. "Yep. I'm done. Have fun with that." She inclined her head toward me before sauntering away with her chin up. Rylen let me go.

Everything blurred as Remy turned on me. I knew Rylen was still behind me. I couldn't have this conversation.

"I don't want to talk about it." I put a hand on the nearest table to steady myself.

"Of course you don't," Remy said. "You never want to talk to me, or anyone else, about anything of actual importance." Her eyes were full of hurt and anger, which bounced around inside of me before seeping in.

"What the hell's going on over here?" Tater asked. I couldn't do this right now.

"I'm getting another drink." I staggered away from them.

"Hey, Amber Tate!" A soldier held up a hand and I high-fived him on my second try. All along the way to the bar people greeted me with smiles. They weren't angry at me. They treated me nice. But still I felt like shit, and I wanted it all to go away. I sucked at life.

"Pepper." His voice came from behind me, filling me with a stubborn frustration.

I made it to the bar and Devon grinned. "One more, baby girl?"

"A shot," I said. "I don't care what it is."

"Amber." Rylen was right next to me now. I didn't look at him, but his presence wrapped around me.

Devon slid the shot forward. This one was clear.

"Don't do it." Rylen's plea near my ear sounded more like a warning. All I could see was Linette up against him, garnering his complete attention this entire night.

I shot it back. It tasted like rubbing alcohol, making my stomach roll. I closed my eyes and slowly opened them.

"Uh-oh," Devon said. "One too many?"

"I'm good." At least, that's what I thought I said. And when I gave a big thumbs up, teetering sideways, he laughed a little too hard.

"Come on," Rylen said.

I stepped closer and peered up at him. "Gonna dance with me now?"

"No."

He took my hand and I blindly followed until we were out in the hall and I realized he was making me leave. I came to a halt like a donkey digging my heels in. "Not goin' bed."

"Amber, come on. Yes, you are."

I faced him with my hands on my hips. "Don't you . . . don't try to . . ." What the hell was I trying to say? It didn't matter, because next thing I knew Rylen swept me up into his arms like a big baby and started marching down the hall. I swung my legs, ready to throw a fit until I heard his gentle voice saying, "Sh. It's all right. Relax, Pepper, I got you."

I lay my head on his shoulder and barely registered the gentle bouncing of his steps up the stairs and down our hall. A minute later I felt him touch my butt, pulling my key from my back pocket. He kicked the door closed behind us and set me on the bed. I started to snuggle down, then shot to my feet, disoriented, as I remembered this bedtime was being forced upon me. I stumbled toward the wall. He caught me by the middle of my shirt, holding the material in his fist, and walked me backward until I was against the wall.

"Relax," he said. "You're all right."

Our aloneness tightened around me like a bubble of hyperawareness.

"Ry," I whispered. My hands went to his biceps, warm and solid. He closed his eyes and opened them again slowly.

"You've probably said enough for tonight," he whispered back.

He was trying to shush me. I shook my head, and it was like slow motion, as if my skull were rocking back and forth on a ship.

"I've lot mores to say." I could hear the slur in my words, the ridiculousness of my lack of control, but I focused on Rylen's pursed, full lips and a sensation of desire overrode the amusement.

He let go of my shirt and put his hands loosely on his hips. "You need to go to bed."

"No." I poked him in the hard chest and leaned forward too fast. I pressed both palms to his chest to balance myself. "God, Rylen" I said, feeling the contours of his pecs and watching my hands as I explored. It took a great deal of effort to lift my heavy head and look into his tired eyes. The comfort of that bluish gray tint was something I wanted to nestle down into. I rose up on my toes and moved my face close to his. So close, I could feel his breaths against my own lips.

"Pepper." Rylen took both my hands from his chest and brought them back down to my sides, putting me firmly back on my feet.

"I love you," I said softly.

"I love you, too." His voice was that of a man trying to appease a child. "Now, let's get you to bed."

"*Don't,*" I said too loudly. I pulled away from his grip and brought my hands up to his neck. This time when I looked at him I felt him soften under my touch. I rose up on my toes again, touching our noses, and he wrenched his face to the side.

"Pepper, seriously."

"Please," I begged.

He took my arms and brought them down again, this time holding my wrists at my sides. God, he made me so mad!

"You . . ." I searched my addled brain. "You're a . . ."

"Don't finish that sentence."

"You're a clit tease!" I shouted.

His eyebrows flew up and then he chuckled deeply. His mouth went to my ear as he pressed me into the wall and said, "I assure you, I'm not." A shiver made me press my pelvis upward toward his. His own hips jolted backward at the touch and he hissed my name in warning. "Amber . . ."

"Kiss me," I breathed.

He pulled back, and his face was guarded. "You're drunker than I thought."

I flung his hands from my wrists, feeling frustrated as the weight of years' worth of emotions pressed down on me. I was sick and tired of not being taken seriously by this man.

"Stop trea'ing me like a kid."

He sighed and dropped his head, as if dealing with me was exhausting. But I couldn't stop. I had so much to say. Damn the slur in my voice. Damn my jelly legs that made me unable to stand straight.

"You don' know," I said. "I don't know how you don't know. How I . . . I love you, with *all* my heart." I fought to make each word distinguishable. I had to get this out. It came rushing to the surface like a messy, muddy flood, and I couldn't hold it back any longer.

"I loved you since I was, like, thirteen. And not like a sister, Ry. Do you hear me?" I clutched his shirt. He lifted his chin enough to eye me. *"Not like a sister,"* I reiterated. The words were so important. Monumental. Life changing.

"Pepper." He spoke with care. "You're drunk."

I clenched my fists in his shirt and screamed through my teeth. His eyes bulged and I dove into the pool of emotions again. "I tried telling you! But every time . . ." I panted, breathing erratically. "You never believed me! Or you . . . you jus' . . . you play it off 'cause you're too nice. But you ha' to listen this time." I shook his shirt. *"I want you."* I tilted to the side and pressed myself back against the wall. "And I's fuckin'brokenhearted-whenyoumarriedher. I feel . . ." I sucked in a breath, trying to hold back tears. "I feel . . . *guilty* 'cause I wanted you when you were married." My eyes fluttered closed, and when my lids felt heavy I blinked them back open with an intake of air.

Rylen was staring at me, frozen. When I stared back, he

abruptly looked down, then to the side, and grabbed his ear, rubbing the lobe. He stayed like that, so still, staring at the floor deep in thought. Oh, God. He was trying to figure out how to let me down easily. This was why I'd never had the nerve to tell him the truth.

I braced myself. "Just say it," I said. "Just fuckin' *say it*."

"Say, what?" He finally looked at me, but his face was fiercely serious. "You probably won't even remember this—"

I opened my mouth and he pinched my lips together, shocking me.

"You hush; it's my turn."

I released the huff of air and felt my eyes glistening. He was going to say the words I'd been dreading for years. It would finally be over with. I had to take it like a big girl. He took my chin and I looked up at him.

"I learned a long time ago that alcohol is only a truth serum to a certain point, and then people say all kinds of shit they don't mean. So, you drink this bottle of water—" he picked something up from the dresser and pressed it into my hands "—and if you've got something to say to me, you say it to me in the morning when you're sober. Got it?"

My jaw dropped open. Fury ensnared me like fire. Dismissed again.

"Tha's it?" I threw my arms out. "Tha's all you're gonna say? After everythin' I jus' . . . you know what, Ry? Fuck tha'!"

He sucked air through his teeth. "Keep talking, Jack."

My words came out all linked together, dragging out. "It's not Jack talking. You never take me seriously. I'm sick o' you."

I shoved him. In a blink I was over his shoulder and tossed onto the bed with a bounce. I shrieked in frustration, my hands in fists.

"I hate you!" I yelled.

"Like I said, tell me tomorrow." His face was hard, guarded.

He opened the door to leave and I shouted, "Stay away from that bitch Linette!" The door slammed and I fell back hard into the pillow, flinging an arm over my eyes. Before a single emotion could register, the bed started to move sideways, then spun like a carnival ride. I pried my eyes open, but everything was blurry from the fast movement. The contents of my stomach were being pushed up by the gravity of the spin. I rolled until I fell out of bed, and stumbled my way to the bathroom just in time to say hello to all of the Jack and rum again.

When I was done being sick, I crawled into the room but couldn't even climb back onto the bed. I passed out on the floor beside it, curled up in a ball.

I woke hours later with a sour pit in my stomach and a rancid taste in my dry mouth. I felt around until my hands landed on the water bottle. With much effort I twisted open the cap and chugged every drop. Then I crawled to the bathroom, pulled myself up at the sink and brushed my teeth to get rid of the horrid taste.

I made it back to the bed and fell asleep on top of the blankets, my face smashed into a pillow.

TWENTY-TWO

A POUNDING PAIN INSIDE my forehead woke me. I kept my eyes closed, assessing the damage. Definite headache and queasy stomach. What had happened last night? Too much whiskey and rum, that was for sure. Just the thought of it made me roll over to my back, just in case I had to dash to the bathroom again. I looked over and saw Remy's small form curled on the other side of the bed, her back to me. She never slept that far away.

We lay there in silence as last night's events slowly unfolded in my memory. Dancing with Josh. Remy and Linette arguing. Being carried back to my room, and . . . oh, my God. I covered my face with my hands. I'd called him a clit tease. Of all the idiotic things to say. I don't think I'd ever used that word before in my life.

But it got worse. I'd said more things to Rylen. I rummaged through the unclear memories and dragged pieces to the forefront to examine them. And then it hit me in the chest with the force of a bullet.

I'd told him I loved him as more than a sister. I'd told him I wanted him, even after he was married. I let out a whimper and Remy rolled over, sitting up to peer down at me. Her eyes traveled over me, and seeing that I was okay, she turned and rolled away from me again.

"Rem?" I whispered.

Something had happened. I tried to pinpoint my time with Remy last night, and then an aching chasm split deep inside of me. I'd told everyone I wasn't a virgin. Something I'd never disclosed to before. I pressed a hand over my mouth, feeling sick again.

Remy deserved so much better than a best friend who kept all of her feelings and experiences bottled up inside.

"Remy," I whispered, forcing each sound from my throat. "I'm sorry."

For a long time, she said nothing, and didn't move. I wondered if she'd heard me. And then she spoke.

"Why don't you trust me? I wouldn't have told a soul."

"I know that," I said, and I did. "I do trust you. I'm just . . . I'm not like you."

She sat up and turned in a rush, her hair wild around her face. "Not a slut like me?"

"What?" I felt the blood drain from my head. "No! You know I don't think that! I just meant . . . I'm not good at *saying* things." I struggled, wanting so badly for this conversation to be over, for Remy to just know my heart and not need the spoken words. But that wasn't going to happen. She crossed her arms, waiting. I had to earn her forgiveness. So I pressed on.

"You're so *good*. You always have the right words. You always care. You put yourself out there. And I'm like this dried up little clam that keeps it all hidden. It's really hard for me, really uncomfortable for me, to verbalize."

God, even now I was sweating and short of breath.

She pushed her waves behind her ears, frowning. "Amber, you weren't . . . raped, were you?"

"No." I shook my head. "Nothing like that. It was consensual, I just regret it. It's embarrassing."

"You don't have to be embarrassed with me. I know you're a private person." She chewed her lip, and it was clear that she didn't want to press but couldn't help herself. "How long ago was it?"

I rubbed my face, not looking forward to rehashing that awful night of my life.

"Remember last summer when I went on that date with Ken?"

Her eyes rounded. "Oh, my gosh, that hot Japanese fire fighter? Yes! It was him?" I nodded, and she couldn't hold back a smile. "So what happened? I mean, never mind. I know you don't want to talk about it." But her eyes were alight with interest.

"It wasn't anything special," I said, much to her disappointment. "We didn't even finish because I freaked out and stopped us." My face heated and I felt dizzy just thinking about it.

Remy pulled a *yikes* face. "Sorry. I know I kinda pressured you to go out with him."

"Not your fault. He was great. It was me. I'm the mess." I fell back on the bed and closed my eyes. Everything from last night was sitting on my chest like a sumo wrestler. "I'm still a mess. Last night . . ."

She practically pounced. "Yes, what happened last night? Rylen came and got me and told me he put you to bed."

"More like he threw me on the bed."

She was clearly trying not to smile. She wanted the details I so badly wanted to forget. I covered my face and spoke against the heels of my hands.

"I tried to kiss him, Remy. And when he denied me . . . I

called him a clit tease."

She slapped a hand to her mouth, stunned, then fell to her side and erupted in laughter. I sat up and glowered down at her, although, to be honest, getting it all out was kind of therapeutic.

"Shut up," she sputtered. "You did *not*."

"Oh, it gets better. I told him I loved him as more than a sister, and that I'd always loved him, even when he was married."

She stared at me hard, as if to gauge if I was serious, and then she stood up and started jumping on the bed, air boxing, kicking her feet up like a cheerleader as she tried to keep her squeals as quiet as possible. Then she crashed into a heap next to me, right in my face. "What did he say?!"

"He said *'Tell me when you're sober,'* and then he threw me on the bed and left."

"Oh," she breathed. Her eyes were still glistening with joy. "That's good. You know that's good, right?"

I looked down at my hands. I didn't know that at all.

"He's a gentleman, Amber. Do you know how rare that is? Any guy I ever tried to kiss when I was drunk was like *hell yeah!*—not about to turn me down. He respects you." Her voice took on a sort of envious awe.

"I know," I whispered. I did know he respected me, but my mind wasn't so sure about his reasons for turning me down and not giving me any feedback about what I'd divulged. Rylen *was* a gentleman, which meant he'd want to let me down when I was sober, too.

"You're totally going to talk yourself out of telling him, aren't you?"

"No," I said defensively. I couldn't look at her.

"Amber, the world is ending." She growled, exasperated. "Let yourself have some happiness before it's too late. *Tell him.*"

She didn't wait for me to respond. She got up and daintily stomped to the bathroom to take her shower.

I laid in bed most of the day feeling like crap in all ways. Remy took pity and brought my lunch to me. While I was relieved she and I had made up so quickly, the Rylen thing was going to take a lot more courage. Remy was right—I couldn't let it drag out. Tomorrow was not guaranteed. But God, I'd never been more nervous or humiliated.

I showered when Remy went to help prep for dinner. I didn't know yet if I'd have the guts to go. I was leaning toward heading straight to my night watch shift without eating, but rations were small and snacks were a no-no. I couldn't really afford to skip a meal.

Still, when it came time to go down I was pacing the room, biting my thumb nail, my stomach in tight, twisted knots. I shook my hands out, reached for the doorknob, felt a surge of panic, then backed away and paced until dinner time was over and my shift was about to begin.

I really hated myself.

The second I left the safety of my room, my nerves skyrocketed, leaving my skin prickling and my eyes darting for signs of Rylen. My empty stomach, still recovering from its abuse last night, was angry as hell. This was going to be a very long night.

I kept my head down in the hall, stairwell, and down the tunnel. I responded robotically to everyone who greeted me along the way.

"Hey." Tater's voice hit me as I spilled out of the tunnel. I immediately searched the vicinity for Rylen, heart pounding, but he was nowhere.

"Hey," I said. He'd let his curly hair grow longer than the Army would have allowed before. It was like he was a teen again, except his taut face and adult scowl.

"You missed dinner," he pointed out.

"Yeah, and I'm about to be late for my shift."

"What's going on with you?" He eyed me. "You look . . . *tired.*" In other words, I looked like shit.

"Nothing," I lied. "Everything's fine. I gotta go." I gave his arm a squeeze and jogged away.

Nothing was fine, and my shift was going to suck.

I spent far too many hours being ribbed by the guys in the watch tower—everything from my so-called highly seductive dances, to my stomach growling every time it got quiet. How nice that my misery entertained them.

"For real," Mark said. "Every time you danced the guys were taking mental videos for monkey spanking later."

Who says that?! Only Mark Mahalchick. The other two guys laughed uproariously, though they tried very hard to do it quietly.

"Would you shut up already?" I mumbled, earning more laughter.

On our way back inside after the shift, Mark draped his arm over my shoulders as we walked down the long hall.

"You know I'm just messing with you, right?"

"Yeah, yeah." I patted his hand and stopped at Texas Harry's door. "I'm going to check on him."

"I visited earlier," he said. "Told him all about your dancing skills."

Oh, great. Just what I needed. I cracked open the door and saw that Tex was sleeping soundly, so I closed it again. I'd be back in seven hours for my med shift.

Mark and I walked quietly through the deserted common area and down the long tunnel together. When we came up the steps and into our hall of the hotel, Rylen's door opened and my heart stopped as Linette walked out. My entire world tilted.

Her hair was mussed and her clothes rumpled. She halted when she saw us, and then a wicked glean filled her eyes as she focused on me. I literally could not breathe or school my face out of its frozen state of shock.

"First Lieutenant," Mark greeted politely, albeit carefully.

"Mahalchick." She squared her shoulders and walked past us.

It wasn't until she was down the hall around the corner that I inhaled shakily and found my body could not move.

"Uh, that was . . . unexpected," Mark said. I couldn't respond. "You okay?" he asked.

"Yeah," I whispered. "I'll see you later." I walked as stiff as a mannequin to my door, but didn't open it. I waited until Mark disappeared into his room. Then I stood there in the silent hallway for what felt like an hour before I moved robotically to the door where Rylen, Tater, Devon, and Matt shared a room. I lifted a weak hand and knocked.

After a long moment, the door opened a crack, and a gorgeous face peered out. Rylen's face.

TWENTY-THREE

MY HEART. WHEN I saw those eyes, gray as smoke, and his shirtless state, that chili pepper tattoo, something huge that lived inside me died, leaving a dangerous hole—a hole that acted as a vacuum sucking everything into it. It happened so fast. All hope I'd had vanished into the depths of that hole. Any positive feelings, gone.

He must have seen it on my face, because he suddenly opened the door further, revealing the small towel wrapped around himself. Oh, God.

"You saw her come out, didn't you?" He held the towel with one hand and used his other palm to rub his face. He chuckled darkly. "And you think . . ."

"I don't think anything," I lied. Horribly. I felt confused, and my chest was tight. "I don't know why I'm here. I need sleep." I turned, but his voice wrapped around me.

"Get in here."

I turned. His eyes were everything, a beam that caught me and saw too much of me. He opened the door all the way and

I peered into where Linette had been. My head gave a stubborn shake. I wanted to dissolve.

"Pepper." His voice dropped an octave. "Get. Your ass. Inside."

I crossed my arms and hurried past him, into the warm space that smelled of men. I stood awkwardly at the end of the first bed while Rylen went in the bathroom and came back out in shorts. I was shaking so hard. This was the part where he'd break me. After all these years, I just wanted him to get it over with.

He faced me, his arms crossed over his chest to mirror me. "I'm not fucking Linette, okay? D was with her roommate last night, so she needed a place to crash."

My heart dropped and reared back up like an untamed animal released from its cage, relieved and alive again. I looked away. "Not my business."

"Isn't it? Then why are you here?"

"I . . ." My arms tightened over my chest. "I wanted to say I'm sorry you had to deal with me last night."

My heart pounded and embarrassment heated through me like a hot blade. I wished I could read his mind. Every ounce of trepidation and nervousness I'd ever felt around Rylen pummeled me harder than ever as my words from last night hung between us. It was all out there, and I had to deal with it.

"And to thank you for getting me back to my room." My brain hurt and I was so nervous that my words came out raspy.

He watched me, arms still crossed, eyebrows up in expectation. He was not going to throw me a bone here.

"What do you want me to say, Ry? I feel really stupid."

His jaw worked, side to side, like he was getting angry. "You remember me taking you back to your room?"

"Yes," I whispered. My heart thumped rapidly, mixing with the white noise in my mind. Rylen and I were on the cusp of something. Something there would be no coming back from. Things between us would change today, for better or worse.

"Do you remember anything you said?" he asked, his voice husky.

A single word shook its way from my throat. "Yes."

He wanted something from me, I could feel it, but my head was such a disaster. Years' worth of self-consciousness rose up to block my path. I could take the leap into the dark precipice, and be done with these feelings once and for all. Or I could let myself slide back into the nothingness of the supposed safety of silence I'd lived in for so long. Miserable safety.

"And you've been avoiding me ever since," he said.

"*No.*" Big fat lie. "I was tired, and I didn't feel good."

When time stretched on and passed in silence, Rylen nodded, stone-faced.

"Well," he said. "Glad you're feeling better."

He moved for the door, as if to kick me out, and panic clutched my chest. "Wait!"

He halted with his hand on the doorknob. I watched him slowly turn his head to meet my eyes. The tension that zinged between us at that moment made me fight to breathe. I'd never been more nervous.

"I'm sober now," I said. He completely froze, eyes still locked on mine. A tremble coursed through my system. *Deep breath.*

Rylen let go of the doorknob and took several slow, prowling steps toward me until we were mere feet apart. "And?" He wanted the words. I was bad at words. Plus, his eyes seriously looked like they could summon a storm at that moment. I felt it all around me—the *whoosh* of wind on my skin and in my ears.

"And I . . ."

"You what?" His voice was deeper than usual, filled with something I'd never heard from him before, something he'd held back from me until this moment: power, strength, and something that sounded unmistakably like . . . lust. He stared at me so hard I could scarcely make myself continue.

"I want you." It was out of me like the push of a powerful tide. There was no controlling it, no taking it back.

He came at me with two panther-like strides until he was hovering over me, forcing me to walk backward until my legs bumped the bed.

"Finally," he breathed, almost angrily, and then his mouth was on mine, his hand cradling the back of my head with firm ownership as his other hand slid around my back and yanked me to him.

A sound somewhere between a moan and a cry rose from deep within me at the feel of his lips and hands. I clutched him around his back, grasping. My mind abandoned all sense of politeness and I raised a knee as if I might climb him. He grabbed my ass with both hands and I held on tight as he lifted me and laid me on the bed with a bounce, then climbed above me and lowered his hips.

"Rylen . . ." Was this real?

His body was flush against mine, his weight rousing a glorious heat that spread out from my core. This was definitely real, and we were needy, so needy. My calves wrapped around the back of his thighs as our mouths moved together, his warm tongue tasting me. When he lifted his face and rested his forehead against mine, we were both panting for air.

My chest rose and fell, feeling like my heart had exploded in a shower of stars. *Rylen is in my arms.* I let out a laugh of surprised disbelief.

"I can't believe this is happening," I said against his mouth.

"Neither can I," he breathed.

He lowered his face to mine and kissed me again, this one long and slow. Then he kept his lips close to mine as he said, "I half thought you were coming here to tell me you didn't mean it. It took all my will-power not to go to you today and get it over with so I could quit obsessing."

Him obsessing over me? "You're crazy!" My laugh sounded maniacal. "I've wanted this for years."

"Years?" he asked skeptically. "How 'bout when I came home that summer you turned seventeen and you were all of a sudden a damn woman? You got pissed when I tried to kiss you."

We'd been over this. "I wasn't mad at you. I was mad at Tater for interrupting us. And it was me who tried to kiss you."

He chuckled, shaking his head. "Not how I remember it."

"You were drunk." My turn to smile.

Regret filled his eyes. "I wish you would've told me."

Holy freaking crap. "I tried! I gave you a *lot* of hints."

He turned his head to the side, smiling bashfully. "For future reference, men need things spelled out. Hints don't work."

"Well, that's really inconvenient."

"Yeah, well, you didn't exactly catch on to my hints either," he said. "I almost kissed you outside at that cabin."

"*What*? Once again, I was the one who almost kissed you!"

He shook his head. "I felt like an asshole for thinking about you when . . ." When Livia had just died. I ran my hand over his cheek.

"You're not an asshole. You never were, and you aren't now."

He moved a lock of hair from my face. "I hate to say it, but I probably wouldn't have let us get involved before, when you were younger, even if you had told me how you felt. I always knew you were destined for something bigger. I would've felt like I was holding you back."

There it was. I shook my head and let myself run my hands up the short hair at the back of his head. "You always thought that about yourself, Ry, that you weren't good enough, but you were wrong. We can do big things, together."

Ry grinned softly down at me. "The past is the past, okay,

Pepper? I never want you to be afraid to tell me something again."

"Or you."

"Or me."

I nodded, feeling his hair slide between my fingers. Emotions welled up inside of me. After all this time, here we were, holding each other like it was the most natural thing ever. Like there hadn't been years of no-touching-tension between us up until two minutes ago. It was surreal.

When Rylen's mouth came down over mine again, all words and worries fled. His lips were the perfect amount of supple. His knee pressed down between my thighs until I opened up for him and he lowered his weight between my legs, making me moan when I felt his hard bulge rub the crease of my jeans. He pressed against me and I grabbed his waist, pulling him down harder, wishing there were no clothes between us.

Rylen stilled and turned his head aside, letting out a huge breath like he was trying to stay in control of himself. Then, to my disappointment, he rose and moved off me, onto his side, propped on his elbow, looking down at me in a heated way that made my disappointment disappear. His hand slipped under my T-shirt and pressed hotly against my stomach. My back arched into his touch. He watched me, as if mesmerized. And then his fingers flicked open the button of my jeans.

I inhaled sharply and stared at him.

"I seem to remember you calling me a certain name," he said. His tone was full of menacing promise that made my pulse quicken. My face flushed when I realized what name he was talking about.

"I really have no idea where that came from." I laughed nervously as he pulled my zipper down. "I've never used that phrase in my life."

"Mm-hm. That may be, but I feel the need to redeem myself

from the accusation, just the same."

"Ry . . ." I sucked in another breath as he sat up and tucked his fingers into the sides of my jeans. He looked down at me seriously. My heart was beating as if I'd run a marathon.

"Lift your hips."

When I hesitated out of sheer nervousness, he whispered, "Trust me."

So nervous. So nervous. So nervous.

Without taking my eyes from him, I lifted my hips. His intense gaze was so satisfying that it sent a hot zap through my blood. My jeans were tossed to the floor, my panties still in place. A second later and he was at my side again, kissing me so well I could've passed out from bliss. His warm hand roamed my waist, down my hip, to my outer thigh. My breathing hitched as his hand moved inward over the swell of my inner thigh, but instead of touching my center, he went back around my leg to my hip and back over my stomach, leaving me yearning. I let out a moan of aching, trying not to wiggle, and he grinned.

"What's wrong?" he asked.

"Now you're definitely being a tease."

He chuckled and nibbled my lower lip as his hand dipped beneath the elastic of my underwear. I held my breath. Rylen's lips stilled on mine as his fingers slid down and discovered how wet I was for him. I almost felt embarrassed until he shut his eyes and let out the most masculine groan I'd ever heard. That sound alone nearly made me overheat. His fingers slid back up and moved with just enough pressure over the sensitive folds and nub that I'd accused him of teasing last night.

I bit my lip to try and stay quiet, but I couldn't help but raise my hips for more.

Rylen whispered a curse under his breath and his hand moved faster. I couldn't stay still. I pressed my hands over the top of his and moved my hips, breathing hard.

"Oh, my God. Ry . . ." His hand moved faster, pressing harder.

"Fuck this." Rylen sat up, ripped my panties down my legs, and then his mouth was there. My entire back arched upward and my head flew back at the feel of his hot lips on my most tender spot, his tongue flicking and tasting with exquisite pressure. Then I felt the heaviness of his finger pushing into me, and the combined stimulation was like a flame to a bomb inside of me, lighting one after another nerve, detonating bursts of pleasure so intense they walked the edge of pain. I grasped his hair as I cried out, unable to stay quiet any longer. Rylen firmly held my hips in place as I bucked until I finally stilled, quivering from the inside.

I was so sensitive when he made his way back up to me, that my body convulsed with aftershocks. He gave me the utterly sexy look of a man who'd staked his claim and was damn proud of himself. I couldn't help but giggle, especially when I tried to lift my hand to his face and found my arm was like a noodle.

"Okay, I take back what I said," I whispered.

Now it was his turn to chuckle. When I caught my breath, I sat up and pushed his shoulder so he was laying down, and then I straddled him and kissed him. I was still so sensitive that my body trembled when I touched my nakedness against the hard heat of his track shorts. His eyes took on a smoky darkness when he felt me rub against him.

I wasn't ready to stop. I was nervous, but this was Rylen. Slowly, I took the bottom of my T-shirt and raised it over my head. His clouded eyes took in the sight of me as he ran his hands from my hips up my waist. I fought the jitters and reached back to unclasp my bra and toss it away.

Rylen sat up with me still on his lap, his hands behind my back, and lifted me enough to take one of my breasts into his mouth. I whimpered as his tongue swirled around it and pulled back, sucking and releasing my nipple with a gentle *snap* until it was a hard bud. He gave the other equal treatment, and I was shocked by how turned on I was again. I couldn't control the eager, passionate sounds that continued to escape me.

I looked down at Rylen's sexy torso. He'd lost some of his bulk, but his lean muscles were defined. I ran my hands over him. I greedily touched him like I'd wanted to for so long. And I wanted to touch much, much more of him. I slid down his legs just enough to rub him through his shorts. Holy, shit. Rylen fell back with a guttural hiss and grasped the tops of my thighs.

A rattling sound from the entrance had me scrambling to get off his lap, but he held me in place and shouted, "Fuck off!" toward the door. Someone was trying to use their key to get in, but Rylen had flipped the inside lock.

"Dude!" Tater shouted through the door. "Some Airman from Nellis just showed up, half dead, and we can't find Amber!"

TWENTY-FOUR

I JUMPED OFF HIM and snatched up my clothes, pulling them on with shaking hands while Rylen did the same.

"One sec!" Ry called. One minute later Rylen flung open the door. Tater's look of shock, then revulsion, then righteous anger would have had me laughing any other time, but right now I just shoved past him and sprinted to the stairs.

"The fuck, Fite?" Tater said.

"Not now," Ry told him.

We sprinted all the way to the med room, where Captain Ward had wrapped a very pale redheaded man in a warming blanket. Two soldiers stood against the wall, weapons out. The dentist's eyes were freaked when he looked at me.

"Hypothermia. Possible frostbite in his fingers and toes."

I forced back a cringe. Burns I could handle. Frozen extremities were not something I'd ever had to deal with. I grabbed his largest medical book and thumbed through until I found information and treatment options, which I quickly skimmed.

"I'll run him a warm bath." I ran two doors down where a

medical tub was kept, but never used. Its primary purpose was for hot or ice baths for physical therapy. I cranked the water on until it was around 105 degrees, and let it fill, water restrictions be damned. Then I ran back to the room.

"We need to undress him and carry him to the bath. Once his body is pinkish red he'll need to be dried in warm cloth and immediately kept warm with blankets." Tater, Rylen, and Captain Ward undressed him. I noted absently that he was definitely human. The guys carried him while I went back to the tub to double check the water and turn it off.

They brought him in and carefully lowered him up to his neck. Several of his toes and fingers were whitish with black along the edges.

The man's teeth chattered and he panted. *"Hurtsss."*

"I know," I said. "It'll feel better soon." I hoped.

"He's talking now," one of the soldiers called into the hall. I looked up to see First Sergeant come in. All of their guns were drawn.

"Do you guys have to have weapons out in here?" I asked.

"He hasn't been cleared yet," First Sergeant explained.

"Well," I said, "I think it's safe to say he's an unarmed human who's not going to fight right now."

First Sergeant gave a curt nod to the soldiers, Rylen, and Tater. "Wait in the hall." But he remained, watching us work, his sidearm at the ready.

I dunked a washcloth into the warm water and ran it over the man's cheeks and ears. He shivered so hard some of the water vibrated out in small splashes. When the water began to feel tepid, I drained some as I added more warm. After ten or fifteen minutes his violent shuddering slowed. I raised his limbs one by one, nearly to the surface without taking them out. My heart began to settle at the sight of most of his fingers and toes turning pink again. But one pinky and the tips of two toes on both feet remained discolored.

Frostbite was like a cold burn. His extremities would likely blister and be discolored, possibly losing sensitivity to cold and heat.

The man struggled to speak. "Will you . . . have to . . . amputate?"

"Not likely," I said. "Unless there's gangrene. For now, we'll just keep an eye on them."

First Sergeant moved his chair next to the tub. I knew he was about to question him, and there was nothing I could do about it. What I wasn't expecting was his method.

"Sit back, Tate," he said. I scooted back.

Top pressed his gun to the man's head, making me suck in a breath. The dentist went completely still.

"How long until the others arrive?" First Sergeant asked. My heart galloped. *The others?*

"Just me." The man's teeth had stopped chattering, but he looked ready to pass out, and his voice was weak.

"Your ID says you're from Nellis, which has been taken over." He cocked the gun, and my insides began to shake with nausea.

"I escaped . . . no one . . . followed."

"What exactly did you escape?"

The man struggled to talk, his voice scratchy. I wanted to give him a drink of water, but didn't dare interfere.

"The DRI. I heard . . . your signal."

"You've been there at Nellis all this time, with the DRI?"

"Yes, sir," he whispered.

"Why did you leave?"

The man closed his eyes, his head drooping. "I thought . . . they were . . . fighting the enemy, but I was wrong. I think . . . I think they *are* the enemy. They . . . they're killing people." His eyes opened and he turned enough to eye First

Sergeant pleadingly. "If you're with them, kill me. I won't let you use me."

This guy wasn't with them. Nobody's act could be this good.

"How exactly have you been used?" First Sergeant asked, never softening, never lowering his weapon.

The man was quiet. His head fell forward. First Sergeant pressed the gun harder into the side of the guy's temple, making me wish I'd left the room with the others.

A quiet sob, almost like a choking cough, issued from the man, and he shook his head. "Just kill me."

First Sergeant's hard face remained impassive, but he lowered the gun to his thigh. "What's your name?"

The man paused a long time before answering. "Michael King."

"Rank?"

"Ca—captain."

First Sergeant gave a nod to the dentist, Captain Ward, who then got up and left the room, I assumed to pass along the man's identity to someone who could check the military database. Two minutes later, Linette stepped into the room with her arms crossed.

"Fighter pilot," she said.

Both mine and First Sergeant's eyes flew to the man. My heart was suddenly in my throat with trepidation.

"Tell me what work you've been doing these past two months, son."

The man shivered. Shook his head side to side. Then his chest began to rise and fall too quickly, his breaths turning from ragged pants to gasps. He grabbed his chest. I leapt to my feet and took his head in my hands, feeling down to his jumping pulse.

"Sh. Michael King, right?" I murmured. "It's okay, Michael." I eyed the First Sergeant and whispered, *"Panic attack."* He could fake the hyperventilating, but the out-of-control pulse told me this was authentic. I gave Top a pleading look and his lips pursed.

He sighed. "Let's get him dried and dressed." Relief flooded me.

Captain Ward, Tater, and Rylen came back in to help me, while the armed soldiers watched from the doorway. We got Michael dried and dressed, and the dentist and I bandaged his toes and fingers. Then we wrapped him in blankets and got him comfortable in one of the medical beds in another room. He was given hot tea and chicken broth, then locked in the room.

To my surprise, I looked up and found the chaplain coming down the hallway. First Sergeant greeted him.

"We need to find out what this man's done, and what he knows about Nellis and the DRI there. He's a fighter pilot. Captain Michael King. He's tired and injured—came in with hypothermia and frostbite—but find out as much as you can before he's allowed to rest."

"Yes, sir," the chaplain said.

Once he disappeared into the room, First Sergeant looked to the dentist and me. "Captain Ward, you're on shift now. Tate, come back at sixteen hundred for the evening shift.

"Yes, sir," we both said.

I walked down the empty, long hall with a lightness in my heart that didn't match our circumstances. Despite whatever disturbing situations surrounded the new guy's arrival, and the fact that we were all hiding underground from aliens, I was hope-filled in a way I couldn't ever remember being.

It was because of Rylen.

Because the secret I'd held in for so long was out there, and he hadn't turned me away. Just the opposite. It made me want to laugh, or maybe cry. I wanted to run and tell Mom . . .

I paused and rested a hand against the wall.

Are you watching, Mom? I closed my eyes and sent up the silent words. Peace and joy spread through me as I imagined her beaming face, knowing she was beyond happy that Rylen and I had found one another in this madness.

"Amber?"

My face quickly lifted to Tater, standing only a few feet away and surveying me with worry. "Are you okay?"

"Yeah." It came out as a whisper. I blinked away the extra moisture from my eyes.

His worry turned to something different. He crossed his arms and turned serious.

"I don't know what's going on with you and Ry, but I know him better than you when it comes to girls. He's not the kind to hook up if he doesn't care, and he's still feeling like shit about Livia. Don't mess with his emotions."

"I'm not," I said. His words hurt, but also drew my respect. "I love him."

His shoulders relaxed. A perplexed, skeptical look crossed his face. "Since when?" It came out like he didn't believe me.

"Since I was thirteen."

"*Thirteen?*" His arms uncrossed as he stared.

"Mom knew," I told him. "Remy knew too. I just . . ." I looked down at my fingers. "I didn't think he'd ever feel the same."

"Oh." He crossed his arms again, but dropped the stand-offish attitude.

"And what about you and Remy?" I asked.

He shrugged, shook his head. "Not happening. She's going through this 'born again' thing anyway. She doesn't want to be with me."

"You mean sleep with you?" Now it was my turn to cross my arms.

He scowled. "Whatever. I'm not even talking 'bout that.

She's the one who feels like she can't be with a someone without having sex."

"I think she needs to know that you want more than that."

"Well, I don't," he said. "I'm not getting married or having kids just for the DRI to fucking take them away too."

I raised my eyebrows and felt myself soften. "Are you going to those classes with her still?"

He scoffed and shook his head, but said, "Yeah."

"Good. That's really good, actually."

He gave a shrug. "I'm not a complete asshole, you know."

"*Yo se.*" *I know.* I reached up and put my fingers through his thick, but soft waves of hair. Mine was straight, like Dad's side of the family. Tater got Mom's awesome hair. Her wide, dark brown eyes.

"I miss them," I whispered. The raw truth of those simple words fissured something inside of me, and I fought to shove it all back into that crack and seal it up before I broke wide open.

"Me too," he whispered back.

I gulped down the rapidly building moisture until I knew I wasn't going to lose it. Then I took a deep breath and let it out.

"I'll see you later," I said. He yanked a lock of my hair before walking away.

I followed behind him out into the common area. It was still early, but a few people milled about the room. The scent of grits wafted from the kitchen. I watched as Tater passed Rylen sitting in an old loveseat, and the two of them fist-bumped. Tater headed to the tunnel, probably to shower before breakfast.

Rylen remained seated, but his eyes drifted over to me, and I stopped in my tracks while he looked at me in a way he'd never looked at me before. His eyes roamed me, and the look on his face was wholly unguarded, not bothering to be careful. I waited for him to shield those lustful feelings, to snap back into the polite boy-next-door that I was used to seeing, but he had let down his guard in that moment in a way that made me think he was imagining exactly what he'd been doing less than two hours ago.

There was a wild sort of predatoriness about his gaze that made me quiver at the core, though I knew I couldn't be much of a great sight. I wore my skinny jeans, that were now faded and slightly loose, with sneakers and Sean's ARMY sweatshirt that he said I could keep. My hair was in a ponytail.

You would have thought from his blatant staring that I was in a skirt and heels. Or naked again. I swallowed hard and slowly made my way over to him. His dimmed eyes rose to mine.

"Sit with me 'till breakfast?" he asked. But I swear his deep voice rumbled something more like, *"Straddle my lap 'till breakfast?"* and I blushed as I quickly sat.

"What'd you learn about that guy?" His abrupt change of tone and subject left me reeling and cooling.

"Um, he's a pilot."

His eyebrows rose and fell. "What else?"

"Nothing, really, except that he was under the DRI, and he's . . . I don't know. He has a lot of guilt about working for them. He escaped. I think he's for real."

"Let's hope," Rylen said.

Yes. It was terrifying to imagine what would happen if this compound were infiltrated.

"How many of us do you think are left?" I asked. "Humans? Do you think there are other places like this?"

"There are," he assured me, but he didn't expound. I resisted the urge to ask how many, and if we were in contact with them. He was privy to more information than most of us, and I knew the reasons. If I were captured and tortured, the information wouldn't be safe.

"We have a chance to beat them," Rylen whispered. "It's just a matter of timing, and the element of surprise. It all has to line up perfectly."

I swallowed hard, wondering what kind of crazy planning was going on behind the scenes. How could we possibly beat them? The thought of what we were up against, and the state of the world, had me scooting closer to Rylen's strong body. He took my hand in his and twined his fingers through mine. We both looked down at our hands, and the sight made my lungs flutter with a shaky breath of disbelief.

"Is it weird to you?" he asked.

I felt suddenly shy. "Yeah. I really never thought it would happen."

We continued to watch our hands. His thumb trailed up and down my skin, and his voice was low.

"When I used to get your letters, I fully expected you to tell me about some boyfriend, or say you were engaged. I thought some smart, lucky guy would snatch you up. Or maybe some asshole that Tater and I would have to get rid of." I snorted at this. His low rumble softened further. "I never thought there was a chance for me."

"I told you in one of those letters that you were the only guy for me." I looked at him now. "You have *no* idea how much nerve that took. And then you blew it off."

His eyes were wide with disbelief. "I swear, I thought you were fucking with me."

I smiled wryly and shook my head.

"My mom would be happy, you know." I glanced down at our joined fingers. "She always hoped for this. She was one of the only people who knew how I felt."

His gaze turned wistful. "I loved her. Your mom . . ." He shook his head, like there were no words. "Both your parents. They were the ones who made me believe I could be some-body."

I swallowed hard and looked in his gray eyes. "You always

were somebody."

He looked away. Still, all these years later, this grown man clearly didn't quite believe his own worth. I wished he could see what I saw when I looked at him.

The door to the tunnel opened, and the breakfast rush began making their way in. I tried to pull my hand away, but Rylen's fingers tightened on mine. I met his gaze, his locked jaw of stubbornness.

"You don't want people to know?" he asked.

"It's not that." I hated how private I was—how any little bit of PDA made me self-conscious—even holding hands. Especially with so many of the people in this compound being lonely and single, missing their loved ones.

"After seeing every one of these men watching you dance," Rylen said, "I'd like them to keep their distance."

Though his voice was full of jest, his eyes darkened with a jealous seriousness. Rylen Fite wanted to publicly claim me. And I could feel eyes on us as people passed.

J.D. gasped and hit Sean's arm. They both smiled at us.

I sensed other's voices quieting as they took in the way we held hands, facing one another, sitting closely. Like a couple.

Oh, my God. Rylen and I were a couple. A jubilant laugh bubbled in my chest and I bit my lip against a smile as I gazed up at him.

The grin he gave me was sexy, lazy even. He bent his head and nuzzled his mouth against my ear, whispering, "You tasted good this morning."

His erotic words caused a immediate full body reaction in me, from a throb in my core to my tingling toes and heated face. I pressed my forehead to his shoulder and let out a short laugh of surprise. I never in a million years imagined Rylen saying something naughty like that.

"You're bad," I muttered. He pulled back enough to see my

face, which I kept turned down.

"I made you blush, Pepper." He sounded proud. I let out another laugh of embarrassment. What other shocking things was this quiet, intense man capable of?

"Um . . . hey?" A sweet voice stood nearby, and we both looked up at Remy, whose smiling eyes gobbled up the scene before her.

"Hey," I said, pulling back just slightly. My cheeks were still warm. I tried not to laugh at the look on Remy's face—I knew she was about to burst at the sight of us together.

She grasped her hands in front of herself and asked, "Are you guys coming to breakfast?"

We stood and walked together to our regular table, where I sat between Rylen and Remy, with Tater on his other side. Everyone at the table looked between Rylen and I, noting, grinning, but nobody said anything. A sense of comfort filled the space.

For the first time in these months of darkness, I felt a ray of hope. Not just for myself personally, but as I looked around at the people at our table, and the people in this room, every one of us a hard worker willing to fight for our way of life. And I thought about Rylen's words that we had a chance. I desperately wanted that to be true.

I tried to eat slowly, but my body was famished from skipping dinner last night. After I finished the small breakfast and weak coffee, I downed two glasses of water to trick my stomach into thinking it was full.

"You working tonight?" Rylen asked me as everyone stood to go.

I nodded.

"Get some rest," he said.

I nodded again, and my tummy flipped, wondering if he would kiss me right here in front of all these people. But he didn't. With a squeeze of my fingers, he left toward the door of secrets, and Remy cleared her throat next to me. I turned to her and had to press my lips together at her bug-eyes staring a hole through me.

"Well?!" she said impatiently. "Don't even try not to tell me! I've been waiting too long for this moment. Not that it's about me, but I have to live vicariously through you!" She bounced on her toes. This was the least I could do for her.

I grabbed her hand and pulled her to the empty loveseat on the other side of the room. And then I forced myself to tell her the conversation that led to our feelings finally coming out and being accepted.

She stared hard. "And then?"

I squirmed.

She prompted, *"And then you had sex?"*

"No." I sighed, smoothed back my hair. I needed to fight this instinct to keep every detail to myself. "Not yet. We just made out and *thenhewentdownonme.*"

She grasped my hands and bounced on the springy cushion, making it squeak.

"All right, enough," I said laughing. "I need some sleep."

Remy pulled me into a tight hug and I held her back. When we let go, she headed to work and I headed to the tunnel. Back in our room, I slept for six much-needed hours until it was time to get up for my evening med shift.

I stared at the shelves of prescription drugs, alone in the supply room, and I felt nervous. The clinic here had a large supply of birth control, and it had grown after the recent pharmacy raid. But I'd never been on birth control. I took several of the boxes out and began to read through the pamphlets, deciding on the shot that would last three months.

I readied the vial and needle, and swabbed my arm with an alcohol pad. Then I pressed my lips together and administered the shot to my left upper arm. It stung, and I exhaled loudly when it was finished. The informational packet said that my periods would get lighter and eventually stop. But now that I thought about it, I hadn't had a period in two months. That was normal, I supposed, considering all that my body had been through. I tossed the needle in the sharps container.

Weird, I thought as I rubbed my stinging arm. I was probably going to be sexually active soon. The thought made my blood rush with nervous excitement. Rylen. Me and Rylen. Together . . . naked.

The door opened and I jumped. First Sergeant eyed me.

"Sorry to startle you. Captain King has been cleared." Ah, the new guy. "I'll need you to check him over to make sure he's ready to be shown to a room."

"Sure." I got up and followed him into Michael's room. The man was sitting on the edge of his hospital bed, dressed in camo pants and a white T-shirt. There was color under his freckled face now that complimented his shock of red hair, but his green eyes were sort of blank when they looked at me.

"Hello," I said. He didn't respond, so I went on, getting my stethoscope and equipment ready. "I'm Amber Tate. Paramedic. Army brat."

He gave a small nod, his shoulders hunched. I took all of his vitals. Then I checked his fingers and toes. A couple had begun to blister.

"This is a good sign," I told him. "They're healing, but they'll look worse before they look better. Just keep them really clean." I made a bag with sterile bandages and a cleaning solution for him to take with him. "Come see me or Captain Ward any time if you need something."

"Thanks," he said quietly.

Top led Michael King from the room, and I couldn't help but feel sad for the man. The darkness surrounding him was thick. I didn't want to know what demons he was battling; I just hoped he was strong enough to beat them.

I went down the hall to Texas Harry's room. He was sitting up in the bed with his monstrous calves hanging down, arm dutifully held up by a sling. His face was the picture of boredom and annoyance as he eyeballed me.

"Get me outta here, Mama Tate."

I smiled. "Let me see what I can do."

I took all of his vitals and was happy about how well everything looked.

"I think I can safely discharge you, if you promise to take it easy on that shoulder and arm."

"Yep." He quickly hopped down, wincing.

"I mean it, Harris. I will kick your ass if you reinjure it."

He saluted me with his good arm.

"Want another dose of painkiller?" I asked him, feeling generous since the run had replenished our stock.

"Nah." He ran a hand down his beard. "Save it for the pansy asses."

I rolled my eyes and he grinned before strolling out.

I stripped the sheets from his bed and was walking down the hall when First Sergeant stepped out of a room and halted in front of me.

"What are you smiling about, Tate?"

Had I been smiling? His gaze was humored.

"I guess I'm having a good day?"

"Well, it suits you." He gave an approving nod and moved on.

And this time when I made my way to the laundry room

at the end of the hall, I embraced the small smile on my lips, fully aware of its presence, and grateful that there was anything to be happy about.

TWENTY-FIVE

I WAS HALFWAY THROUGH my shift and bored enough to read about suturing techniques when the door to the med room opened. The sight of Rylen's handsome face and stark gray eyes sent a zing singing through me.

"Hey," I said, shutting the book and trying not to grin like an idiot.

The hallway was silent behind him as he slipped in and closed the door. It was the middle of the night.

He leaned against the door. "Working hard?"

"Hardly working." I pushed the book away. Nerves shot through my belly as Rylen pushed off the door and his presence filled the room, energizing my blood. He paced before me with his arms crossed.

"That new guy," he said quietly. "I want you and Remy to keep your distance from him."

My eyebrows pushed together in curiosity. "Why?"

"He's just got some skeletons."

"Don't we all?" I backed up to the exam bed and hopped up

on it, my feet dangling. Rylen moved closer and put his hands on my knees, sending a shiver up my thighs.

"Yeah, but, let's just say his skeletons would . . . clash with others' skeletons."

Huh? I was about to dig for more information, when he grasped my lower thighs and pulled me to the edge, stepping between my legs. Our conversation fled my mind. The intensity of his eyes took up every bit of space in my head. When his body met mine, a rush went to my core and my breaths became shorter.

"I'm on the clock," I whispered.

"Yeah, me too." He wrapped his arms around my back and I slid mine over his shoulders. It was still so strange and exhilarating to be able to touch him like this.

His mouth hovered over mine, his warm breaths skirting my lips. "Want me to leave?"

"No," I whispered. My nails dug into his hair as I pulled him to me. God, his mouth was so perfect on mine. One of his hands roamed up my back to my neck where he cradled the base of my head as he leaned forward, making me cling to him, wrapping my legs around his waist as he held me at an angle. The kiss grew hungry and hurried. If he were to slide a hand down my pants right now, I would immediately come apart. No kiss had ever done that for me. No kiss had ever made my body beg for so much more, and right now it was crying out to be covered in him.

My mind was harried when Rylen's mouth pulled back and he pressed his forehead to mine, our panting breaths mingling between us.

"I wasn't planning for that to happen. It was supposed to be a quick break."

He had to get back to work. I gave an unhappy whimper and fought the urge to resort to dirty tactics to get him to stay longer. But what I was craving should probably not be done in an unlocked room when Top could walk in at any second. The thought was sobering. I unhooked my feet from his back and tried not to pout.

Rylen leaned in and sucked my bottom lip into his mouth before releasing it and giving me a look of sheer ravenous promise. The thrill of that look was still crashing through me when he closed the door behind himself. I closed my eyes and took two deep breaths, trying to calm the blood flow that had me yearning for things I couldn't have right then.

Damn him.

I was worthless the rest of my shift, still marveling at this change of events, the shiny newness of it, imagining what it would be like to be with Rylen in all ways. In other words, I was turned on at work for hours.

Damn him.

By the time Captain Ward relieved me of my shift, I was a bundle of taut nerves. I didn't know how I'd be able to get to sleep in this state. It was only five in the morning, so Remy would still be sleeping, which would help cool me down when I got to the room. I would hunt down Rylen right now if he wasn't at his shift for another couple hours.

I walked down the chilly tunnel with my flashlight on, lost in thought. When I neared the end I heard a strange sound coming from the other side of the door—a voice, but it sounded like a distressed moan, like someone was in pain. I rushed forward and pushed the door open, only to stop dead in my tracks. Linette was sitting on top of one of the dryers, yanking her shirt down and turning a glare to me. Josh stood between her legs. He turned his head, eyebrows up in a menacing way that was meant to scare off the intruder, but when he saw me he gave a wry grin.

I pushed the door to the tunnel closed and walked through

the room without a word. Linette's husky giggle followed me up the stairwell, until she was suddenly silenced, I'm sure by Josh's mouth.

Well, then. I was sufficiently cooled down now, and ready to nap until breakfast.

The stars aligned that night after dinner, and everyone gathered in the hotel lobby. It had quickly become my new favorite place on earth. Someone had set up a ping-pong table and dart board. Aside from the covered glass, the room had a sense of normalcy that we were lacking in daily life. The ceilings were higher. Music played lightly overhead. It seemed to be the only place where people dared to laugh and relax a little. We'd brought a pack of cards to play with Remy and Tater after their meeting.

An old business room off the lobby was being used for the Grief Support Group. We'd watched Remy and Tater walk in, along with the chaplain, seven other men and women, and the new guy with his head down. Captain Michael King. He always looked like he was wasting away. I made a mental note to make sure he was at the meals.

Rylen starting acting nervous when he saw him go in. He scooted to the edge of the loveseat we shared, and watched the closed door, tugging his earlobe.

"What's wrong?" I asked.

"Hm?" He tore his attention from the door. "Nothing." He made an effort to relax back into the chair, but his attention was still on the Grief room.

"Seriously, what is it, Ry? The new guy?"

He ran a hand over his cheek and down his chin. "Yeah, I, uh . . . I kind of wish he wasn't in there."

"Why?"

Rylen shook his head.

"Why can't you tell me?" I pressed.

"He's done classified jobs that are best left unspoken."

"Like what? I won't tell anyone."

Rylen ran a thumb over my chin, the tip touching my bottom lip. "It's stuff I wish I didn't even know." He nodded toward the door. "Top told him he should go, 'cause those meetings are confidential—they have an understanding that what's said in that room stays there—but I'm hoping he doesn't share too much."

Geez, what kind of things has this guy done? He seemed so normal, but he'd definitely been broken by his time with the DRI. I decided to change tactics.

"Rylen . . . what do you do all day at work?"

He scooted closer to me and twined his fingers with mine. "Well." He leaned his head toward mine and said in a low voice. "I'm working on getting a Bael airship to fly."

I gasped and stared at him. "You're serious?" I hissed.

"Yeah. But so far we've had no luck." He put a finger to his lips to show it was our secret. I realized he was breaking major rules by telling me this. I wanted to ask a million questions, but having that information actually scared me a little. Plus, I doubted he'd tell me any details.

We held hands, both of us lost in our thoughts. I tried to imagine what the ship looked like, and what types of technological advances they had over us. Could we learn from them and adapt enough to fight them?

A weird feminine yelp came from the Grief room, causing Rylen and I to both tense. The voice was choked as she shouted something.

"Is that Remy?" I asked.

"Fuck," Rylen breathed. His face paled. We both stood and moved to toward the door, just as a raging male voice let out a cry, followed by a crashing sound, screams, and shouts.

"Tater!" I said. Rylen was already running. He barreled into the room with me right behind him. I could not believe what I was seeing. Tater had Michael King on the ground, pinned, with his hands around his throat. Tater's face looked crazed. Remy stood beside them, screaming for them to stop.

The chaplain and Rylen both struggled to pull Tater off the man, whose face had gone deep red. When Tater released him, Michael didn't bother trying to get up. He just lie there, back arching, gasping for air.

"You killed them!" Tater shouted. My brother thrashed and they held him tighter. "Fucking idiot! *Why*? You had to know it was innocent humans down there!"

What . . . ? His words slithered into me like a poisoned serpent, and I began to shake and burn. He couldn't mean what it sounded like. I rushed forward and stood in front of Tater, taking his face in my hands to calm him. His eyes finally focused on me, full of tears, and he sagged in the arms of the men holding him.

"He dropped the bomb on them, Amber. This fucker . . . he killed them."

"He . . ." I glanced down at Michael, and a sickening sense of wrongness filled me. "He dropped the bomb?" I shifted my eyes from Tater to Remy to Rylen, whose tight features and locked jaw told me it was true. This pilot had been dropping bombs on townspeople. He'd killed my parents, and grandmother, and Livia. He'd killed Remy's parents. She collapsed into a chair, shuddering. Another woman dropped to her side to console her.

My gaze slowly moved to the man on the floor, who was sitting up now, still gasping.

"Amber," Rylen warned. I barely heard him. My feet were already moving, taking me to this human whose hands had flown the plane and released the bombs. He'd done it. *He'd done it.*

The room took on a deadly stillness. The chaplain and another man had gotten Michael King to his feet. He peered at me, cowering slightly, looking like absolute shit.

"You knew you were bombing humans?" It came out of me as a whisper.

The room was so quiet. This man and I were both shaking, trembling, this man who'd stolen my family with one flick of his finger. Even the chaplain watched, his face pained, and he didn't try to intervene.

"I was told the encampments were outliers. Resisters of peace. The people who poisoned the waters." His voice was so weak as he continued. "But you're right to hate me. Because even after I began to question it in my mind—to question the sheer numbers of people at those sites—I was too cowardly to question them directly. I knew they would kill me. I knew the only way I could stop being used by them was to escape."

I couldn't even respond. My mind screamed *murderer*, but my heart felt debilitating pity, as if his remorse were mingling with my own, our brokenness forever linked.

"I'm sorry," he whispered. "If I could do it all over again, I would refuse. I would have let them kill me." Tears slid down his cheeks.

"I believe you," I said weakly.

Without another word, I turned to Remy and held out my hand. She took it. I looked at Rylen and nodded to the door. He and the chaplain moved Tater toward it. In the lobby, we ignored the stares of everyone who'd heard the commotion and come to check it out. The four of us went to mine and Remy's room, and together we sat. Each of their unguarded faces mirrored my brokenness.

Seeing the face of the person who'd killed our families, and knowing he'd been a blind part of the Bael race's plans, left us bleeding all over again. There would be no funerals. No court trials. Michael King would have to live this miserable existence with the rest of us. We would not try to punish him.

Instead, we talked about our families. We told stories, ridiculous reminiscing that had us in stitches of laughter, wiping tears. But there was something healing about the tales of our loved ones who we'd never see again in this lifetime. Something soul-nourishing and cleansing about bringing them back to life through our memories, reminding ourselves they would always live on in us. Through us.

Our hearts were raw and tender by the time Tater and Rylen left for their own room. I let Remy snuggle me as we fell asleep, thankful the four of us still had each other.

TWENTY-SIX

THE NEXT MORNING A meeting was called for the entire compound following breakfast. Everyone who wasn't on watch duty was expected to attend. As we made our way through the super secret doors and into the large meeting room, First Sergeant pulled Tater, Remy, Rylen, and me aside.

"I want you each to know that the only reason we allowed Captain King to remain was because we sincerely believe he was following orders under the pretense that he was working for the right side, and that he left them under peril of his life when he realized things weren't as they seemed."

We all nodded, and he continued. "I'm sorry for how things came about yesterday. We've asked King to keep his distance—"

"Sir," Tater interrupted. "With all due respect . . . I'm not ready to make nice with him, and I might never be, but you have my word I won't go after him again."

First Sergeant searched my brother's face before saying, "All right then." He gave Tater's shoulder a hard pat and looked at

Remy and me with sad eyes. "You girls okay?"

All we could do was nod again. We might never be "okay," but we wouldn't cause anymore scenes.

By the time we finished our conversation the room was bursting at the seams. It was the same room we'd been in when we learned about Bael, but this time everyone was present. People were standing in the back. All chairs were taken, and some had propped themselves on the long tables. The four of us stood against the side wall.

The screen came on, and Top used a clicker in his hand. Someone dimmed the lights in the front of the room. A topographical map filled the screen.

"This is Dugway," First Sergeant said. He pointed to the entrance where we'd originally come in with the watchtower overlooking it. He pointed to the Army hotel on the outskirts of base where we all stayed. He pointed out the side exit of the compound inside the base where Remy went out each night to get to the greenhouse. Beyond that was a much larger structure he pointed at now.

"This building housed the laboratories where bio and chemical warfare was once tested and stored. It has since been imploded, however our chemist—" he inclined his head to an older man in the front row who I'd often seen attending grief meetings, "—had the forethought to take necessary records and antidote samples, which he works on every day to restock our stores."

Next, First Sergeant pointed to a series of aircraft hangars. "In these we have three choppers, and two cargo planes. Enough to carry everyone in this safehouse if the need arises. We've got pilots ready for each vessel." He peered around the room, meeting the gaze of three men, including Rylen, and one woman. My heart gave a great pound as I looked up at Rylen and received a *don't worry* wink from him.

No way. How long had it been since he flew a plane?

"We also have one fighter jet which Captain King has agreed to fly as a defensive measure to ward off any air or ground attacks while our troops exit."

A murmur of whispers rose up and the four of us shifted our stances uncomfortably. Could Michael be trusted to protect us in his frame of mind? First Sergeant obviously thought so, but it was scary. Also, it could be a suicide mission, Captain King against all of whatever might come. If the DRI . . . er, Baelese, caught wind of what was going on here, they would most likely pull out all the stops to take us down.

I looked over to where Michael sat, hoping we'd make eye contact so I could show him we weren't hostile, but he kept his unfocused eyes squarely forward as Top went on.

"The problem we face if we're attacked during the night, is getting everyone from the hotel to these hangars in a timely manner. In the past week we've instituted measures outside of base to slow any threats—tire cutters on the roads and hiding rocks with armed soldiers farther out in surrounding fields. Our hope is that if we are attacked, we can keep them at bay long enough to give everyone time to get to these hangars.

"Here's the thing." He paused and let his deadly serious eyes roam the faces in the room. "When the alarm sounds, you have eight minutes to get to the hangar. Eight. At the eight minute mark, those aircraft must leave or risk losing everyone. I do not want a single one of you left behind. I don't care if you're in the shower and you have to run out butt-ass naked and soaking wet. When you hear the alarms you stop what you're doing and go. Move quick, but not panicked. Move as a team. Got it?"

"Yes, sir," we all murmured in chorus. My heart was in my throat, fluttering wildly at the thought of attack.

"All right then. Everyone's dismissed except you two." He pointed over at Remy and me. We looked at each other with surprise. The room cleared out, but Tater and Rylen remained.

Ry's forehead was pinched with worry. "Mind if we stay with them?"

Top glanced at us. "Fine." The four of us sat.

He cleared his throat and I crossed my arms tightly over my chest. "Captain King was not privy to insider information, but there were things he overheard during his time under the Baelese leadership. He revealed more last night to the chaplain after the, uh, episode." He cleared his throat again and lifted a piece of paper with notes.

"What does it have to do with Amber and Remy?" Rylen asked.

"It's specific to females. Females who were out there, in towns, after the war began. Females who had contact with DRI." We all listened, their faces as baffled as mine. "There was talk of population control, one race among humans, and infertility shots given to masses of women at clinics."

Population control. Infertility shots. A dizzy spell smacked into me, and Remy grabbed my arm. We looked at each other, and her face reflected the absolute horror seeping through me.

"They gave me a shot," she whispered.

"Me too."

Her voice broke. "But they were for the Red Virus, right?"

"That's what they said . . ." My voice trailed off as I remembered how those shots had affected us. We'd both been violently ill. We'd had cramps like menstrual cramps, but far worse. And come to think of it . . . I haven't had a period since then." I assumed my cycle had stopped due to stress and lack of caloric intake.

"*Amber.*" Remy's hand tightened on my arm as her face took on a plastic sheen, then she bolted to the trashcan in the corner. I sprinted after her, getting to her side as she coughed and vomited. My own breakfast was halfway up my esophagus.

Tater and Rylen were right behind us as I pulled her hair back.

"I'll get some paper towels," Tater said. He ran to the bathroom down the hall.

While Remy got sick, gasping through moans, and my own stomach and mind turned, and turned, and turned, I felt Rylen watching me. His eyes were loaded with emotion and questions. Tater was back now, handing Remy a paper towel that she used to wipe her mouth. She sat back on her heels and covered her face. She trembled, but didn't cry.

"We don't know for sure," I said, but Top's words ripped through me like a jagged knife. What if it were true? Remy would not be having children someday. And neither would I. Not that either of us was in any rush with the state of our world, but someday . . . who knows? The point was, they took that choice from us. They made us unable to repopulate.

"Maybe that's not the shot you guys got," Tater said, as he crouched beside Remy.

"God damn it," First Sergeant muttered, his voice filled with anger. "I'm sorry to do this to you. I don't know what this intel means. I don't have any information on whether it's something we can reverse."

"We have two types of ultrasound machines," came another voice from the doorway. The dentist.

Top looked at us apologetically. "I told Captain Ward about it and asked him to wait outside."

"We can have a look," the dentist said. "Run blood tests. If the two of you want." He looked at Remy and me. She and I shared a glance and she gave a nod.

"Okay," I whispered.

"You all go," Top said. "Take the day off."

He disappeared into the hall, and the four of us stood there like shells of ourselves. I didn't want to think about this. I didn't want to mourn people that didn't even exist yet. I didn't want to imagine the possibilities that were no longer mine to imagine. Rylen's eyes were boring into me, but I couldn't look up. Once upon a time I'd let myself imagine having babies with him. No, I couldn't look at those eyes, knowing I could never mother his children. A shudder ripped through me as we left the room and moved down the hall.

Try as I may to ignore Rylen's presence, he took my other hand in his and held it. He was warm, solid, steady. And he knew me. I didn't have to admit how broken I felt at that moment, because I was certain Rylen knew.

We decided to go straight to the clinic rooms. I found the upright ultrasound machine, and the transvaginal ultrasound machine. A quick read through of manuals told me the transvaginal one was going to show us what we needed to see: a closeup of our ovaries.

Tater hitched a thumb toward the door. "I'll wait out there."

He and Rylen left us.

"Should we wait for the dentist?" she asked.

"Um, no. We'll figure it out. I'm going to let you go first. You'll lay back, and um, hold the device, you know . . . inside yourself." Her eyebrows flew up skeptically, and I charged forward. "And I'll tell you when to hold it still while I read the monitor. Team effort."

"Okay," she whispered. I turned to get everything ready as she took off her pants and got on the table, covering her hips with a towel. She waited patiently while I looked through manuals and books. I found a picture of what normal ovaries and fallopian tubes looked like. I stared at the tiny dots of follicles, or eggs. Then I took a deep breath and handed Remy the transducer probe with a glob of lube on the end.

She made a face and I sighed. "It's going to send out sound waves that will bounce off your ovaries and give me a picture.

Just try to relax. I won't be looking at you; I'll be watching the screen."

"Do you know how to read that thing?"

"I'm a quick learner." Honestly, people attended classes and schooling to become experts at reading these things. I had no idea if I'd be able to decipher it.

She lay back and exhaled loudly. I stared at the screen. Fuzzy images began to show. After five minutes of squinting at squiggly lines I was feeling frustrated with myself. So much for being a quick learner.

Voices in the hall distracted me, then a light knock. I got up and opened the door a crack.

"Are you using the probe?" Captain Ward asked.

I nodded. "It's hard to read."

"I actually borrowed one from the clinic during my wife's two pregnancies," he said sheepishly. "I know how to read it if you'd like."

"Yes!" I pulled him into the room and shut the door. He came right over and sat in the stool by Remy's knee, taking the monitor.

Within seconds he said, "It's not in far enough. Do you mind? I'll be gentle."

"Okay," Remy whispered.

He reached under the towel and Remy stared up at the ceiling. I stood beside her and took her hand.

One minute later the dentist went very still as he stared down. He looked up first to me, his eyebrows scrunched, then his eyes slid to Remy. We squeezed hands.

"Your ovaries are . . . not what they should be. They appear to have aged and shrunk. I'm sorry, Miss Haines. There are no eggs left."

TWENTY-SEVEN

IT'S GOOD THAT WE had the rest of the day off. I opted not to have an ultrasound done on myself. I already knew the results would be the same. I nearly laughed at the irony of the birth control shot I'd given myself days before. What a waste.

We told the guys we wanted to be alone, but they brought us lunch and dinner. I couldn't let my gaze linger too long on Rylen's pleading eyes. He so wanted to comfort me, but my heart was too flayed. If I cried, it would be ugly, and I might break shit. I couldn't let loose what was inside me.

I kept thinking of the image of Remy's ovaries on that screen, shriveled like raisins. Remy who would have been such a wonderful mom.

No matter how hard I tried not to think about it, an inferno built inside of me, a burning rage against the invaders of our planet. The destroyers. They had conquered us, and it all happened so quickly. We were too trusting in our nature, as humans, we let them take control despite our reservations. I had ignored my instincts.

Never again.

I couldn't sleep that night. It was like fire ants ran beneath my skin. At two in the morning I slipped from bed and went down the hall and stairs, relishing the spooky quiet all around me. I made my way to the empty gym and stepped onto the treadmill. I started at a jog and lost track of time. My legs still itched, so I turned up the speed and raised the incline. I needed to burn that itch away. I panted for air, savoring every strain of my muscles, every bead of sweat that ran down my face and back. I wanted to run faster and farther.

But what I really wanted was music. I wanted headphones with heavy metal that would blast every last pitiful thought from my head as it all bombarded me. *They killed your family. They've ruined your body.* The thought of my reproductive system being slaughtered by them . . . it was a violation of the worst kind. I desperately needed to feel alive and in control, but something was missing that I'd never be able to retrieve. They'd taken it without a single thought or repercussion. I still remembered the lady's face who'd given me the shot. The out-of-place questions she'd asked me and her blatant dismissal of my worth.

I was sprinting and panting so hard I could barely see the panel before me. With a shock, I realized my eyes had filled with tears. I punched the power button and jumped off, collapsing into a pile of gelatinous muscles, weeping inconsolably.

And before I could register the door opening, Rylen was crouching next to me, gathering me into his arms right there on the floor, his voice against my ear, "I'm here, Pepper."

No, oh, God. I tried to pull away and hide my face. Through disgusting sobs, I asked, "What are you *doing* here?" I so didn't want him seeing me like this.

"I heard your door and followed you," he said, like *duh*. "I was worried."

"Well, don't be." I slashed at my eyes with my sleeve. "Leave. Please."

"Don't push me away, Pepper. I'm not scared of your tears."

Another coughing sob wrenched from my soul. "I'm so disgusting, just leave."

I wasn't even sure what I meant specifically. I felt disgusting in every way. On the outside I was sweating profusely on a gym floor and my face was drenched with tears, my nose runny. On the inside I was shriveled. Like an old woman. Not good enough for a virile, strong man.

"I'm not leaving you," he said into my damp hair.

I sucked in a ragged breath. "I can't give you babies."

He gave an ironic laugh. "The last fucking thing I want in this entire world right now is a baby. That is never, ever going to be a problem for me, Pep. I swear. All I want is you. Just as you are."

He held me tighter and I moved my arms around him, pressing my wet cheek into his shirt. When I'd finally cried all my tears, I became distinctly aware of just how soaked through I was with sweat.

"I'm fine. You should go." I tried to pull away, but the stubborn bastard wouldn't let me. "I mean it, Ry. I smell bad."

He chuckled, then completely took me by surprise by laying me back on the floor mats and kissing me with a burst of passion that made me realize he couldn't care less how I thought I smelled. He broke away from my mouth and kissed my cheeks, then my eyelids, whispering my name between each kiss. I wanted to cry all over again, overwhelmed by the tenderness of his attention.

I opened my legs and he nestled his hips between them as I wrapped a foot around his thigh, tugging him against me and finding him completely turned on. We stopped moving and stared into each other's' eyes. He brushed my long, wet bangs off my forehead.

"I'll take you back to your room," he said thickly.

But I shook my head. "No. You won't."

Rylen's eyes stormed over. He looked around us at the small room and exercise equipment on gray mats.

"It's fine," I whispered. I took his face in my hands and raised my head to kiss him. At the brush of my lips he was focused again, his mouth moving over mine as our hips moved in sync, rubbing, driving us both to panting. I put a hand on his hard stomach and pushed until he raised himself enough for me to pull my damp T-shirt over my head.

"Pepper . . ." He glanced toward the door. "There's no lock."

"Then we'd better hurry."

"But the floor's—"

"Shh." I put a hand over the large bulge in his running pants, and his eyes closed, his mouth opening in a shocked inhale. I let go of him and sat up on my knees to face him. His eyes dipped down to where I was pushing my yoga pants and undies south, over my hips, to my knees. I pulled them off, then tossed my bra on top.

I was completely naked in the public gym. A thrill of rebellion shivered through me, and I reached for Ry's shirt, yanking it up over his head. His eyes were completely smoky now. Gone were the warnings and worries. His stomach flexed as my fingers grazed the line of elastic slung low on his waist. I leaned forward enough to press my breasts to his chest and take his mouth as I pushed his shorts down. Then I looked down.

Every ounce of pent-up passion I'd felt for Rylen over the last few days came rushing back at the sight of him naked, hard, for me. And so human. I took him in my hand and he crushed his mouth to mine, laying me back on the mat again.

He sat up on his knees between my legs and looked down at me. His gaze felt like a soft finger tantalizing every inch of skin it touched. My nipples peaked as he watched my chest rise and fall quickly. My stomach tightened while he took in my belly button. His hands landed on the tops of my thighs, hot and strong, his fingers digging in just enough to make me arch my back. I watched as he took himself in his hand and rubbed my nub with the hard, round head of his cock.

A moan tore from my throat. "Yes." I bucked my hips but he grabbed my hip in his free hand to hold me steady.

He watched me as he rubbed himself slowly down my folds, both of us gasping when he came into contact with my wetness, around my waiting opening, and back up to the bundle of nerves that was throbbing wildly.

"Please," I begged. "Oh, God." I tried to reach for him, but he was too far away. I could only reach his knees, which I dug my nails into until he lowered himself to align with me. He waited until my eyes fluttered up and were watching his, and then he pressed his entire length slowly into me. With every inch I sucked in air until I was full. So full.

When our bodies met, his eyes closed and he brought his hands to the sides of my body, lowering his weight onto me. I arched my hips as far as I could and we stayed like that for a minute, pressed together, breathing hard, every inch of him inside of me. I swear I could feel him pulsating with self-restraint.

"Rylen . . ." He lowered his face to mine, his lips trembling against my cheek, and I whispered, "Don't hold back."

A guttural sort of growl rumbled through him and I felt his hips ease off mine a fraction, only to slam back down and grind into me. My head flew back. He did it again. My back slid against the mat, grains of dirt digging into my skin, but I barely felt it. Every time Rylen rammed his hips into mine, he rubbed against that bundle of nerves, grinding his body to mine as if he couldn't get deep enough.

I tried to stay quiet, I really did, but I could feel those nerve endings building power each time our bodies met. His hips came down against mine over and over and over, faster and faster, until we had somehow moved up the entire length of the mat and my head was banging into the wall, but we didn't care.

"Yes," I breathed, clutching his back, reaching down for his ass, hitching my legs around him. "Yes."

And then he did something fucking magical that made the breath stick in my lungs. Deep inside me, he stopped pulling out even an inch, and just started rocking his hips against mine. I moved mine circular while he pressed, pressed, pressed as hard as he could, and the explosion detonated inside of me, spreading out like wildfire.

Rylen crushed his mouth to mine, probably trying to quiet my uncharacteristic sounds, which were considerably louder than his own. I felt him ignite inside of me, and I wanted to cry at the rightness of it, shattering and breaking together. We stayed like that for a long while, the two of us catching our breath as one.

At the same time we both seemed to notice the intrusive wall that my head and neck were pressed against at an awkward angle.

"Um, whoops," I said. A giggle escaped my throat, and the sound of it surprised me.

"Sorry about that," he said, grasping my hips and scooting me down a few inches. He smiled down at me, and I wound my fingers in the back of his short hair, pulling his face to mine.

"I love you, Ry."

"I love you too, Pepper."

In the far distance we heard a door open and close, and our eyes flew wide. We jumped up, hissing at the sudden lack of contact, then ran around the room laughing as we yanked our clothes back on. Nobody came into the gym room. It was probably just someone heading to their shift, but we left anyhow. Rylen walked me back to my room. We kissed for a long time in the hallway until we both started to get worked up again. I was about to consider asking him to sneak to the grief room in the lobby with me so I could climb all over him, but he took the gentlemanly high road and showed me to my door. It was almost four in the morning, and as I went inside I got a whiff of myself.

I smelled *so* bad. I almost laughed again at the fact that Rylen was unfazed by it. I pressed my lips together as I grabbed a change of clothes and decided to get my daily shower right then. The warm water slid over me, a sensual reminder of Rylen's hands and mouth. I sighed as I turned the water off, the five minutes ending far too quickly.

A small, unfamiliar smile graced my lips as I dried myself and got dressed. Today was a new day. And I could handle it.

TWENTY-EIGHT

I WINCED AND SAT up in bed.

"What's wrong?" Remy sat up next to me, sounding groggy.

"My back." It stung. I stood and went to the bathroom with Remy behind me. I turned and lifted my shirt enough to see red irritation and small scratches. Then it hit me and I breathed, "*Oh*." I dropped my shirt.

"Oh, my gosh! Amber, what happened?"

I smiled and a small laugh slipped out. Remy looked at me like I'd lost my mind.

"It was . . . me and Rylen . . ." I pulled my hair over my shoulder and fussed with it. She continued to watch me and wait. "We were at the gym during the night, at like two in the morning, and we ended up . . . on the floor."

Her eyes grew with a slow gradualness that made me giggle again.

"That—" She pointed at my back. "Is from the gym floor?"

"Yeah. Mat burn or something." I shrugged and looked at

the ends of my hair.

She grasped my shoulders. "You had sex on the gym floor?!"

Now I laughed outright. "Yeah?"

"And?" she asked, giving me a shake.

"And what?"

"*How was it?*"

I pulled my bottom lip between my teeth to fight the giddy loco I was feeling.

Remy fell back against the sink and threw her head back. "Uuuugh, I'm not even going to lie. I am so freaking jealous."

"You know," I said, crossing my arms, "I think Tater would treat you right if you let him. Someday. When you're both ready." I couldn't believe I was saying it, but I believed it. Despite Tater's claim not to want to marry someday.

She crossed her arms too, and gave a small shrug. "I would just ruin it. The way I'm feeling . . ."

"I don't think so, Rem," I whispered. "Things are different. I think your whole outlook on life has changed, and so has his. I don't want you to be afraid to have a little happiness. Even if it's with my brother."

She nudged the bath mat with her toe. "We'll see."

I blushed the entire way through breakfast with Rylen at my side, unable to stop thinking about our time together, especially when he kept stealing serious glances that made me want to combust. I felt like the entire table could feel the heated tension between us. I know Remy could. She kept clearing her throat and taking sips of water, trying not to smile.

"You all right over there, Remy?" Matt asked from across the table.

She gave a high pitched laugh and said, "Yep!" Then she took another sip before shoving a last bite of blueberry muffin in her mouth with a forced smile. Matt chuckled and shook his head as Tater watched her curiously.

"Yeah, what's going on?" J.D. asked. "Why's everyone acting so weird?"

I gave a clueless shake of my head.

Texas Harry was back with us, in a sling like a good boy. He downed the last of his coffee before looking at Rylen. "Where'd you go at two in the morning, man? I heard doors closing and looked out to see your ass going down the stairs."

My blushing cheeks inflamed.

"To the gym," Rylen said, straight faced.

"The gym? For what?"

Rylen kept his cool. "What do people normally go to the gym for, Tex?"

"Release," Mark said in a profound tone.

Remy coughed on her water, shoving back her chair to bend forward. Tater patted her back.

"She knows?" Rylen murmured to me.

"Yep," I muttered back. He chuckled into his coffee.

"I just meant, you already went that afternoon," Texas Harry said.

"Yeah," Rylen told him. "Couldn't sleep."

Tex shrugged with his good shoulder, like that was acceptable enough. Really, I knew he was asking because people in the compound were warned against overuse of the gym due to strict food rationing. They didn't want anyone overdoing it when there weren't enough calories to warrant it.

This convo needed to steer away from the gym. "How you feeling?" I asked Texas Harry.

He gave me a thumbs-up. "Just dandy." *Liar.*

"Come see me later to have your bandage changed."

He nodded.

We all stood to leave, and Rylen clutched my hip, pulling me closer and kissing me—a long, soft peck. To my humiliation, our entire table let out catcalls, howling.

"Oh, my God," I said as Rylen chuckled.

Remy's lips were pressed together in glee, and Tater had a bemused expression, mouth quirked to one side. "That's just weird."

"See you after work," Ry said.

I walked away from them feeling a gushy sense of happiness I'd never experienced in my life. I couldn't wait to get to the med room where I could smile all I wanted and not have to hide it. This kind of joy seemed out of place in the compound.

Keeping my eyes down, I nearly collided with someone at the entrance to the hallway. I looked up at Linette and stopped when she blocked my way.

"You're welcome," she said.

"For what?"

"For giving you the push you obviously needed." She peered over my shoulder to where Rylen was disappearing into the forbidden door. I rolled my eyes and started to walk past until she said, "You should have heard how he talked about you when he was being questioned."

I looked at her again, and she was serious. My heart expanded just a little.

"He didn't quite know how to categorize you in his life, but it was clear he loved you. Still . . . if you didn't make a move soon, I would have." She smirked and walked away, to the forbidden door where she punched in a code. Freaking Linette.

Well, at least I wasn't smiling like a dumbass anymore.

My shift was almost over when a soft knock revealed Rylen's face. My tummy swirled with thoughts of making out at work again, but his face was tense. He came in and shut the door.

"What's wrong?" I asked.

"Captain King . . . they've got us working together. Flight simulations."

My stomach plummeted. "For the fighter jet?"

Rylen nodded. "I'm copiloting."

Copiloting? I pinched the skin between my eyes the way Dad used to.

"No, Ry. It's too dangerous. He's a loose cannon." Being in the fighter meant Rylen and Michael would be flying *at* the enemy, while the rest of us were flying away. "If DRI attacks, they'll bring fighter jets of their own. And those big ass guns that can shoot down planes from the ground."

"Shoulder-fired missiles," he said, almost to himself.

"Can't one of the other pilots do it? You can fly a passenger plane."

"Pepper." He stepped closer and took my clammy hands. His gray eyes held mine with sincerity. "I would be doing it to steer them away from you. To keep you safe."

"No!" I pulled my hands away and backed shakily into the counter. "I need *you* to be safe too!"

Rylen moved forward and enveloped me in his strong arms. I held him around the waist, breathing him in, squeezing him like I could keep him safe by sheer willpower.

These aliens were determined to break us before they exterminated us. "I hate them," I whispered.

Rylen held me tighter. We stood there clinging to each other until my shift ended.

TWENTY-NINE

REMY

AT NINE O'CLOCK, *EXCUSE me*, twenty-one-hundred, Linette opened the hatch door for me like she'd done every night I worked. We both wore coats with scarves wound around our lower faces and necks as we climbed the cellar-like stairs into the freezing, starry night. She checked all around with her eagle eyes, a big gun over her shoulder, while I made a beeline for the greenhouse thirty steps away. My feet crunched over old snow, now hard and icy as I speed walked, praying I wouldn't slip like I did too often.

When I made it inside and shut the door, Linette sank back down into the hidden entrance and shut the cellar-like door. She would open it again for me in three hours.

The greenhouse was just warm enough from residual daylight heat to make me take off my jacket and scarf. I hummed while I made my way down the long length of the room, my eyes adjusting to the dark as I went. Several veggies were ready to harvest, and my fingers itched to pick them. I pulled the crates out from under the table. I had to lean down and take the cherry tomatoes in my fingers to gauge their darkness against my pale skin. I picked from all six bushes until only half-ripened ones were left. I would get those in two days.

Next I picked curly-edged romaine lettuce and cucumbers. I could not wait to see everyone's faces tomorrow when we fixed these salads with diced canned ham and croutons I was making from scratch. I wouldn't have touched canned ham six months ago to save my life, but now it was a delicacy.

Once everything was picked, I walked the length of the greenhouse to see if there were new sprouts, and to reseed any pots that weren't growing. The feel of soil on my fingers soothed me, and I found my mind wandering to the conundrum of Matt and Jacob. I hadn't had a chance to tell Amber what happened that afternoon while she worked. A bunch of us were hanging out in the lobby. When it became loud and crowded, Matt pulled me into the grief room to "ask me something." I should have known better. He's a guy, and I knew guys. As sweet and kind as he'd always been, he was bound to take advantage of a moment alone, and he did. He kissed me, and for one second, I let him. Then I pulled away, and I didn't have to explain why.

"Tater," he said with an uncharacteristic, sardonic laugh.

"Don't say it like that," I whispered. "I know he's . . . messed up. But he's been through a lot."

"So have you, Remy, and you're not being a bitch to everyone you care about."

"Everyone reacts differently to tragedy." I didn't have it in me to fight, but I needed him to understand. "Matt, look. I'm glad to have you—"

"As a friend." He shook his head. "I got it. Thanks." I'd never seen him get upset with anyone. It was unsettling. Had I led him on *by being too nice? That was the tricky thing with guy friends. But it was unfair. I was sick of feeling guilty. Guilty for drinking too much, hooking up too much. Now guilty for being too nice. Screw that.*

"Don't be like this," I told him. "All I can offer is friendship. Take it or leave it."

I stormed out with him shouting an apology behind me, only to run straight into Tater, who'd apparently seen us go in and was coming to . . . I don't even know what. I stopped, and Matt nearly ran into my back. We both looked up at Tater's locked jaw and crazy eyes.

"You guys finally together?" Tater asked with faux calm.

"No," I said, feeling more and more pissed off. This game Tater was playing with me had my emotions in turmoil. He didn't want me with Matt, but he wouldn't talk to me or look at me most days, even though he'd taken such good care of me while I was sick. He had no right to be angry. "You know what?" My hands made little fists as I swiveled my head between them. "I'm not with anyone, and that's how it's going to stay."

I don't know how they responded, because I'd pushed past them and didn't look back. The whole thing had left me feeling like crap. Honestly, there was too much going on to be worried about guys, but I couldn't help it. Relationships were what life was about. And when I looked at Tater I saw all aspects of him: the boy he'd been with his family growing up, the laid back, funny man he'd been before the war started, and now the standoffish man he'd become after seeing our families murdered and getting blood on his own hands.

I knew him. I knew what he was capable of, and I couldn't help but hope he could have that life back when all of this was over. I wanted us to laugh again, for him not to be afraid to embrace the love he felt, instead of denying himself and living in fear of losing again.

I swiveled my wrist to catch the moonlight on my watch. I had an hour left. Time to water everything and clean up. I lugged the first crate of veggies in my arms and quickly brought them to the door. Then I went back for the second. As I was picking it up, and pivoting to turn, a head-splitting sound blasted through the air, like a horn blowing straight into my ear. I screamed and turned too quickly, trying to run, but tripping over my own stupid feet. A nasty *pop* sounded from my ankle as it twisted, and pain ratcheted up my leg, stunning me. With the heavy crate in my hands, I fell sideways, banging my hip into the side of the crate and whacking my head on the table ledge. All I saw were stars as the bleating siren continued to fill my ears.

AMBER

It happened while I was playing Yahtzee in the lobby with Tater and Josh. Sean and J.D. had left minutes before, arguing about something. I was pretty sure by now that their constant bickering was foreplay. Or foreplay to future foreplay.

While Josh was grabbing water, Tater whispered to me, "Hey, did, uh, Remy say anything about earlier?"

I peered at him. "No, I haven't talked to her. Why? What happened?"

He shook his head, and Josh jogged back, sitting with his legs spread wide. Tater's mouth was clamped shut now. I'd have to ask Remy later.

I rolled the dice. Two sixes along with my other three sixes. "Yes!"

"You're cheating!" Tater said to me. "*Chuleta!* There's no way you can get two Yahtzees in one game when none of the rest of us got any!"

I smacked my thighs. "I cannot cheat at throwing dice! You watch me like a hawk the whole time."

"What's chuleta?" Josh asked.

"It means porkchop," I said. His eyes scrunched, and I laughed. "Don't ask. Our grandma always used it like an expression." I looked at Tater. "Stop being a sore loser."

He opened his mouth to retort and the strangest sound came out, so loud I flinched. The guys were on their feet in half a second, their faces suddenly sober and frightening to see. I was half a second behind them processing what was happening before I jumped up too.

The siren. We were under attack.

I imagine if I were in a civilian place, like a mall or something, there'd be somewhat of a stampede. Mass hysteria. And although I definitely felt near hysterics on the inside, the calmness of the soldiers around me quickly put me in check. We moved as one, exactly how Top had instructed, and we moved fast.

It was a blur. Leaving the lobby, sprinting through the halls, down the stairs, through the tunnel. Sean was just ahead of us, pulling J.D. by the hand.

"Remy," I said when we burst through the tunnel. "Rylen!"

"They're both working," Tater said through panting breaths. "They'll get there before us."

"Oh, God," I said, nearly panicking now. "Rylen's going to the jet! We have to stop him!"

Tater broke formation, yanking me to the side against the wall as everyone sprinted past.

"Don't, Amber!" He shook me. "¡Cálmese!" *Calm down.* "He has a job. Let him do it! Now, come on." He yanked my arm and we slid back into the running ranks.

The worst, most sickening sense of fear entrapped me as I ran. I never got to say good-bye to my parents. And now I wasn't going to see Rylen before he boarded that jet to try and give us all a chance to escape. A sob broke from my throat, but it was a dry, fearful sound. Even my tears were too afraid to come out.

We filed smoothly into the forbidden door and someone at the exit stairs ahead shouted, "Five minutes! Move your asses!" Another man was shoving guns of various types into soldiers' hands as they ran past. Tater got one. I didn't.

We picked up speed, slowing the slightest bit as we all had to sprint up the steps and out into the night. A blast of cold air slapped me, but I barely felt it. My eyes went straight to the greenhouse where Remy would have been working. To my relief, it appeared empty. Tater was right. Since she'd been out here, she was probably one of the first ones to run to the aircraft hangar.

It was a dead-on open air sprint the rest of the way to the hangar. We burst through the tall, metal doors, which were being opened from ground to ceiling. Engines were roaring and propellers were whirring. Top was at the bottom of the stairs of the first plane, waving people up.

"Is Remy on this one?" I shouted to him.

He shook his head, circling an arm to tell everyone, "Go, Go, Go!"

Tater and I ran to the next airplane.

"Did Remy Haines board?"

The man shook his head. "No women onboard yet."

Tater and I shared a look of confusion that turned to panic. We looked all around us at the people spilling into the hangar, running up the stairs. We ran to both the choppers, no Remy. I shook out my hands at my sides.

"Tater, where the hell is she?" We were back to Top's plane now.

"Thirty seconds!" he shouted.

"Still no Remy?" I asked. Top shook his head.

Tater motioned something to the First Sergeant, and shoved me forward. Top grasped my upper arm hard. And then Tater was running out of the hangar.

"Wait!" I screamed and tried to yank away, but Top literally picked me up off my feet and carried me, kicking and screaming, up the stairs.

"Tater! No! Tater, come back!"

"Don't let her off!" Top told the people on board as he unceremoniously dumped me inside. Devon's arms wrapped around me, not leaving a single crack for me to pry myself loose. I sank into the floor of the plane as the doors closed, wracked with violent sobs.

RYLEN

I didn't like the look in Captain King's eyes when we got to the jet. He wasn't focused. He looked fucking insane. We didn't have time for this.

"Dude," I said. "Are you up for it?"

He blinked, but his eyes still freaked me out. "I can fly."

"I know you can fucking fly, but can you focus on this mission?"

His jaw locked. "I'm not afraid to die."

"Good for you, man, but I have no intention of dying today." I grasped my helmet and shoved it over my head. "Do *you*?"

He put his on too. "We might have to."

What the fuck. I grabbed him by the shoulders and shoved him into the leg of the jet. "This isn't a fucking kamikaze mission, King. You're not gonna throw our asses at them."

His lips pursed. "If you'd seen what I'd seen—"

I shoved him harder. "This isn't time for your personal revenge!" *Fuck this.* "I'm flying. You're copilot."

I shoved away and sprinted for the stairs.

"You can't do that!" he shouted behind me, but I was already jumping into the cockpit.

"Watch me."

REMY

I blinked and pushed up, then screamed when I tried to stand. The siren was still ringing in my ears, and the direness of the situation hit me with a surge of panic. How much time had passed? I turned onto my hands and knees and crawled. A rush of adrenaline drowned out the pain in my knees, head, and legs as I scrambled down the concrete path to the door. I grabbed the handle and pulled myself up. I couldn't see from one of my eyes, and when I reached up I realized I'd cut my head. Blood covered my eye. I wiped it with the back of my hand and blinked.

I yanked the door open. In the distance, I saw one person running, and a plane was pulling out of the hangar. They were leaving! Sheer, blood-stopping panic filled me.

"*Wait!*" I screamed.

The person running, who was now halfway to the hangar, spun and looked at me. I couldn't make them out with one clear eye, but I definitely heard her voice say, "Fuck!"

I tried to run to her, but oh my gosh, that foot—I couldn't put pressure on it without collapsing—so I dragged it as I moved forward. Linette got to me and shoved a hand under my arm.

"One of the choppers is waiting for me. We've got to move!"

We'd gone about five quick steps when she halted and my breathing stopped. On the left, a group of people in all black with dark weapons were coming around the side of the old bio warfare building, all stealthy-like. I knew instinctively they weren't with us. Linette yanked me back against the side of the greenhouse. We stood there two seconds, hoping they'd move along, but they didn't. I think we both came to the same conclusion. There was no way we could get past them to the hangar. And it would take less than half a minute for them to shift this way and see us.

"*Psst.*" The quiet sound came from the side of the building across from us. A shadowy figure stood with his back against the wall, gun up. I froze until his head peeked out to glance back at the DRI figures in black.

Tater! Why wasn't he on a plane? He motioned to the bunker's cellar doors.

"Back down," Linette whispered. And although her voice and body were fluid and confident, I saw a shadow of fear across her face when she turned back to the bunker doorway and moonlight hit her.

An ear-splitting *whoosh* vibrated the air around us—our fighter jet taking off like a rocket. A blur.

The three of us rushed forward, crouching, and were down the hatch in seconds. Linette locked the door and we followed her as she ran down the once-forbidden hall. The farther we went, the more trapped I felt. Our situation came crashing down around us. We'd missed the planes, and Baelese were swarming the area. How could we possibly survive this?

A blast shook the ground beneath us and I choked on a scream.

"Bye-bye spaceship," Linette said.

I followed blindly through the twists and turns of the underground maze. Linette whipped a door open and shoved me in. I stopped, stiff at the sight of jail cells before us. I looked and saw a man in a pile on the ground in the last cell, lying in a puddle of blood.

"Go! Come on!" Linette rushed me into a cell and I backed against the wall, holding myself around the waist.

I tried so hard not to look over at the man in the other cell. Who was that? The blood was shiny and fresh. Linette handed her gun to Tater, who ran over and put both their guns on a table, before running back to us. Why were they getting rid of their guns?

Tater closed us into the cell, locking it with a *click*, and then stood, listening.

"Why are you locking us in?" I hissed.

Linette crouched before me and took my chin. "Listen to me. You're about to have to put on the best damn act of your life. The three of us are prisoners of the troop that was here, prisoners because we were on the side of the DRI. We were on the side of change. We didn't want to go against them. We didn't believe they were bad, and so we were locked up. Following me so far?" I was too stunned to nod.

"They're coming," Tater whispered. "They're opening and closing doors down the hall."

Linette never looked away from me, and I swear it was her steadiness that kept me from crumbling in panic at that moment. She spoke faster.

"We are brainless. We're going to be fucking thrilled they're saving us. We're going to swear allegiance and do whatever we have to do to be found useful to their cause. We'll keep our eyes and ears open. And then we're going to take those bastards down from the inside while the others plan an attack from the outside."

I managed a tiny nod.

Linette turned on her knees and grasped the bars. I couldn't move. I felt trapped in the spiral of a twilight zone. *This isn't happening. It can't be happening.*

The door flew open, making me jump, and three men filled the doorway, dressed in what looked like SWAT team uniforms. They spread out, guns pointed at us. All three of us raised our hands. I was still on the floor, my legs feeling like jelly. A well-dressed woman in a black pantsuit sauntered in and her eyes took in everything. A creeping sensation overcame my flesh as I watched her jerky movements, knowing what she was.

"You're here," Linette said. Her voice had transformed from

confident to meek. "Are you DRI?"

She eyed Linette without answering, and her gaze moved to the next cell. Her jaw tensed.

"He's one of you," Tater said, sounding scared. "DRI. They came in and killed him when the sirens went off."

"And who are you?" the woman asked.

"Prisoners," Linette said, still on her knees, peering up.

"Why have you been imprisoned by your own kind?"

"We wanted to contact the DRI," Tater said. "We wanted to work with you, to help find outliers, but they said no. They said you all were the enemy. That's when we knew they were the outliers you warned us about. So the three of us tried to leave, and they stopped us. Locked us up."

Words bubbled up inside me and came out as a shaken whisper: "I knew you would come." And I did. I think I always knew this place was too good to be true. I'd even held back from getting too close to Jacob.

The woman looked at me, stared at the tears that trickled down my face as I peered up like the lamb that I was, all laid out for slaughter.

"Can we help you?" Linette begged, sounding convincingly fanatic. "Will you get us out of here? Please?"

The Baelese woman's eyes scanned until they landed on the key ring on the wall. She nodded to her nearest soldier. "Cuff them and bring them with us."

RYLEN

It'd always been my dream to fly a fighter jet, but not like this. Not with Amber and the others down there, running for their lives. I imagined I'd work my way up the ranks and take online courses, eventually become an officer so I could fly. But I always imagined the people I loved would be safe at home. I'd been in such a damn hurry to join the military when I was eighteen. I should have listened to Mr. Tate. Tater and I were just dumb ass kids when this war started. Back when we thought we knew who the enemy might be.

We couldn't have been more wrong. About everything. All of us.

I nosed the jet back around toward base with Captain King behind me in the copilot seat. He outranked me, but that shit didn't matter anymore. I'd read everything about this jet that I could get my hands on, and I'd been in the simulator countless times. Still, nothing could prepare me for the cold fear I'd feel knowing who I was directly protecting. Knowing what was at stake.

I finally, for the first time in my life, felt stable, and it was because of her. All these years. I hadn't let myself believe there was a chance. I wasn't going to lose her now.

"What do you see?" I asked King through our helmet mics.

"DRI in all black, crawling all over the base like fucking roaches. None of our people in sight."

I exhaled heavily. "Good." They'd made it to the hangars.

Now that I knew Amber was safe on a plane, I could concentrate.

King was turned, watching behind us. "Passenger Carrier One is up." The first plane had taken off.

I searched the perimeter of the base. "Three white vans at the entrance and something smaller. Jeep, maybe?"

"Let's take them out," he said.

"Not if there's a chance they've taken any of our people prisoner," I responded, glad as fuck that I'd forced him out of the pilot seat. Top's orders were to take out any enemy aircraft or ground vehicles that were directly stopping our people from getting to the hangar or trying to stop our planes and choppers from leaving. King always wanted to blow shit up—even on simulations—but I wasn't taking any chances.

"Carrier Two's in the air," Lennox called.

A *blip* sounded from my radar screen and my pulse shot up. "Incoming!"

Not one, but two enemy jets were heading straight for us.

King let out a howl I'd heard in times of war—the wicked sound of thrill when it came down to killing or being killed. But that was all right. I was in control, and being killed was not an option.

"Let's take 'em down," I said.

AMBER

My face was glued to the small window and my heart was inconsolable. The higher we climbed, the more a frosty layer grew around the bottom of the window. I could see nothing but white ground, mountains, and clouds. The entire plane and all fifty passengers were eerily quiet. Top stood in front, staring blankly at us, his mouth clamped shut.

Dreadful imaginings ran rampant in my mind, despite my desperate attempts to hush them. Images of Remy being dragged from the greenhouse by DRI, Tater shot on sight, Rylen's jet bursting into flames and crashing down. Would I ever know their true fates? Once again, my heart seized and I fought to breathe, covering my face as I brought my knees up in the seat.

Devon sat next to me, with Shavonta on his other side. Now and then he'd give my knee a pat, but he mostly acted as if he was unfazed by my sounds of despair. He respected my need to freak out. I didn't know if any of the rest of our gang was on this plane. I couldn't bear to look around.

At one point I heard Shavonta whisper, "Do we know where we're going yet?"

"Nope," Devon whispered back. "Top's waiting 'till we're clear of air signal."

I didn't care. I didn't care about anything. I just wanted to be back at the bunker with my brother and Remy, come what may, or in that cockpit with Rylen. I bit down hard on my thumbnail. So many people here had lost everyone they loved. How did they do it? How did they manage to sleep and sometimes even smile? I found it hard to believe I'd ever have those desires again. That my body would ever find rest again.

"Ladies and gentleman," Top called out over the sounds of engines and propellers. "We're clear. Thank you for your expedient exit from the base. I can now tell you we're on our way to Anchorage, Alaska. I've been in contact with an underground bunker there since day one, and they welcome us. From there, we will forge a plan of attack. My estimation is that we will act this spring. Mere months away. There's no time to lose. They've got another ship due to land by the end of the year. You with me?"

A round of "Hooah!" filled the plane, giving me a chill.

"It looks like all but a few people made it aboard—"

"Who didn't make it?" I asked.

Top shook his head. "I don't know yet—"

"What about the fighter jet?" I sat on the edge of my seat. It was a stab to the chest to see his face fall.

"We have to keep all lines of communication closed, so as not to be tracked. It's a waiting game now."

I sat back heavily, my hands trembling as I brought my thumbnail to my mouth.

"And for those of you feeling like shit, like there's not much to live for anymore . . ." He gazed around the cabin with steel eyes. "I find that vengeance is a damn good motivator."

Some chuckles and more "Hooahs" rang out, and I clung to his words.

Vengeance. Yes. I would play my part in bringing them down. I'd do whatever I could to keep the Baelese from succeeding in this takeover. They'd ripped everything, *everything*, from me. I wouldn't let terror and loss kill my spirit, not while there was still breath in my lungs and blood pumping through my heart.

I pressed my hand against the window and stared out at the dark night as one hot tear slid down my cheek, and I made a promise to my family. Remy. Rylen.

"I won't let it be for nothing."

TO BE CONTINUED . . .

In the final book,
UNDONE, Coming Fall 2017

ACKNOWLEDGMENTS

TO ALL MY SWEETIES (my readers), group hug!!

Thank you to my family and friends—the usual suspects—for their love and constant encouragement. Especially my daddy, Jim Hornback, for his help with all of the military stuff in this series.

Thank you to Ann Kulakowski for the cheerful wakeup calls to get my booty in gear.

Thank you to my early readers for their valuable feedback: my friends Meredith Crowley, Jill Wilson and Hilary Mahalchick, bloggers Jaime Arnold and Jessica Reigle, and author-friend Cindi Madsen. I would have been lost without you guys on this one!!!

Thanks also to my proofreader, Nichole Strauss of Insight Editing Services, and my formatter Christine Borgford of Type A Formatting. You guys are so wonderful to work with!

Thank you KP Simmon of Inkslinger PR for your love and support!

I feel like I need to give a shout out to Twitter for keeping me humble by refusing to give me that little blue verified checkmark. Hehe.

And thank you Jesus for getting me through another book. I still can't believe this is my life.

Dream big, dreamers.